Here is #14 in the compelling series about that famous and unforgettable, slightly tarnished hero Travis McGee. People just don't read Travis McGee novels, they devour 'em. There just isn't another quip-making, crime-punching, girl-watching boat bum anywhere like McGee.

"John D. MacDonald is the great American storyteller. McGee is for me."

—Richard Condon

"A crime writer who never lets the customer down."

—Saturday Review Syndicate

"John D. MacDonald, long one of the most creative and reliable writers of paperback originals . . . can create a series character just as well as he does everything else in the suspense field."

—New York Times Book Review

"When it comes to electrifying suspense stories, teeming with action, tingling with taut-stretched plot and boiling over with original and acidly etched characters, there just isn't anyone around doing the job better than John D. MacDonald."

—State Journal Register
Springfield, Ill.

Fawcett Gold Medal Books
in the Travis McGee Series
by John D. MacDonald:

THE DEEP BLUE GOOD-BY
NIGHTMARE IN PINK
A PURPLE PLACE FOR DYING
THE QUICK RED FOX
A DEADLY SHADE OF GOLD
BRIGHT ORANGE FOR THE
SHROUD
DARKER THAN AMBER
ONE FEARFUL YELLOW EYE
PALE GRAY FOR GUILT
THE GIRL IN THE PLAIN
BROWN WRAPPER
THE LONG LAVENDER LOOK
A TAN AND SANDY SILENCE
THE SCARLET RUSE
THE TURQUOISE LAMENT
THE DREADFUL LEMON SKY
THE EMPTY COPPER SEA
THE GREEN RIPPER
FREE FALL IN CRIMSON

THE SCARLET RUSE

by John D. MacDonald

FAWCETT GOLD MEDAL • NEW YORK

A Fawcett Gold Medal Book

Published by Ballantine Books

 Published in the United States by Ballantine Books, a division of Random House, Inc., New York, and simultaneously in Canada by Random House of Canada Limited, Toronto.

ISBN 0-449-12640-4

Manufactured in the United States of America

First Fawcett Gold Medal Edition: July 1973
First Ballantine Books Edition: August 1983

I have learned that the countless paths one traverses in one's life are all equal. Oppressors and oppressed meet at the end, and the only thing that prevails is that life was altogether too short for both.

—Don Juan as quoted by Castaneda

Oh, goddamnit, we forgot the silent prayer!

—Dwight D. Eisenhower
[at a Cabinet meeting]

THE SCARLET RUSE

One

After seven years of bickering and fussing, the Fort Lauderdamndale city fathers, on a hot Tuesday in late August, killed off a life style and turned me into a vagrant.

"Permanent habitation aboard all watercraft within the city limits is prohibited."

And that ordinance included everything and everybody from the Alabama Tiger aboard his plush *'Bama Gal*, running the world's longest floating houseparty, all the way down to the shackiest little old pontoon cottage snugged into the backwater mangroves.

It included Meyer, the hairy economist, living comfortably aboard his dumpy little cruiser, *The John Maynard Keynes*, low in the water with the weight of financial tomes and journals in five languages and chess texts and problems in seven.

It included me and my stately and substantial old barge-type houseboat, *The Busted Flush*. The edict caught me off balance. I had not thought I was so thoroughly imbedded in any particular environment that being detached would be traumatic. Travis McGee is not hooked by things or by places, I told myself.

But, by God, there had been a lot of golden days, a lot of laughter and happy girls. Moonrise and hard rains. Swift fish and wide beaches. Some gentle tears and some damned good luck.

Maybe that is what made the gut hollow, an old superstition about luck. Long long long ago I stepped on a round stone in darkness and fell heavily at the instant that automatic weapons' fire yellow-stitched the night where I had been standing six feet four inches tall and frangible. I had two souvenirs from that fall—an elbow abrasion and the round stone. I still had the half-pound stone after the elbow healed. I kept it in the side pocket of the twill pants. Then they leapfrogged two battalions of us forward by night to take pressure off some of our people who'd dug in on the wrong hill.

Our airplane driver didn't care for the attention he was getting and kept his air speed on the high side as he dumped our group. I came to the end of the static line with one hell of a snap, and there was such a sharp pain in my ankle I thought I'd earned another Heart. I pulled the shrouds around, landed on shale, favoring the right leg, rolled and unbuckled, unslung the piece, and listened to night silence before I felt my ankle. No ripped leather or wetness. Pain lessening. Then I missed the round rock. When the chute popped, the rock had popped the pocket stitches, and it had gone down the pant leg, rapping the ankle bone on the way out, hurting right through the oiled leather of the jump boots. And I felt at that moment a terrible anxiety. "My rock is lost. My luck is lost. Some bastard is sighting in on me right now."

Later I realized that I had made some bad moves during those next five days before they pulled us all back.

This was the same feeling. I'd clambered up onto the sundeck of the *Flush* so many mornings at first light and had looked out at my world from the vantage point of Slip F-18 and known who I was. True, the great panorama of the sky had been dwindled over the years by the highrise invasions. But it was my place. I'd taken the *Flush* out a hundred times and brought her back and tucked her, creaking and sighing, against the piers, home safe. Safe among her people and mine.

I guess there weren't enough of us, all told. The City Commissioners authorized a survey and found out there were sixteen hundred people living on boats within the city limits. That isn't much of a voting block in a place the size of Lauderdale. And boat people are not likely to act in unison anyway.

We'd all been pretending it would be voted down, but they made it unanimous.

So all day Wednesday, little groups formed, reformed, moved around, broke up, joined up again, aboard the watercraft at Bahia Mar.

Meyer lectured an embittered audience aboard the *'Bama Gal,* standing on the cockpit deck amid a decorative litter of young ladies, quaffing Dos Equis, spilling a dapple of suds onto his black chest pelt.

"They say we have added to the population density. Let us examine that charge. Ten years ago perhaps a thousand of us lived aboard cruisers and houseboats. Now there are six hundred additional. During those ten years, ladies and gentlemen, how many so-called living units have appeared in this area? Highrise, town houses, tract houses, mobile homes? They were constructed and trucked in and slapped together and inhabited without thought or heed to the necessary water supply, sewage disposal, schools, roads, police and fire protection. All services are now marginal."

"Fiffy thousand more shore people, maybe, huh?" said Geraldine, mistress of the old *Broomstick.*

"They say we have created sewage disposal problems," Meyer intoned. "Doubtless a few of the live-aboard people are dumb and dirty, emptying slop buckets into the tide. But for the majority of us, we have holding tanks, we use shoreside facilities, we want clean water because we live on the water. Thousands upon thousands of transient cruisers and yachts and houseboats stop at the area marinas every year. Hundreds of millions of dollars' worth of marine hardware, paying a high ticket for docking privileges and bringing ashore a lot of out-of-town spending money. And we all know, we have all seen, that it is the transient watercraft which cause a sewage disposal problem. They do not live here. They take the easiest way out. They do not give a damn. But will the City Commissioners pass a law saying transients cannot stay aboard transient boats? Never! Those transients are keeping this corner of Florida green, my friends."

He was applauded. Yay! We would march on City Hall. They would see the error of their ways.

But Johnny Dow put the whole thing in perspective. He cleared his throat and spat downwind, turned away from the rail and said, "*Ad valorem,* goddamnit!"

"Speak American," said one of the Tiger's playgirls.

"They hate us. Them politicals. You know what they make their money on. They come from the law and real estate and selling lots and houses. *Ad valorem.* We not putting dime one in their pockets. They drivin' past seeing folks live pretty free, not needing them one damn bit, and they get scalded. We're supposed to have property lines and bushes and chinch bugs and home improvement loans. Jealous. They all nailed down with a lot of crap they don't like and can't get loose of. So here we are. Easy target. Chouse us the hell out of town forever and they don't have to see us or think about us. Figure us for some kind of parasite. Scroom, ever' damn ass-tight one of them. Can't win this one, Meyer. We're too dense, and we make sewage. Easy target. Neaten up the city. Sweep out the trash. *Ad valorem.*" He spat again, with good elevation and good distance, and stumped across the deck and down the little gangway and off into the blinding brightness of noontime.

Meyer nodded approvingly. "Scroom," he murmured. The end of an era.

We walked together back to the *Flush* and went aboard. We sat in the lounge, frowning and sighing.

Meyer said, "I saw Irv. He said something can be worked out."

"Something can always be worked out. Sure. If a man wants to live aboard a boat, something can be worked out. If he can pay the ticket. A man could buy a condominium apartment right over there in that big hunk of ugly and make it his legal and mailing address and stay there one night a month and aboard all the other nights. Can something be worked out for all the people who get hit by the new law?"

"Hardly."

"Then it isn't going to be the same, old friend. And do we want any part of it, even if I could afford the ticket?"

"You short again?"

"Don't look at me like that."

"You in the confetti business? You make little green paper airplanes?"

"I have had six months of my retirement in this installment, fella."

He beamed. "You know, you look rested. Good shape too. Better and better shape this last month, right?"

"Getting ready to go to work, which I seem to remember telling you."

"You *did! You did!* I remember. That was when I asked you if you would help an old and dear friend and you said no thanks."

"Meyer, damnit, I—"

"I respect your decision. I don't know what will happen to Fedderman. It's just too bad."

I stared at him with fond exasperation. A week ago he had tried to explain Hirsh Fedderman's unusual problem to me, and I had told him that it was an area I knew absolutely nothing about.

Meyer said, "We have thirty days of grace before we have to move away, boat and baggage. I just thought it would be a good thing to occupy your mind. And I told Hirsh I knew somebody who maybe could help out."

"You got a little ahead of yourself, didn't you?"

He sighed. "So I have to make amends. I'll see what I can do by myself."

"Stop trying to manipulate me."

"What are you talking about?"

"Take a deep breath and say it. If it's what you want, take a deep breath and say it."

"What should I say?"

"Take a wild guess."

"Well . . . Travis, would you please come with me to

Miami and listen to my old friend Hirsh Fedderman and decide if you want to take on a salvage job?"

"Because you ask me so nicely, yes."

"But then why was it no before?"

"Because I had something else shaping up."

"And it fell through?"

"Yesterday. So today I need Fedderman, maybe."

"He is a nervous ruin. He's waiting for the roof to fall in on him. If it would be okay, how about this afternoon? I can phone him?"

Two

Fedderman asked us not to arrive until quarter after five, when both the female clerks in his tiny shop would be gone for the day. I put Miss Agnes, my Rolls-Royce pick-up, in a parking lot two blocks from his store. He was in mainland Miami, a dozen blocks from Biscayne and about three doors from the corner of Southwest Eleventh Street.

There was a dusty display window, with a steel grill padlocked across it. Gold leaf, peeling, on plate glass, said ornately "FEDDERMAN STAMP AND COIN COMPANY." Below that was printed "RARITIES."

Meyer tried the door, and it was locked. He knocked and peered into the shadowy interior and said, "He's coming."

I heard the sound of a bolt and a chain, and then a bell dingled when he opened the door and smiled out and up at us. He was a crickety little man, quick of movement, quick to smile, bald rimmed with white, a tan, seamed face, crisp white shirt, salmon-pink slacks.

Meyer introduced us. Fedderman smiled and bobbed and shook hands with both hands. He locked the door and led us back past dim display cases to the small office in the rear. There was bright fluorescence in the office and in the narrow stock room beyond the office. Fedderman sat behind his desk. He smiled and sighed. "Why should I feel better?" he asked. "I don't know if anybody can do anything. The whole thing is impossible, believe me. It couldn't happen. It happened. I can't eat. I can't sleep. I can't sit still or stand still since I found out. Mr. McGee, whatever happens, I am glad Meyer brought you to hear this crazy story. Here is—"

I interrupted him. "Mr. Fedderman, I try to recover items of value which have been lost and which cannot be recovered by any other means. If I decide to help you, I will risk my time and expenses. If I make a recovery of all or part of what you have lost, we take my expenses off the top and split the remainder down the middle."

He nodded, looking thoughtful. "Maybe it wouldn't fit perfect, because what is lost isn't mine. I understand. Let me tell you."

"Go slow because I don't know a thing about stamps and coins."

He smiled. "So I'll give you a shock treatment." He took a desk-top projector with built-in viewing screen from a shelf and put it on his desk and plugged it in. He opened a desk drawer and took out a metal box of transparencies and fitted it into the projector. He turned off the light and projected the first slide onto the twelve-by-fifteen-inch ground-glass viewing area.

A block of four stamps filled the screen. They were deep blue. They showed an old-timey portrait of George Washington. The denomination was ninety cents.

"This was printed in 1875," Fedderman said. "It is perhaps the finest block of four known, and one of the very few blocks known. Superb condition, crisp deep color, full original gum. It catalogs at over twelve thousand dollars, but it will bring thousands more at auction."

Click. The next was a pair of stamps, one above the other. A four-cent stamp. Blue. It pictured three old ships under sail, over the legend "Fleet of Columbus."

"The *only* known vertical pair of the famous error of blue. Only one sheet was printed in blue instead of ultramarine. In ultramarine this pair would be worth . . . twenty-five dollars. This pair catalogs at nine thousand three hundred and will bring fifteen at auction. The top stamp has one pulled perf and a slight gum disturbance. The bottom stamp has never been hinged, and it is superb. Quite flawless."

Click. Click. Click. A couple of crude bears holding up an emblem, with "Saint Louis" printed across the top of the stamps and "Post Office" printed across the bottom. A block of six brownish, crude-looking five-cent stamps showing Ben Franklin. There were no rows of little holes for tearing them apart. A twenty-four-cent stamp printed in red and blue, showing an old airplane, a biplane, flying upside down. And about a dozen others, while Fedderman talked very large numbers.

He finished the slide show and turned the bright overhead lights back on. He creaked back in his swivel chair.

"Crash course, Mr. McGee. I've showed you nineteen items. I've bought them for a client over the past fifteen years. Right now there is another twenty thousand to spend. I am looking for the right piece. Another classic. Another famous piece."

"Why does he want them?" I asked.

Fedderman's smile was small and sad. "What has he put into these pieces over fifteen years? A hundred and eighty-five thousand. Plus my fee. What do I charge for my time, my advice, all my knowledge and experience and contacts? Ten percent. So let's say he has two hundred and three thousand, five hundred dollars in these funny little pieces of paper? I could make two phone calls, maybe only one, and get him three hundred and fifty thousand. Or if I spent a year liquidating, feeding them into the right auctions, negotiating the auction house percentage, he could come out with a half million."

Meyer said, "As the purchasing power of currencies of the world erodes, Travis, all the unique and the limited-quantity items in the world go up. Waterfront land. Rare books and paintings. Heirloom silver. Rare postage stamps."

"Classic postage stamps," Fedderman said, "have certain advantages over that other stuff. Portability. One small envelope with a stiffener to prevent bending, with glassine interleafs for the mint copies, you can walk around with a half million dollars. These classics, you can sell them in the capital cities of the world, cash money, no questions. Well, some questions for these items because all the old timers like me, we know the history, which collections they've been in over the years—Hines, West, Brookman, Weil. We know when they changed hands and for how much. For each item here there is a certificate from the Philatelic Foundation saying it is genuine. The disadvantage is they are fragile. They've got to be perfect. A little crease, a little wrinkle, it would break your heart how much comes off the price. These, they never get touched with a naked finger. Stamp tongs if they ever have to be touched. They are in a safety deposit box."

Meyer encouraged Hirsh to tell me how he operated. It was intriguing and simple. He and any new client would take out a lock box set up to require both signatures and the presence of both parties before it could be opened. He used the First Atlantic Bank and Trust Company, four blocks from his store. When he made an acquisition, he and the client would go to the bank and put it in the box. The reason was obvious—as soon as Fedderman explained it to me. He made a formal legal agreement with each client. If at any time the client wanted to get out from under, Hirsh Fedderman would pay him a sum equal to the total investment plus five percent per year on the principal amount invested. Or, if the client desired, he could take over the investment collection himself, at which point the agreement became void.

"It's just to make them feel safe is all," Fedderman said. "They don't know me. They don't know if the stamps are real or forgeries. I started it this way a long time ago. I've never closed one out the way it says there in the agreement. But some have been closed out, sure. There was one closed out six years ago. About fifty thousand he had in it. I got together with the executor, and we auctioned the whole thing through Robert Siegel Auction Galleries, and a very happy widow got a hundred and forty thousand."

"They can get big money that easily?" I asked.

Fedderman looked at me with kindly contempt. "Mr. McGee, any year maybe twenty-five millions, maybe fifty millions go through the auction houses all over the world.

Maybe more. Who knows? Compared to the stock exchanges, very small potatoes. But if the merchandise was available, the stamp auctions would be twice as big. Three times. That is because shrewd men know what has happened to classic merchandise during forty years of inflation. They'll buy all they can find. You put money in a Swiss bank, next year it's worth five percent less. The same money in a rarity, it *has* to be five percent more because the money is worth less, and the demand adds more percent. So in true rarities these days, the increment, it's fifteen to twenty percent per year."

"How many clients do you have right now?"

"Only six. This one and five more. Average. Sometimes ten, sometimes three."

"How much do you invest in a given year?"

He shrugged. "Last year, over five hundred thousand."

"Where do you find the rare stamps to invest in?"

"All over the country there are dealers who know I'm in the market for the very best in U.S., British, and British Colonials. Those are what I know best. Say a dealer gets a chance to bid on an estate. It's got some classics which make it too rich for him. He phones me and he says, 'Hirsh, I've got here in a collection all the 1869 pictorials in singles used and unused, with and without grills, with double grills, triple grills. I've got special cancellations on singles and pairs, and I've got some blocks of four. Some are fine, some superb, average very fine.' So maybe it's Comeskey in Utica, New York, maybe Tippet over in Sarasota, I fly there and figure what I can use and maybe I add enough to the pot so he can bid in the whole collection, and I take the '69s, and he takes the rest. Or I get tipped about things coming up at auction and move in and make a buy before they print up the catalog. Or there is a collector tired of some good part of his collection, and he knows me. Or a dealer needs some ready cash on stuff he's had tucked away for years, watching the price go up. I deal fair. I never take advantage. Three years ago a collector wanted to sell me his early Bermuda. He had some fakes of the early Postmasters' Stamps from Hamilton and St. George. At eighteen and twenty thousand each and looking like some dumb kid printed them in a cellar, no wonder there's fakes—lots of them—around. He threw in fifteen or so fakes he'd picked up over the years. I sat right here and went over them. One bothered me. It was Stanley Gibbons catalog number 03, center-dated 1850. The W. B. Perot signature was way off. Too far away from the original. Know what I mean? The rest of it was so damned perfect. Would a counterfeiter be so stupid? Not with several thousand dollars at stake. Okay, so maybe Perot was sick or out of town or had a busted hand that day. It took six months, but I got an authentication out of the Royal Philatelic Society, and I sent the collector my check for nine thousand, which was the best offer I could get for the stamp at that time. I put the stamp in a client investment account. You wouldn't believe the kind of word of mouth advertising I got out of that."

The whole thing seemed unreal to me. He claimed to have made fifty thousand last year as a buying agent for the investment accounts. But here he was in a narrow little sidestreet store.

"Your problem, Mr. McGee, I can see it on your face. You think all this stamp stuff is like bubble gum wrappers, like maybe baseball cards, trade three of your players for one of mine. It doesn't seem like grownups, right? Let me show you how grownup it can get, okay?"

He opened an old cast-iron safe, took out a little file drawer, took out some glassine envelopes. With small, flat-bladed tongs he took out two stamps and put them in front of me.

"Here, look at these two through this magnifying glass. These are both the five-dollar Columbian Exposition of 1893, unused. Printed in black. Profile of Columbus. Catalog seven hundred. For stamps like these, the retail should be a thousand each. Quality. Perfect centering. No tears or folds or bends. No short perforations. No perforations missing. Nice clean imprint, sharp and bright, no fading. A fresh, crisp look. Right? Now I turn them over. Keep looking. See? Full original gum on each. Nobody ever stuck a hinge on either one and stuck it in an album. Perfect? You are looking at two thousand dollars retail? Wrong! This one is a thousand dollars. This other one is *schlock*. I'll show you."

He got out a pistol-grip light on a cord, turned it on, and turned off the overheads. We were in almost complete darkness. "Black light," he said. "Look at the stamp there." Two irregular oval areas glowed. One was the size of a lima bean, the other the size of a grain of rice.

Fedderman turned the lights on again. "Let me tell you what is maybe the history of this piece of junk here. Back in 1893 maybe some uncle goes to the Exposition and he brings back a fine gift, all the stamps, and maybe a souvenir album. So a kid licks this one like putting it on an envelope and sticks it in the album, along with the others. This one maybe had one straight edge, where it was at the edge of the sheet when it was printed. Okay, maybe it spends thirty, forty years in that album. Finally somebody tries to soak it off. Hard to do after the glue has set. They don't get it all off. Some of the stamp comes off on the album paper. That leaves a place called a thin. A nice centered stamp like this with no gum and two thins and a straight edge, nothing else wrong, it goes for maybe a hundred and fifty, hundred and a quarter retail, perhaps ninety bucks wholesale. Okay, last year or the year before, somebody buys this dog along with some others of the same kind of high value dogs. They take them to Germany. Right now, working somewhere in West Germany, there is a pure genius. He makes up some kind of stuff to fill the thins. He gets the gum from low-denomination Columbians. He puts it on perfect, no slop-over between the perfs. And he reperfs the straight edge perfect as an angel. I'm telling you, back around World War One, Sam Singer was the stamp doctor in this country. Then there was a fellow in Paris named Zareski who was pretty good, especially faking cancellations. But this German is the best yet. Very dangerous. And I'm showing you why I'm worth the ten percent I get for doing the investing."

Suddenly he slumped, sighed. "Sure. Hirsh Fedderman is so damned smart. When you think nobody can take you, somebody takes you."

"Tell Travis what happened," Meyer said.

It took Fedderman a few moments to pull himself together. "Eighteen months ago, a little longer ago, I guess, this man phones up, his name is Frank Sprenger, he wants to have a talk with me about investing in stamps. He says he heard about me from so and so. I knew the name. Excuse me, I don't like to give out names. It's a confidential relationship. So I drove over to the Beach, and he's got a condominium apartment, like a penthouse, in the Seascape. It's in the afternoon. There is a party going on, girls and laughing and loud music and so forth. Sprenger comes and takes me into a bedroom down a hall and shuts the door. He is big and broad, and he has a great tan. He has a great haircut. He smells like pine trees. He is not going to tell me what he does for a living. It is entertainment, maybe. Like with girls or horses or importing grass. Why should I care who I deal with? The protections are there. I do a clean business and pay my taxes. I give my sales talk. He listens good. He asks the right questions. I show him a sample of the agreement and a sample receipt like I sign to show the total investment and a sample inventory list like he can have if he wants. He says he will let me know. He finally lets me know it is yes. We meet at the bank and set up the box, and I sign the agreement, and we get it notarized. He says he can't say how much or how often, but it will usually be cash and is that okay? I tell him okay. He gives me forty thousand in cash in a big brown manila envelope right there, and I put it in my business account. Who wants to walk these streets with money like that? He had the two fellows who came with him waiting in the car. I'm alone. The items I showed you, that's not Sprenger's account. Sprenger said he didn't want anything well known, any special item that dealers would know on sight. I said it would make a little more volume. He said okay, but keep the volume down."

"Did his request mean anything to you?" I asked Federman.

"What do you mean?"

"He planned to turn over cash in unpredictable

amounts for merchandise which couldn't be traced. Did you make any guesses about him from that?"

"Guesses? A man can do a lot of guessing. Why should I care? I can prove the money turned over to me from my copy of the receipt and from my deposit record. I can show where it went, show my percentage for my own taxes. Suppose it isn't his money. Suppose he's getting ready to run. Any time he wants, he can meet me at the bank, give me back my signed agreement, take the merchandise home."

"What did you invest in?"

"Superb unused blocks of four without plate numbers. High values. Columbians, Trans-Mississippi, Zeppelins. Some larger multiples, like a beautiful block of nine of the two-dollar Trans-Miss, mint, sixty-five hundred it cost me. Same kind of purchases of Canadian Jubilee in the high-dollar values. Also some older stuff when they were perfect singles, used or unused, like a nice mint copy each of Canada numbers one, two, five, seven, nine, and thirteen. Twelve thousand, five hundred right there. Value." He leaned toward me. "It is the most valuable stuff, Mr. McGee, on a size and weight basis, the world has ever known. Some years ago Ray Weil and his brother, Roger, bought a Hawaiian stamp at auction for forty thousand. Very thin paper. Some newspaper guy in New Orleans, I think it was, figured out that it came to one and a half billion dollars a pound."

"I'm impressed."

"It doesn't come with bubble gum."

"I said I'm impressed, Mr. Fedderman."

"Call me Hirsh, please."

"Hirsh, I want to know what happened. How did you get taken? Or did you get taken?"

"You know those early Canadas? The way I came onto them, there was this old guy up in Jacksonville, he—"

"Hirsh!"

"Okay, I'm sorry. They were switched."

"What do you mean?"

"I mean what I said! Sprenger did a lot of business with me. A *lot!* I had to really hustle to find the right stuff. I know the figure by heart. Call it nineteen months. Three hundred and ninety-five thousand. My ten percent on top of that. Four hundred and thirty-four thousand five hundred, that's what he has in it. Cash every six to eight weeks. Right now I've got about nineteen hundred and fifty dollars of his money to spend. It can't come out perfectly even, right?"

"It was switched, you say?"

"Let me show you something," he said. He got up and trotted out of the office into the store and came back in a few minutes and closed the door again. He put a slim, handsome album in front of me. It was in a black, fiber, dust case. The album was of padded blue imitation leather. The pages had transparent slots for stamps, and Mylar interleafing.

"This is a brand made abroad. Lighthouse. Same color and size as Sprenger's. I provide it, after making the first investment. Right here on the front bottom corner, in gold, his book says Frank A. Sprenger. I get it done at the luggage place in the next block. This size fits nice in a middle-size safety deposit box. Here is the procedure. I buy something for Sprenger's account. Mary Alice keeps the records on the investment accounts. Mary Alice McDermit. Missus, but separated. She's been with me almost five years. Very sharp girl. Okay, I turn the item over to her, and she fixes up a Hawid or a Showguard mount or mounts and posts the price from the invoice in the ledger, on the page for Sprenger's account. She puts the item in the safe, and then when Sprenger can meet me at the bank, Mary Alice comes along too, and we take the box into one of the bigger rooms where there is room for three to sit down at a table. I show Sprenger what I bought for him and answer questions if he has any, and Mary Alice puts the item or items in the album just like this one as we sit there. Then it goes back in the box, and we get an attendant, and it gets locked into the hole in the wall and we leave."

"He comes alone?"

"He comes alone into the bank. Yes. There is usually somebody else in his car."

"The stamps were switched?"

"Listen. Almost two weeks ago, the seventh. Thursday. He was able to make it at eleven in the morning. I walked over with Mary Alice. I had some Zepps and some early colonials. Barbados and Bermuda. Solid investment stuff. Thirty-three thousand worth. Too much to keep here. Okay, it was like always. We went in. I showed him what I had. No questions. Mary Alice put them in the stock book. She wondered if she should put the Barbados on an earlier page with other Barbados. She looked back at that page. She had to turn some pages to find what she wanted. I got a look at the pages. Meyer, like I told you, I thought my heart was going to stop. I've got eyes like an eagle. Fifty years I've been looking at stamps. Across a room a diamond dealer can tell a good stone. Right? I'd bought prime merchandise for Sprenger. And I am looking at junk. It is not so obvious Mary Alice could tell. Sprenger couldn't tell in a year. What am I looking at? Bad centering. Some toning and staining. Some pulled perfs. Instead of very fine to superb, I am looking at good space fillers, if that. I felt for a minute like the room was spinning. What saved me, I didn't have any breath to say anything. Then my mind is racing, and I get hold of myself. When Mary Alice has put the new buys in, I take the stock book and leaf through it, saying something about Sprenger will never be sorry he made the investment. It is worse than I thought. Blocks reassembled from singles. Repairs. Scratches. Little stains. Not counting what Mary Alice had just put in, I had bought three hundred and sixty-two thousand dollars worth of standard classics. Mostly superb condition. Total catalog would run maybe three hundred and twenty-five. I was looking at stuff that was one fifth and one sixth and one tenth catalog anywhere. Sixty-five thousand at the best. Somehow I got the strength to walk out of there on my own legs. You think I've had a night's sleep since then?"

Meyer said, "Hirsh got in touch with me."

"It had been too long since I saw you last," Fedderman said. "What is the matter with the world? Old friends don't see each other. What I wanted, Meyer, was to borrow your mind. Such a logical mind! I get excited, and I can't think two and two."

"I listened to the story," Meyer said, "and it made me wonder if Frank Sprenger might be the kind of barracuda who'd steal his own property and make Hirsh pay him for the loss. The deposit box is in a busy bank. Hirsh here is not an unusual type. His signature isn't complex or ornate. Sprenger would know the way Hirsh usually greeted the different vault attendants. Sprenger had an inventory list of everything in the investment collection. I asked Hirsh if defective duplicates would be hard to find. He said some of them would take awhile, mostly no. So it began to seem plausible that Sprenger had somebody accumulate the same items, and then they went to the bank together and switched, took the good ones out of the stock book, and put the defective ones in. Somebody successfully passed as Hirsh Fedderman."

"You like that assumption?" I asked Meyer.

"I don't like it any better than you do. It is a very touchy thing. Hirsh goes there often. Somebody gets uneasy and steps on the silent alarm, and Frank Sprenger is in a special kind of trouble. Anyway, it didn't happen."

"Vault records?" I asked.

Fedderman beamed at me approvingly. "I keep a careful record of every time I go to the vault. I made a list. I went to see my friend Mr. Dobson and gave him the list and asked him to find out if I'd been there more times than on the list, because maybe I had forgotten to write down a visit, and that's why my inventory was sort of messed up. There was no extra visit at all."

"And your next guess?" I asked Meyer.

"Hirsh's practice is to turn the items over to Mary Alice McDermit. She keeps the records, puts the items in mounts. I suggested the switch took place in this shop, item by item, before they even got to the bank. Hirsh went up in blue smoke."

"Not her. Believe me! Anyway, I always personally showed the new items to Sprenger. I couldn't help seeing if they had turned to some kind of junk. Could she make the switch right there in front of both of us? No! A stock book like this one has double-sided pages. It holds a lot. Here is the inventory list. To add up to that much without buying well-known pieces, there are almost seven hundred items. No. That's ridiculous. Even if she wanted to do it, there's no way."

"Next guess?" I asked Meyer.

"The next thing was try to talk you into taking a look. You said no. Today you said yes."

I frowned at Fedderman. "What happens if Sprenger decides to ask you for cash money, according to your agreement?"

"Don't even say it out loud! I have to find four hundred and fifty thousand. Where? I can sell out my investments. I can empty the bank account. I can borrow. I can liquidate inventory. Maybe I can make it. Then I can get some salvage from that junk, pay back the loan. Maybe I end up naked like the day I was born."

"What if he wanted to cancel and the stamps hadn't been switched?"

"No problem. You have no idea how hungry the auction houses are for prime merchandise. I could borrow, interest free, seventy-five percent of anticipated auction prices. That would be close to four hundred. I would come out ahead on the whole deal. The older an investment account is, the better off I am if the client wants out. If a client wanted out, I would have to advise him he'd be better off selling the items on the open market. I'd handle that for him without commission. It's part of the agreement. I'd get him the best price around."

"When did you look through that stock book previously, Hirsh? Can you pinpoint a date when everything was in order?"

"I tried. Four times this year I met Sprenger there. February, May, July, September. It was in February, or it was November last year, I looked through the book. Everything looked good. I think it was February, but I can't be sure."

"So . . . it couldn't happen, but it did."

"I . . . I just don't know what I . . ." His voice got shaky. His face started to break up, and he brought it under control, but for a moment I could see just how he had looked when he had been a boy.

"I'll think about it and let you know," I told him. It wasn't what I had opened my mouth to say. Meyer knew that. Meyer looked startled and pleased.

Three

Meyer and I strolled through the golden sunshine of evening, and through the residual stink of the rush-hour traffic, now considerably thinned out. We walked a half-dozen blocks to a small, dark bar in an old hotel. Elderly local businessmen drank solemnly, standing along the bar, playing poker dice for the drinks. At first glance they looked like an important group, like the power structure. But as eyes adjusted to the dimness after the hot brightness outside, the ruddiness became broken veins, collars were frayed and dingy, suits cut in outmoded style, the cigar smoke cheap, the drinks especially priced for the cocktail hour.

They talked about the market and the elections. Maybe once upon a time it had been meaningful. They had probably met here when they had worked in the area, when the area had been important, when the hotel had been shining new. So now they came in from their retirement at this time of day, dressing for the part, to nurse a couple of sixty-cent drinks and find out who had died and who was dying.

We carried our drinks over to a table under a tile mural of an improbable orange tree.

"So Fedderman got in a bind, a bad one, and he took Sprenger's money and bought junk and pocketed the difference," I said. "All along he knows there is going to be a day of reckoning, and because Frank Sprenger sounds hard case, it could be a very dirty day. If, by getting help, he can give himself the look of being a victim, he could save his skin."

Meyer smiled. "I went down that road. It doesn't go anywhere. Not because he is an honest man, which I think he is, but because he is a bright man. He buys for old customers, not under any special agreement. They take his word on authenticity. He could slip junk into those collections, and there would be no recourse against him. He is bright enough to know that you don't fool around with the Frank Sprengers of this world. Maybe you shouldn't deal with them at all. He rationalizes by saying that what he does is honest. He likes action. Sprenger is a lot of action. Fedderman likes having big pieces of money to invest. He likes phoning London and talking to his friends at Stanley Gibbons."

"How do you know him?"

"Ten years ago I invented an economic indicator I called the Hedge Index. Activity in works of art, antiques, gold, silver, coins, rare stamps. I felt it could be done on a sampling basis. Fedderman was one of the people who agreed to help. He was absolutely candid. No tricks, no lies, no exaggerations. When I had the bugs ironed out, I ran the index for two years and then published a partial report. There was a direct correlation between rate of inflation and hedge activity, with the hedge activity being a lead indicator of major rises in the announced cost of living by about ninety days. It's been picked up by the big boys and refined. I wanted the kind of built-in warning they used to have in France. When the peasants started buying gold and hiding it, you knew the storms were coming."

"Are they coming, O Great Seer?"

"What do you think we are standing out in the middle of with neither spoon nor paddle? Anyway, I've dropped in on Hirsh when I've been in the neighborhood ever since I gave up running the index. I said something to him once about having a friend in the salvage business. It was in connection with a customer whose valuable collection had been stolen. That's why he phoned me when this came up."

"If he's such a specialist and so bright, why isn't he rich?"

"He's seventy-two years old. His wife died of cancer twenty years ago. He gives a lot of money for cancer research. Both his sons emigrated to Israel and married there. He has seven, I think, grandchildren. He visits once a year. He gives to Jewish Relief, Bonds for Israel. He's set up an educational insurance policy for each grandchild. He's big in the temple. Special work and special gifts. He runs the store because he likes it. He's used to it. His work is his hobby. He's very proud of his reputation for fair dealing. He's proud of having so many good friends scattered around the country. He overpays his help. He lives in an apartment hotel, so called. He knows everybody within four blocks of his store in any direction. Why isn't he rich? I think maybe he's as rich as he wants to be."

"Maybe he ought to sell the business and retire and leave for Israel next week."

"That's the last thing Hirsh would ever do."

"If he could do it, he would have already done it."

"Right."

A huge old man came lumbering over to our table. "Don't tell me," he said. He bent over and peered into my face. "Don't tell me. You were six years witha Steelers. Then you got traded to the Eagles. This your second year witha Dolphins, right? Like fourteen years in pro ball. You lost the speed, and you're not as big as the ones coming up, but you got the cutes, boy. You got the smarts. You got those great patterns and those great fakes. In a minute I'll come up with your name. You'll see. Who's this with you?"

"One of the trainers."

"Trainer, eh? Good! Worse thing you can do is consort with a known gambler, right? They'll throw your ass out of the league."

When he reached for a nearby chair, I stood up quickly and said, "Nice to meet a knowledgeable fan, sir. See you around."

"Any minute now I'll remember your name, fella."

"Want some help?"

"No. I don't need any help. I know you good."

The sun was gone when we went out into the muggy evening. Meyer sighed as we started toward the parking place and said, "You look like a hero, and I look like a known gambler."

"Nature plays fair. You're the one with the good head."

"The good head says you are going to try to get a line on Sprenger first."

In September the Amalgamated Lepers of Eurasia could negotiate special convention rates at any one of fifteen brassy hostelries along Collins Avenue. Bellhops even smile when tipped.

I found a handy spot for old Miss Agnes and told Meyer to be patient. I could work it better alone, and it might mean several hotel lounges before I could put anything together. I tried the Fountainbleu first, that epic piece of decor a *Saturday Evening Post* journalist once described as looking like "an enormous dental plate."

When my eyes were used to the gloom, I spotted a bar waitress who used to be at the Eden Roc. Kay. Nice eyes, big smile, fat legs.

"Hey, where you been hiding, McGee?"

"What are you doing working here?"

"Oh, I run into kind of a personal problem the other place. It was better I should try another place. It's okay here."

"How are the twins?"

"In the second grade! Would you believe?"

"I bet they're beautiful."

"They are, if I say so myself, but they're hellers. Look, I got to go take care of my station."

"Come back when you get a chance. I want to ask you something."

"Sure."

When she came back to the bar and touched me on the shoulder, I turned on the stool and said, "I was trying to get a reading on somebody. I was looking for somebody like Brownie."

She leaned warmth against the side of my thigh and said, "I know. But they say he's dead."

"How long?"

"A year, maybe. He just stopped showing, and when somebody checked his place, there was nothing there. So nobody got a postcard even, and they say he was dropped in the ocean, and somebody cleaned his place out so it would look like he left. Maybe he had too many readings on people. You know."

"Is Willy still over at the Contessa?"

"Sure. He knows all, that guy. But he won't say."

"Maybe he owes me one."

"If he does, he won't remember. You know how he is."

"I'll give it a try."

"You come back, hear? I'm off at nine tonight."

"Wish I could, Kay. I really do. But this one is priority."

The desk tried to brush me off. I told the cold-eyed old man to check with Mr. Nucci before he made it final. He went over and murmured into the phone, studying me as he talked. He hung up and came over and told me that if I would go to the Winner's Circle Bar, Mr. Nucci would join me there in a few minutes.

It was more like twenty minutes before he slipped onto the stool beside mine. He wore a brown denim suit with lots of pockets and ropes and zippers, and a yellow velvet shirt, open to the umbilicus. His face was bland-brown, hairless as his brown smooth chest. Sleepy eyes, languid manner, a thin little mouth, like a newborn shark.

Willy Nucci started as a bus boy and now owns more points in the Contessa than anyone else. This is an unlikely Horatio Alger story along the oceanfront. He managed it by making various pressure groups believe he was fronting for other, just as deadly, pressure groups. He did it by expert intelligence work, brass, guile, persistence, and hard work. Nearly everyone thinks he is a front for New Jersey money, money that comes down to be dry-cleaned and flown back or flown abroad. I am one of the very few people who know Willy is clean and that he owns the biggest piece of the hotel. Maybe the IRS knows.

The motif of the bar is horse. Everything except saddle horns on the bar stools. In season it is a good place for the winners to spend and the losers to cry.

"I kept you waiting," Willie said in a flat voice. Statement of fact. I nodded. Silence is the best gambit with Willy Nucci, because it is one of his useful weapons. He makes people edgy by saying nothing. It's always handy to use the other man's tricks, because he never knows if he is being mocked.

I outwaited him, and finally he said, "It's your dime, McGee."

"Look at the edge of my glass."

He leaned toward it, tilting his head, and saw the little pale pink smear of stale lipstick. He called the barman over and chewed him in a small terrible voice. The man swayed and looked sweaty. He brought me a new drink, delivering it with a flourish and a look of splendid hatred.

"What else is bothering you?" Willy asked.

"I have a name, an address, a description, and I want a fill-in."

"I don't know many people anymore. The Beach keeps changing."

"You *have* to know, Willy."

"All I *have* to do is run this place and turn a dime on it for the owners."

"Willy?"

He gave me a quick, sidelong glance. Silence. A barely audible sigh.

"Willy, there is a young lady with a lot of energy on the paper in Lauderdale, and she keeps after me, saying she wants human interest stories about playtown, USA. She digs pretty good. She knows how to use courthouse records."

He got up slowly, looking tired. "Come on, damn you."

We went out past the guard and the empty pool and up the stairs to the roof of the cabana row of the Contessa Hotel. These are the days of exotic bugs, induction mikes, shotgun mikes. People like Willy Nucci talk in the open, at night, near surf roar or traffic roar. Or they rent cars and turn the radio volume high and drive around and talk. They never say anything useful over the phone, and they put in writing the bare minimum information required by the various laws and regulatory agencies.

We crossed the recreation roof to the ocean side and stood side by side, leaning on the railing. Freighters were working south, inside the stream. The sleepy ocean whacked listlessly at the little bit of remaining beach, with a little green-white glow of phosphorescence where it tumbled.

In my Frank McGee voice instead of my Travis McGee voice, I said, "When Willy Nucci quietly acquired his first small percentage of the Contessa Hotel, it was laboring under the crushing burden of a sixth and a seventh mortgage. Today, hiding behind a bewildering maze of legal stratagems, Mr. Nucci is not only the principal owner, but he has managed to pay off most of the indebtedness—"

He responded, his voice rising with exasperation. "Look. Okay. I wanted to tell *somebody*. I wanted to brag. We had a lot of time and nothing to do, and neither one of us figured we had a chance of getting out of there once it was daylight and they could use those goddamn rifles."

"Wouldn't you like other people to know?"

He calmed down. "Sure I would. But it would cost me. I get nibbled pretty good. The unions, the assessments, the graft, the public servants on the take, the gifts you make like insurance premiums. But there's restraint. They have the idea that if the bite gets too big, some very important muscle is going to come down here and straighten some people out. If they knew it was just Willy Nucci, owner and operator, there would be a big grin, and they'd smack their lips and move in very tight and close. I don't have much margin to play with. I've got sixteen years invested. The books look good right now. Last season was good, and this one will be better. You might as well know this too. I'm going to try to move it this season. I can come out well. And cut out of here. How come I always run off at the mouth to you, McGee?"

"I win friends and influence people."

He frowned at his private piece of ocean. "You could have used what you know, but you haven't. Except you use it to leverage me."

"Not often."

"I make this the third time. In three years. Maybe this time I can't help you."

"The man is big and broad and suntanned. Officially or

unofficially, he's in a penthouse at the Seascape. He moves around with some fetch-and-carry people. Frank Sprenger."

Silence. He pinched the bridge of his nose. He looked up at murky stars.

"Willy?"

"I don't know how much you know about the way things are. For all I know you think that soft, romantic crock of shit, *The Godfather,* was for real."

"I thought it was real, like a John Wayne western."

"There's hope for you. All the action is divided up. There are independents, and when they get big enough, they are absorbed or smashed. There are three neutral areas. Places where anybody can go who is part of the national action and not get pressured. Sanctuaries. Miami, Vegas and Honolulu. There are hits sometimes, but outsiders, amateurs. Discipline situations. 'Do not crap in your own nest' is the motto. There's enough for everybody in the sanctuaries. That's how come you have maybe nine different groups from elsewhere, owning lots of pieces of property and pieces of action along the Beach here. Like there are twelve groups operating side by side in Vegas. Other areas are strictly territorial. That's how come all the trouble in New York lately. Now suppose every one of the nine organizations operating here sent down their own bag men and bankers and enforcers? It would get too hairy. People would start pushing. People would push back. It would stop being a safe place for the topside people to come and relax, and it would hurt trade. So there's been a working arrangement for maybe thirty years. The local group has their own operations, like a franchise area, but you can see how it wouldn't be fair to cut the out-of-town groups out of the picture entirely because a certain substantial piece of business comes through their owning certain situations here."

"Example?"

"Okay, say that Minneapolis has substantial points in a couple of hotels and owns a steak house franchise and a taxi company. The local group will be scoring from every part of the operations. Hookers and games and drugs at the hotels on top of linen service, union dues, kickbacks, dozens of angles. And they will work the steak houses and the taxi company pretty good too. So it works almost like a money-room skim. The extra costs of doing business get built into the books as legitimate expenses, and then out of the unrecorded cash flow, an equal amount gets bundled up and couriered to Minneapolis. The profit is minimized, which cuts taxes, and the rebate is under the table, ready for more investment."

"And somebody has to be the bookkeeper and enforcer, somebody everybody agrees on, to see that the skim is honest?"

"For the last six years, Frank Sprenger. Phoenix. Before that it was Bunny Golder, for years and years. He died of a stroke. I heard that some kinky girlfriend got him smashed and then ran a sharpened piano wire into his brain through the corner of his eye, but nobody ran an autopsy to check it out."

"What is Sprenger like?"

"I'll tell you what he's like. He's like exactly the right man for the job. He doesn't use anything, not even booze or tobacco or coffee. He's a body freak. Not muscle building. Conditioning. He lives like a good heavyweight six weeks away from a title shot. Except for women. He takes care of more than his share. He spends a lot of time cross-checking the action. He's found some people clipping off a little as the money went by them, and they are not seen around anymore. I hear the local group has stopped trying to con him, because it isn't safe or healthy."

"What's his cover?"

"Investment consultant. He has a second-floor office on Lincoln Road. He's in the yellow pages. He pays his taxes. I think maybe he has some legitimate clients. He's a careful man."

I waited until I thought of the right kind of hypothetical question. "Willy, I want you to listen to some stuff I am going to make up and tell me if it could happen. Let's say that in the past year and a half Frank Sprenger has been buying important paintings. He has been using an expert and paying a fee for his judgment. Four hundred thousand worth of art. It's been going into a storage warehouse. Possible?"

"Sure," Willy said. "Especially if it's on a cash basis."

"Say it is."

"Money makes more problems every day. You hear how they want banks to report everything over five thousand? Now they are beginning to crack the Swiss and get the numbers. The islands used to be good, but what's going to happen to the Bahamas, the Caymans, Jamaica the next couple of years? It's very hard to set up a corporation and feed cash into it in such a way you can get past an audit. You put cash in a jar in your back yard, it isn't working for you. It's shrinking all the time it's buried. Dry-cleaning money gets more expensive all the time. One way they are using lately is you buy yourself a broker, one who'll fake back records for the sake of the commission and a little present. Then you set up a buy five years ago for something that has gone up like eight hundred percent. Then you have the sale records faked too and pay capital gains, and what you have left is legitimate and you can invest it legitimate. You have to be your own fence, for God's sake. So why not paintings? I like it. He would be handling it for one of the out-of-town groups or individuals. He handles investment money right here. The local group has legal talent he can use. Raw land has been good. Pieces of home-building outfits have been good. In-and-out marinas have been good."

"How much would he be supervising in a year? I mean, how much would the total skim be, the amount he'd be watching?"

"McGee, this has to be absolutely horseback. I could be off, way way off."

"Take a guess."

"Well . . . working it backward and saying that the total take for the Florida group in this area is seventy-five million with fifteen million expenses, and maybe twenty-five percent of the net is reimbursed on account of special ownership . . . Sprenger keeps an eye on maybe fifteen million."

"And *invests* that much?"

"Oh, hell no! The groups mostly have got their own way of handling a cash rebate. It goes back by messenger. Frank might have to find a home down here for one mil, or one and a half, or even two."

"Okay. Now here is the final suppose. Suppose that right now all those paintings in that bonded warehouse are fake."

He snapped his head around, eyes wide open for the

first time that evening. "You have some weird sense of fun there, McGee."

"Think out loud."

"Well . . . Sprenger wouldn't know it. He wouldn't get into that kind of a con. Unless, of course, he had orders to spoil somebody's day. But I don't think they'd use him for that. He's too good doing what he does. Okay. Sprenger doesn't know. Then he's dead."

"Literally?"

"Literally. Because there are only two choices when the news gets out. Sprenger is either getting cute or getting stupid. And they can't take a chance either way. The only reverse leverage he has is what he knows. So he has to be taken dead before he can get a chance to use it. It's a standard risk. A man like Sprenger makes as much money as the president of Eastman Kodak. He accepts the occupational risk. If he goofs, he gets more than fired. And if he goofs and has any small chance of covering himself before the news gets out, he would gut his brother, peddle his sister and feed his father and his godfather to alligators, a hunk at a time, to earn that small chance."

"Why are you so sure Sprenger will do what he's told to do?"

"Where have you been? They never let anybody close to the money unless they've got a good lock on him. Sprenger will always be some kind of errand boy. Somewhere there is something in writing or on tape or on film that some prosecutor can't ignore. Like with the talent they own. Nobody goes looking for a new manager if the one you already have owns your ass."

In silence he looked down at the eroded beach. He said dolefully, "They want to pump umpty-seven billion yards of sand in front of all the hotels, a big beach like in 1919 they had. Bond issues, big assessments, more taxes, just so all the clowns can go parading by on public beach land for maybe two years before a hurricane takes it all back out to sea. And after next season this old crock hotel will need a quarter mil of maintenance and redecorating. With luck I'm out by April."

"Willy?"

"Uh?"

"You've got me wondering. You have to get a rebate from Sprenger."

"I should sidestep it and give up the edge?"

"But how?"

"Maybe there is a little spin-off group of like investors in St. Louis, and maybe they have sixteen points. So a hundred percent of the skim goes there, and they take twenty-two percent instead of sixteen, in return for running it in and out of some accounts before it ends up in something which could be called maybe Acme Management Associates or Scranton Development Corporation."

"Which could be you?"

"Not entirely, but mostly. There's no other way I can go and still make out. You can't fight the establishment."

"Funny thing to call it."

"Why? It's the way things are. They put a night bell captain on. I don't have to pay him a dime. What's your pleasure? Hash-candy from Calcutta? A Greek virgin? Table-stakes poker? Cuban cigars? A quick abortion? Mexican gold? An albino dwarf? If you can afford the ticket, you've got it. I can't get rid of him. The cops probably know he's dealing. But if they charge him, if the case is airtight, it still goes all the way to jury, and after the jury is picked, it takes two phone calls. Or three. Cash money if you vote to acquit, Pancho. And if Alfred gets convicted, you'll come home from work some day and find something that'll give you a weak stomach the rest of your life. Who stands up to that? Nobody. The klutz with no connections cops a plea, and they process him into the slammer. Alfred, my special employee, will never do a day of time unless he gets smartass and they want to settle him down. Nobody really gives a goddamn anymore, McGee. Everybody wants to keep his own ass safe from harm." He paused and made a sound which was like a suppressed gag. Maybe it was laughter. I'd never heard Willy Nucci laugh before, so I couldn't tell. "Even me," he said. "Especially me."

Four

I felt guilty about leaving Meyer alone for so long. I had no way of knowing Willy was going to make ZsaZsa sound like a mute. I always feel guilty when I keep Meyer waiting. And there is never any need for it. He never paces up and down, checking the time. He has those places to go, inside his head. He looks as if he was sitting and dozing, fingers laced across his middle. Actually he has walked back into his head, where there are libraries, concert halls, work rooms, experimental laboratories, game rooms. He can listen to a fine string quartet, solve chess problems, write an essay on Chilean inflation under Allende, or compose haiku. He had a fine time back in there. If you could put his head in a jar of nutrient and keep him alive forever, he would wear forever that gentle, contented little smile.

He came reluctantly back to the lesser reality of here and now and, as I drove north up A-1-A, he told me he had a confrontation with urchins. They had a needle-sharp icepick and thought a protection price of five dollars per tire was a good place to start the bargaining.

"We had a nice conversation," Meyer said.

"You had a nice conversation."

"I told them that theirs was a profession mentioned in the first writings of mankind over thirty centuries ago. Roving bands of barbarians would demand that a village pay tribute, or they would sack it."

"They listened to the lecture?"

"A discussion, not a lecture. Questions and answers. There is a parallel, of course, in Vietnam, where the Viet Cong would spare villages in return for food, shelter, and information. And I told them about the Barbary pirates extracting tribute from our merchant vessels. Then they went away finally. After they were gone, I remembered we hadn't decided on any dollar figure. I guess they forgot."

"Three of them,"

"Age twelve, thirteen, and fourteen."

"Meyer, did it ever occur to you that one of those half-size hoodlums could have shoved an icepick into you?"

I could sense he was genuinely startled and upset. "Into me? But why?"

Why indeed? Conversely, why not? I don't know exactly what it is about Meyer. Sometimes, for fun, when we have been at someone's home, I have seen him do his St. Francis bit, when there has been a bird feeder visible from a window. Meyer goes and stands a few feet from the feeder. The birds come back. They look him over. They talk about him. And in a few minutes they start landing on him. Once when we took a runover dog to a veterinarian, the man told Meyer he had good hands. Meyer could hold the dog still. It snapped at the doctor. I have been on the beach with Meyer and five hundred people and had a frantic girl run directly to Meyer to tell him she was hallucinating and please help me, please. It is a rare attribute, but not all that rare. Lots of people have it in varying degrees. Maybe it is an echo of the remote past when we all lived in the peaceable kingdom. We should find out what it is, how to increase the aptitude, how to teach it to others. It is symptomatic of our times that no one is studying this wild card, nobody thinks it important. In an icepick world, any kind of immunity is crucially important. Any avenue of loving kindness needs some directional signs.

I went up A-1-A looking for a place I had not been to in a long time. Meyer had never been there. It was near Hallandale. I know I made the right turn. I cruised a few blocks. Everything looked strange. I put my old electric blue pickup truck next to a gas island where electronic pumps squatted like skeptical Martians. After extravagant admiration, and several questions about Miss Agnes, the attendant let me ask my question.

"Huh? Oh sure. Hell, it's been maybe two years. That old house was right down there where that big red and white chicken is flapping its wings. Chicky-Land. Let me see. It was Rosa and . . . and . . ."

"Vito."

"Right! I took the old lady there plenty of times on special occasions. They could handle maybe twenty-four people, tops. Reservations only. You never knew what you'd get for dinner, but by God it was always delicious and always more than you could eat. They treated you like guests in their home."

"What happened?"

He frowned as he cleaned the high windshield. "Something about the zoning and all. They started giving them fits. Rewire the place, then redo the plumbing, then put in some kind of sprinkler system. Then change the kitchen over somehow. They say somebody wanted that land. Every time something had to be done, they'd have to close until it was all okay and approved. Then Rosa had some kind of breakdown, and Vito went down to a meeting and broke the nose on one of the commissioners. They jailed him, but some of his old customers with clout got him out and got it all quieted down. They went away someplace. I heard one of the commissioners was in the group that bought up that whole two blocks for the shopping plaza and Chicky-Land."

"If you wanted to find a meal that good right now, where would you go?" I asked him.

He took my money and made change as he thought it over. Finally he said, "Damn if we just don't eat that good anymore anywhere. Funny, sort of. Big, rich country like this. Everything starting to taste like stale sawdust. Maybe it's just me."

"We are all living in chicky land," I told him.

Back in the car, heading home, I told Meyer about the little sculpture garden Vito and Rosa Grimaldi had fixed up. White cement statues of swooning maidens and oddly proportioned animals. With a dozen complicated floodlights which all kept changing color, focused on the statuary and the three small fountains and the plantings. "So incredibly vulgar, it was somehow very touching."

"As vulgar as that big red and white electric chicken?"

Meyer is often unanswerable, an annoying habit.

We ate in one of the less offensive steak houses, at a table made from an imitation, wooden hatch cover. They are sawing down forests, strapping thick green planks together with rusty iron, beating hell out of them with chains and crowbars, dipping them in a dark muddy stain, then covering the whole thing with indestructible transparent polymer about a quarter inch thick. Instant artifact.

We talked our way up, over, across and around the Sprenger situation, after I had given him the Willy Nucci perspective.

It was agreed that Sprenger had the contacts to get an accurate reading on Hirsh Fedderman before opening negotiations. So it was possible that he could have set Hirsh up, that by devising a way of switching the rarities, he had invented a way of doubling his money. The stuff had a ready market. And Hirsh would pay instead of run. But it did not seem to be Sprenger's style, even without knowing the man. If he wanted to play tricks and games, wouldn't he rather play them in his own jungle?

We decided that if we could figure out how the switch had been made—and that might involve walking Hirsh and Miss Mary Alice through a typical bank visit complete with philatelic props—it might be possible to work backward from the method to the conniver.

Which would mean letting Mary Alice McDermit know for the first time that important stuff was missing.

"I'd say she's about twenty-seven," Meyer told me. "One of those big, slow, sweet, gentle girls. You know the type? Dark hair, fair skin, blue eyes, expression always on the edge of a smile. A beautiful disposition. Five years with Hirsh. I think I heard him say the other woman had been there fifteen years. She would be close to forty. Jane Lawson. A service widow. Teenage kids, I think. Small woman, quick and cranky and very smart. I don't think Mary Alice has any children. I'm sure of it. She is separated from her husband. This is the way I read that store and the relationship. They are dependent on Hirsh and on the job. He pays them more than they could get elsewhere. So between them they make it up to him by making that little store pay off. It's kind of a family, the three of them. They take care of each other."

We both agreed that any frontal approach to Frank Sprenger had an unhealthy flavor. Nucci had marked him high for hard, high for smart. He was in a slot where he had to be suspicious of any approach from any direction.

Meyer came up with one faintly promising thought.

"Even though those aren't famous rarities he bought for Sprenger, not things any dealer would recognize on sight, maybe there is some kind of way of identifying them. I don't know enough about it. But did you notice that Philatelic Foundation certificate he showed us? There was a photograph glued to it, and an embossing seal used. If just one of those things can be traced . . ."

"There were numbers in the margin of those blocks of four and six he showed us."

"We need to know more about it, Travis."

"Do we?"

He leaned forward and peered at me very intently. "Hmmm. A kind of disapproval? That's what's bothered me most. Why should Travis McGee give a faint damn what happens to an elderly party who isn't too careful whom he deals with and inevitably gets stung? The desirable quality of shining innocence isn't there this time. And is it a total disaster? He has a place to go, people to look after him. You could get involved, but it would be going through motions."

"Sometimes it isn't any more than that."

"Are you saying no?"

"Not quite yet."

"But you might?"

"It is a distinct possibility."

He looked tired. He sighed. He pushed a piece of gristle around his plate and finally hid it under his potato skin. I caught the eye of the redcoat who had served us. He had saved up all his cordiality for the critical moment of check and tip. The service had been indifferent, the orders not quite correct. What do you do? If you are cross, tired, and immature, you take it out on the waiter. The world is not enhanced to any measurable degree by one, or by one million, confrontations with venal, lazy waiters. And it impedes the processes of digestion. So you compute the tip and leave in good order and try to remember never to return.

But it had been one more smear on an already dingy day. All day I had been trying not to think of the eviction notice. But it was in the back of my mind. Willy Nucci had depressed me more than I had been willing to admit. He wanted to get out, and he was not at all sure he could. So, out of accumulations of anxiety, he had talked and talked and talked. The old men in the old bar had depressed me. And children with icepicks are not amusing. And I wished I'd gone to eat at Grimaldis' when Vito and Rosa were in trouble. I might have been able to help. It was easy to see that I had a new remorse. It was one of the night thoughts of the future. If I had only . . . I have a long list of those.

After Meyer had gone to his home afloat, I made myself a hefty nightcap and turned the lights off and went up to the sundeck in a ratty old blue robe and sat at the topside controls, bare feet braced on the dew-damp mahogany. It was a soft night. Car lights, boat lights, dock lights, star light. Sound of traffic and sound of the sea. Smell of salt and smell of hydrocarbons. The *Flush* wind-swayed under me and nudged against a fender.

"Hey, McGee? McGee?" she called from the dock.

I got up and went aft and looked down at Jenny Thurston under the dock lights, in basque shirt, baggy shorts, baseball cap, and ragged boat shoes.

"Hey, is it really true?" she asked.

"Come on aboard. Want a drink?"

"I got most of this here can of beer, thanks."

She came up topside and took the other pilot chair, beside me, and swiveled it around to face me in the night. "I got back around five, and they showed me in the paper, and all of them were bitching about it. I looked for you to check it out."

"It's true enough, Jen."

"Well, goddamn them! Nobody is going to move me ashore, McGee. I was born on a boat. We'll have to find a place where they're not trying to iron everybody out flat. Maybe down in the Keys?"

"Maybe."

"But it won't be the same as here. Never."

Jenny lives aboard a roomy old Chris and paints aboard her. Jenny paints three paintings. One is of a beach with a long cresting wave, sandpipers, and overhanging palms. One is of gulls in the wind, teetering over the abandoned, stove-in hulk of an old dory on a rocky beach. The last is of six old pilings at low tide, with weed and barnacles on the exposed part, with four brown pelicans perched on individual pilings, and two more sailing in to land on the empty ones. She paints them in varying sizes and frames them in different styles, in order to have a useful range of prices. They all sell. They hang in untold hundreds of northern living rooms, all signed in the bottom right corner. Jennifer Thurston.

She is chunky, forthright, salty, and loyal to her friends. She paints as many paintings as she needs, in order to get along. She has pretty eyes and good legs. From time to time, sturdy young men move in with her, aboard the *West Bank.* The average tour of duty has been about three months. The old timers have learned to estimate the probable date of departure very accurately. They detect in the young man a certain listlessness, a sallowness, a general air of stupor.

So we sat in the night and talked about old times and people long gone. Sam Taggert. Nora Gardino. A girl named Skeeter. Puss Killian. Remember when . . . Hey, what about the time . . . Were you around when . . .

It was all nostalgia, sweet and sad, and it was good therapy. Sometimes you need that special kind of laughter.

I went down the ladderway with her and walked aft to the gangplank. I bent and kissed her and felt her mouth sweeten and flower under the pressure when she grabbed hold to make it last longer. She sighed as I straightened, and she said, "Sometimes I wisht I didn't have my rule about sleeping with my friends."

"A lot of the trouble in my life has come from not following your rule, Jen."

"It's always better when you don't have to give a damn."

"Take care of yourself."

"Let's try to see if we can find a place most of the old hands can tie up permanent. You know. Enough room and everything."

I watched her walk away. She slapped her old boat

shoes down with stumpy authority. Her hair had smelled fresh and sweet. I needed a lady to be happy with. Not that lady, though. It had been a long time between amiable ladies. Chauvinist pig yearning for new playtoy, new love object? Not so as you would hardly know it. Reverse of Jenny's dictum: It's always better when you give a damn. But how do you tell a genuine damn from one you muster up to justify tupping the wench? Well, you can tell. That's all. You can. And so can she. Unless, of course, she is just a female chauvinist pig yearning after you as a playtoy, a sex object, and drumming up *her* little rationalizations.

I dreamed about a lady I saw on one of those stamps. Antigua. 1863. Lady in profile in rosy mauve, with an elegant neck, a discreet crown on her pretty head. She turned with a half smile, looking out of the stamp at me, then shook her head, frowned, and said, "Oh, golly. *You* again, huh?"

Five

The First Atlantic Bank and Trust Company occupied the first two floors of its own office building on a noisy corner. The four of us walked from Fedderman's shop to the bank. Meyer walked ahead with Hirsh. I followed with Mary Alice McDermit. Anyone would probably mention that she was tall enough for me. In hardly any heels at all, she came close to six feet. It was a stifling Thursday morning. September can be a seething bitch in Miami. She wore some kind of sunback dress with about five inches of skirt. Maybe six inches. Her glossy black hair bounced to her free stride. Her fair skin had taken a tan the color of weak butterscotch. Her face had good bones, but it was slightly plump, and something about her expression and the way she dressed made me think of a very large twelve-year-old girl.

"I can't believe it," she kept saying. "I just can't *believe* it."

"Hirsh believes it. He got a good look two weeks ago today. The good stuff is gone, except what you put in that day."

"We knew something was awfully wrong. The way he's

been acting. Jane and I talked about it. We tried to find out from him. I just can't believe it."

It felt good to walk with a girl who matched my stride, nice brown knees alternating. Any kind of a close look and that twelve-year-old impression was gone all of a sudden.

She said, "It wasn't any of your really great stuff. You know. Like one-of-a-kind or tied to historical covers or anything. But it was all really first-class, high-catalog material, the kind you can depend on to hold value."

"You like futzing around with postage stamps?"

She gave me a blank, frowning look. "What do you futz around with, huh? Hitting an innocent little white ball with a long stick? Soldering wires together and playing four-track stereo? Slamming some dumb little car around corners, upshifting and downshifting? Are you a gun futz or a muscle futz?"

"I think I know where you're going with that."

"Where I'm going is that there's no list to tell you where you rate on some kind of scale of permanent values and find out how unimportant you are. But I can tell you what nobody ought to be doing."

"What's that?"

"Nobody ought to be sneering at anybody else's way of life."

"Mrs. McDermit?"

"Mmm?"

"Could we set our personal clock back and start over again?"

Her smile was bright, vivid, personal, merry. "Why, you dummy? We're getting along pretty remarkable."

"We are? Good."

"I like people. I really do. Here's the bank."

The safety deposit vault was in the back left corner. There were three people on duty there. Hirsh Fedderman signed the slip and put down the number of his own personal box. They let us all in, and had the three of us wait in the corridor off to the side which led to the private booths and little rooms. Hirsh joined us, with his box under his arm. The attendant led us back to one of the little rooms. There was a table, three chairs. The attendant said he would bring another chair. I told him thanks, not to bother.

The table was butted against the wall. It was narrower than a card table and about half again as long. They moved the chairs to where they had been in an identical little room on September seventh. As I stood with my back against the closed door, Hirsh and Mary Alice sat at the right, Mary Alice nearest me, facing Meyer across the table—Meyer, of course, representing Sprenger.

I said, "Try to make as exact a reconstruction as you can. I'll stop you if I have any questions."

Hirsh said, "I put the box right here, against the wall, nearest me, and I opened it like this and took the stock book out. Okay. Here is the stock book I brought, so . . ."

"Put it in the box and close the box and then take it out as you did before and do with it exactly what you did the other time."

Hirsh took it out and put it in front of Mary Alice and said, "Other clients, I hand them the book. They want to take a look at their money. Not Sprenger. I tried at first. He wouldn't take it. He'd just shrug."

Mary Alice said, "That was when I was taking the new purchases out of my purse, like this. And the inventory sheet. I gave the inventory sheet to Mr. Sprenger, and I put the new stamps, in their mounts, right here, where they would be handy for Mr. Fedderman."

"I took a copy of the list out of my pocket," Hirsh said. "I put it here in front of me, like this. Then I read off the items and found each one and showed it to Sprenger and then pushed it toward Mary Alice."

"By then," she said, "I'd taken the book out of the slip case and opened it up, and as Hirsh pushed them toward me, I would pick them up and slip them into the book like this, into these transparent strips. I used these tongs because you have to have something to lift the edge of the strip. The stamps were in mounts like this, so it was just because it's easier for me, not to protect the stamps, I used stamp tongs."

"Is that the same inventory list?" I asked.

"Exactly," she said. "And I fixed up the right number of mounts and the right size. But these stamps I just put in are junk from the new issue service."

"Go ahead just the way you did with him," I said.

Hirsh tried to smile. "I'd try to give a little spiel. Clients like it. I couldn't tell if Sprenger did or not. We never got loosened up with each other. He'd grunt. He always seemed bored, like I was taking too long. Okay. I'll say the sort of thing I said to Sprenger. It won't be exact, but it will be close."

I watched intently. I had them do a repeat of Mary Alice looking back through the book to see if there was room on a prior page to put the new Barbados stamps with the previous Barbados stamps. I had Hirsh take the book and leaf through it and give it back to Mary Alice. She put it in the fiber slip case and handed it to Hirsh. He opened the box and put the stock book in and closed the lid.

"Then I picked up the box and started to stand up, but he said he had some money. I thought he had it with him so I sat down, but he said he would be in touch and get it to me soon. I haven't seen it yet. We left the room. When I came out of the vault, he was gone. Mary Alice was waiting for me. We walked back to the store. Like always, I would have been kind of depressed. He never said, 'Very nice. Very pretty.' Nothing. You like people to take an interest. But I was too scared to be depressed. I was terrified. My head was spinning. I almost told this girl."

"You should have told me, Hirsh. Really."

"I should worry your pretty head with total disaster?"

She looked at me. "Did you see anything?"

"Nothing at all. Did you always do it that way?"

"Always," she said. "With him and the other clients too. Just like that. Except it's more fun with the others."

Meyer said, "Do either of you remember a distraction? Did anybody yell fire, drop anything, fall off a chair?"

They remembered nothing like that. They had been buoyed by a fragile hope. It seeped away. Hirsh went from looking sixty-two to looking ninety-two. Meyer was somber. The girl bit her thumb knuckle and blinked rapidly.

So we all got out of there. We went back to the shop. Jane Lawson looked at us with anxious query when we all walked in. Hirsh and Mary Alice shook their heads no. Jane looked bitterly depressed. An old man with hair like Brillo sat erect on a stool, using gold tongs with great deftness as, one by one, he examined stamps and replaced them in the stock book in front of him.

"Fedderman," he said, "everything here is perfectly ordinary, quite tiresome, exceedingly unremarkable."

"Colonel, if I had looked through them, I would have known that, right?"

"Yes, but—"

"And then if I told you I had not looked through them, I would be lying. Right? Believe me, that book is exactly the way I found it, in one of the cartons. If it's tiresome, I'm sorry."

"Huh!" said the Colonel.

"What?" asked Fedderman.

"Nothing. Nothing at all."

"Wait. You put this one back crooked. Let me help you. What do you know? Look, Mary Alice. A nice double surcharge on Canada C3. Doesn't that go pretty good?"

"Like about seventy dollars in Scott, Mr. Fedderman."

"See, Colonel? In the middle of all this junk, a nice little error. Let me see. Original gum. Never hinged. Nice centering. To you, Colonel, only forty dollars."

"Forty!"

"I know," said Mary Alice. "That surprises me too, sir. It ought to be fifty-five at least."

"Well . . . put it aside, dear girl," said the colonel.

They meshed smoothly and well, did Fedderman and Mary Alice. She went behind the counter. Meyer and I went back to Fedderman's office with him and closed the door.

"Now what?" Fedderman asked out of the depths of his despair.

"One thing I know," Meyer said. "The impossible doesn't ever happen. Only possible things happen."

"To me the impossible happens," said Fedderman.

"If it isn't you and it isn't Sprenger," Meyer said, "then it has to be Mary Alice."

"Impossible!"

"So we are comparing two impossible things, and it being Mary Alice is not quite as impossible as what happened."

"Maybe I follow you," Hirsh said. "My head hurts. I hurt all over. I'm coming down. I should be in bed with a pill."

"Did she bring that same purse," I asked Fedderman.

"Purse?"

"The one she had today is like a picnic basket made of straw painted white. Did she have the same purse the last time?"

"Yes. No. How should I know? There are five clients. What difference does it make?"

"I wish I knew *if* it made any difference. That junk you saw in the Sprenger collection. Could it have come out of your stock here in the store?"

"What I saw? Some of it, maybe. Very little. I didn't have long enough to study it, you understand. A dealer has a good memory for defective pieces. No, I'd say probably none of it from my stock, or I would have recognized one piece anyway. Besides, it was higher catalog value than what I stock here."

I remembered Meyer's interesting thought. "Hirsh," I asked, "suppose whoever switched the goods has sold the Sprenger items to the trade. Could you identify them?"

He thought, nodded, and gave me a show-and-tell answer. Once again the projection viewer came out. He put a slide box in place and in the darkened office clicked through a half-dozen slides and stopped at a block of four blue stamps imprinted "Graf Zeppelin" across the top. They were a two-dollar-and-sixty-cent denomination.

"This is one I picked up for Sprenger. It was in a Mozian auction catalog last year. It is absolutely superb, and I had to go to fourteen hundred for it. I take an Ektachrome-X transparency of everything I put in an investment account. I use a medical Nikon, and I keep it right here on this mount. Built-in flash. Now you see where the perforations cross in the middle of the block, those little holes? They make a certain pattern. Distinctive. Maybe unique? Not quite. Now look out at the corners. See this top left corner? That paper between the perforations, right on the corner, is so long, it looks as if maybe there was a pulled perforation on the stamp that was up here, in the original sheet. Okay, add that corner to the pattern in the middle, and it *is* unique. Any dealer could look at this slide, go through a couple dozen blocks and pick this one out with no trouble. Individual stamps would be a lot harder, especially perforated. Imperforate, usually they are cut so the margins are something you can recognize. Of course, postally used stuff, old stuff, the cancellation is unique."

As he put his toys away, I said, "Could you get prints made from the slides of the most valuable items and circulate them to your friends in the trade?"

"A waste of time and money. These days, believe me, there are more stamp collections being ripped off than ever in history. Information comes in all the time. Watch for this, watch for that. Hoodlums come in here to the store, and they tell me their uncle left them some stamps in an album, do I want to take a look, maybe buy them? I say I've got all the stock I want. They'll find people who'll buy. But not me. I don't need the grief. After fifty years in the business, I should be a fence? Am I going to look at the stamps the hoodlum brings in and call a cop? Who needs a gasoline bomb through the front door?"

"Then there's no way?" Meyer asked.

Fedderman sighed. "If all that stuff goes back into circulation, a lot of those pieces *have* to find their way into the auction houses. Every catalog, there are pictures of the best pieces. Like if there are two thousand lots listed in the catalog, there could be a hundred photographs of the best items. One day last week I sat in here, I went through a couple dozen catalogs to try to spot any item from the Sprenger account. H. R. Harmer, Harmer, Rooke and Company, Schiff, Herst, Mozian, Siegel, Apfelbaum. Nothing."

"Oh," said Meyer, his disappointment obvious.

"I think I am going home to bed, the way I feel," Fedderman said. "What are you fellows going to do now?"

I said, "I am going to get Mary Alice to help me."

"How do you mean?" Hirsh asked.

"If she knows more than she's told us, the only thing she can do is play along with me."

"But that kind of person," Hirsh said, "she would help if you ask. It wouldn't prove anything."

"Suppose I get to the point where I ask something or do something which would make her back away fast if she was innocent, and she doesn't back away?"

He stared at me, uneasy and upset. "She is a good person. She isn't used to anything rough."

"Rough?" I asked him.

"No offense," he said.

Meyer said, "You look terrible, Hirsh. Travis will drive you home."

"It's not even as far as the bank, but the other way. So I can't walk it?"

"I'll walk with you," Meyer said.

"Why should you bother?"

"Why shouldn't I?"

On the way out through the store, by prearrangement, Hirsh told his two ladies that Mr. Travis McGee was going to do what he could to help out in this terrible situation, and he would appreciate it if they would answer questions and show him things and so on. Meyer told me he would go his own way, do a little research maybe, take a bus probably, and see me at Bahia Mar.

Six

Jane Lawson went off on her lunch break about fifteen minutes after Meyer and Hirsh left. A man came in to buy a beginner's stamp-collecting outfit for his son's birthday. I imitated a browser, leafing through big glassine pages on a countertop easel, looking at incredibly florid stamps from improbable countries, like Ajman, Zambia, and Bangladesh.

I liked the way Mary Alice handled the customer. She was plugging an outfit which, with stamps, album, manual, hinges, and so on, came to $24.95. The man finally said he couldn't go over fifteen dollars. She told him there was a $14.95 kit, but she could assemble something better for him. She took items from stock, added them up, and told him it came to $14.50. Then she threw in another packet of stamps as a birthday present from Mr. Fedderman. She did not patronize the man. She made it seem like a better deal than the more expensive spread.

The narrow store seemed jammed full of merchandise in a bewildering confusion. But as I got used to it, I could see there was a logical order to the storage and display, and see that everything was bright and clean.

After the man left, she moved over to where I stood at the counter and said, "It's sort of a policy in the trade, you know, to encourage kids to collect. But look at what some of these countries are doing. This stuff is just a bunch of . . . gummed labels. And they grind it out in such millions, they'll never be worth more than what they're worth this minute. I've told Hirsh I wish they'd all get together and boycott the countries that take advantage." She turned a page. "Look here. This is a new issue for Grenada; it's an island near Trinidad that used to be part of the British Empire. They've got a contract with some company that grinds out stamps and sends a few of them to Grenada for postal use and sends the rest directly to dealers like us and splits the profit with the government in Grenada. It's just a racket. Gee, I guess we're no better. Our government encourages collectors. Every stamp that isn't used means no postal service is required, so it's practically all profit. People buy all the commemoratives as they come out, in whole sheets and tuck them away like an investment. Some investment! You go to sell them, somebody will take them off your hands like for seven percent discount off face value. That's because they print hundreds of millions of every one." She hesitated. "I guess you don't want to know about stuff like that."

"Why not? If I was looking into a theft of paintings, I'd want to know something about art."

"What are you? Some kind of investigator? I know you are Meyer's friend. He's such a dear, sweet man. We all love him."

Before I could answer, a man came in and was greeted by name. She went back to the safe and brought out five little brown envelopes. The man sat on a stool, took out his own magnifying glass and, one by one, inspected the gold coins. Big coins. Mary Alice waited patiently. Finally he said, "Okay, dear. These three. Tell Hirsh this one is a slider, and I don't like the strike on this one. That makes six hundred and twenty, doesn't it?"

She used scratch paper and said, "Six forty-four eighty with tax, Mr. Sulzer."

He produced six hundreds and one fifty. She made out a receipt and gave him his change. He said, "When are you going to change your mind about some nice Sunday?"

"If I do, I'll let you know, okay?"

"How is he doing locating a 1930?"

"Gee, I don't know. He was complaining about finding one that wasn't the quality you want. I really don't know much about coins, like I keep telling you. If he finds one, I'm sure he'll phone."

Sulzer left. She made a face at me. "He collects double eagles. St. Gaudens, not the Liberty Heads."

"What's a slider?"

"He won't buy anything except B.U. or better. That means Brilliant Uncirculated. The only things better are choice, gem, and proof. This one here, he thinks it could just as well have been called A.U., or Almost Uncirculated. So if a coin is sort of in the middle, where you could maybe honestly call it one or the other, it's what a dealer calls a slider. I don't feel a thing for coins. I mean they're valuable, and they keep going up and all, but I don't want to own them. Let me get these back in the safe with the money."

When she came back I said, "What about some nice Sunday?"

"Oh, he's got a sailboat. And a lot of ideas."

"And you've already got somebody you'd rather go sailing with?"

"Yes, but not the way you mean that. You didn't tell me what kind of investigator you are, Mr. McGee."

"Travis or Trav, Mary Alice. I'm not any kind. I just try to find things people lose. On a percentage basis. Salvage consultant."

"I hope you find the stamps."

"You'll probably be able to tell me where they are."

She bit her lip and tilted her head. "Now that's kind of a rotten thing to say."

"How so?"

"I wouldn't do anything like that!"

"Like what?"

"Steal anything."

"You, dear? I mean you are a bright woman, and you probably saw something or heard something or know something which doesn't seem important at all, but is really very important. When you and I find out what it is you know, then it will tell us where the stamps are."

She frowned at me. "I don't like cute."

"What?"

"You said that the way you said it so I would take it wrong. You wanted me to. You wanted to see me react. Okay, I'm reacting. I don't like that kind of cute. Don't play little games with me. If I'm waiting for you to play games all the time, I won't be thinking of how to help, will I?"

"Good point."

"You did it on purpose?"

"Certainly. Can I take you to lunch?"

"She'll be back in ten minutes. Sure."

"Seems quiet around here. Don't you get bored?"

"Bored! I'm about ten thousand jobs behind right now. I've got a whole mess of new issues to mount. Our mailing is going to be late this month. It goes to six hundred people. I've got three appraisals I'm working on, for estates. I took two of them home to my place, because they aren't all that important moneywise. But the other is back in the safe, and it's pretty nice. It's nicer than Hirsh said it was going to be."

"And if you wanted to, you could pull a nice item out of it and replace it with something cheaper, and nobody would know?"

She turned away from me and began straightening albums on one of the shelves behind her.

"What's the matter?" I asked.

"I'm waiting until I can say something."

I waited. She turned back. "Here is the only way I can say it. Excuse my French, I don't give a goddamn what you would do or wouldn't do. Or what anybody else in the world does or doesn't do. If I steal, somebody knows. Me! That's why I can't, won't and don't. And I am going to have lunch alone, thanks."

"I guess you should. I guess nobody is really worthy of breaking bread with you, dear. We ordinary mortals are unable to tell at first sight just how totally honest and decent and virtuous you really are. At first glance, you look like a sizable and pretty lady, and I have the vague feeling that many pretty ladies have done unpretty things over the last few thousand years. By all means, lunch alone and think clean and honest thoughts, dear."

She went white and then red with anger. She slapped her palm on the plate glass counter top. "But I am getting so goddamn tired of you accusing me of things!"

I yelled too but just a little louder. "So move the scenario elsewhere, you silly bitch! Move it to Chicago. Mr. X, the expert, buys for Mr. Y, the investor. Miss Z keeps the records and handles the merchandise. X, Y, and Z go to the bank a dozen times. The merchandise is stolen and replaced by cheap goods. Who do we blame, dear? X, Y, or Z. You were there! Who? Who? Who?"

She blinked and blinked, and the tears welled and spilled and trickled. She made an aimless gesture, and I took her hands and held them. She looked down and said, "I guess I just . . . I don't . . ."

The door opened, and the pressure on the mat bonged the overhead bell. Jane Lawson peered at us.

"What's going on? Are you crying, Mary Alice?"

"We were just going to lunch," I told Jane.

"Let go and I'll get my purse," Mary Alice said.

After we'd ordered a drink, Mary Alice went to the women's room to repair the tear damage. She came smiling back and sat and sipped and said, "You're kind of wearing, you know? Or maybe it's the whole rotten day. I feel ragged around all my edges."

"It doesn't show."

"On me it never does. I could be dying, and people would tell me how great I look. I always wanted to be one of those mysterious little girls with the hollow cheeks and the sad eyes. I wanted to have a kind of accent. You know. Like Hungarian."

"And all the sad-eyed little Hungarian girls want—"

"I know. I know. You've got a funny look on your face, Trav."

"I just found out I don't have to wonder about one thing that didn't fit too well. I don't have to accuse you again."

"Thanks for practically nothing."

I reached across and touched the bridge of her nose and pulled my hand back. "The answer is right there."

She looked puzzled, took out a mirror, and turned her head toward the light. "Oh. The little groove place, huh? From the glasses. But why would . . . Oh, I think I see. If I inventoried all those things and cut the mounts to size and put them in the book, wouldn't I see they weren't the same when I looked back through the book that day? The answer is, I don't wear my glasses in the bank. The close work is all done. The answer is vanity. Okay. No matter what kind of frames I get, I look like a big goggly owl."

"How about contacts?"

"I can't adjust to the hard ones. You can't get bifocals in soft lenses. I wear them to see close, and then I'd have to take them out to see across the room or drive my car or cross the street. Or wear glasses for distance when I was wearing them."

"Oh."

"Jane says the only thing faster than light is me whipping my glasses off when a customer comes in. I know it's silly. I think my husband made me sort of supersensitive about them."

"How?"

"I shouldn't mention him because I don't like answering questions about him, and so I hardly ever do."

"No questions."

"Thanks. We better order, maybe?"

We ordered. After the food came, I said, "I know you didn't find out until this morning, but you must have *some* idea of how it was done."

"I can't believe it really happened. I keep thinking Hirsh has to be wrong. He's really old. Don't old people get weird ideas sometimes?"

"That would be a pretty complicated fantasy."

"But for me it's easier to believe."

"Why do you say that?"

"Look, it's the detail, the volume. If I had no interruptions and everything right there, it would take a *long* time to take the good items out and put the bad items in. There are thirty-six double-sided pages in that stock book. Seventy-two pages and about ten to go. Okay, that means about ten items per page. I'm pretty quick with my hands. They're kind of big but quick. So I have to take an item out of the horizontal strip and put it aside and then select the item that goes there and put it where it should be. Ten seconds to switch one? Fair guess? So six hundred single stamps, pairs, blocks and plate blocks all in mounts would take six thousand seconds, or one hundred minutes, or an hour and forty minutes. And if I could get very whippy and do it in five seconds, it would still take ten minutes less than an hour. Just exactly how am I going to do that sitting practically touching two men at a little table under a bright light? The goodies *have* to be right there in that book! Or the bank is crooked. Take your choice."

"Would you be able to remember the arrangement, the way you put the items in the book?"

"Sure."

"And you could see well enough to—"

"I'm not *that* blind. I found the Barbados page, and it was too full to take the ones we'd brought that day, even if I'd moved the items closer together. And I like to arrange the stamps on the pages. You know. Spaced to look nice. It doesn't matter to Sprenger. He wouldn't care if we put them in a cigar box, I guess. But they are nice, and they represent a lot of money, and it is sort of . . . a response to the quality and the money to arrange them nicely."

"Do you think if you had your glasses on that day in the bank, you would have seen something was wrong?"

"From what Hirsh said this morning I should hope so! Bad centering. Stains and toning and fading. But not in every case."

"Why not?"

"Well . . . take Barbados for example. Scott 53, the four-penny rose is worth about fifty dollars unused, for a real good one. But Scott 53b in the same condition is worth fifteen hundred dollars anyway. Know what the silly difference is? Well, 53 is perf fourteen on all sides, and 53b is perf twelve and a half on the sides."

"What do those numbers mean?"

"Like fourteen. Those little holes so you can tear the stamps apart, it means there are fourteen holes in a space two centimeters long. You use a gauge to measure, something with the different gauges all printed on it. So you couldn't look in the stock book and tell with the naked eye if you had the ordinary 1875 four-penny rose or the special one. The special one is worth so much more because there were so few of them printed."

"And you certainly have one fantastic memory, Mary Alice."

She laughed. "I'm showing off. My memory isn't so great. I remember that one because I found one. Hirsh bought a collection of Colonials. It was so neat and orderly and well-labeled and mounted that we sort of took for granted the collector had really studied them. Well, it was just sort of luck. I took an ordinary one we had in stock and put it beside the one in the collection because I wanted to see which one was really best, for a customer. And the perforations didn't look right. I used the one stamp to measure the other. After the customer left, I used a gauge. Then, on my own, I sent it off to the Philatelic Foundation in New York, with a fee in advance, and in six weeks it came back with the certification it was 53b. So I put it on Hirsh's desk as a surprise. He put it in Sprenger's investment collection, and he gave me a hundred-dollar bonus. It's really *fun* to find something like that, you know? Like mining for gold, I guess."

Though I had no empathy for her excitement, I liked the expression on her face, the look of enthusiasm. To each his own. I wondered why some man hadn't made a lot of extra effort to keep hold of this girl, The special, bonus size. A lifelong supply of goodies. But she had warned me nicely about asking questions.

I decided abruptly that I was going to take the lady at her own valuation. It is a process of logic, I guess. If she had the art, the style, the exquisite ability to project a total plausibility regardless of what stress I'd put on her, then she would not have spent five years in a funny little stamp store in Miami. Pretense requires vast expenditures of energy. That much guile would have sought better stalking-places.

Besides, I liked the neat little creases at the corners of her mouth. I liked that tricky blue shade of her iris. I liked the genuine big-girl hunger with which she stashed away the medium-adequate meal. I liked the way the black hair had a coarse, healthy gloss and the way she tossed and swung it back out of her way.

"Okay," I said, "you are no longer on the suspect list."

"Are you sure you want to do me such a big favor?"

"I know how impressed you must be."

"Are you suspicious of practically everybody?"

"Practically."

"That must be a hell of a way to go through life, fellow."

"It's only when I'm working. The rest of the time I'm an amiable, trusting, innocent slob."

"Isn't it steady work?"

"It could be, but I don't let it. When I get a few bucks ahead, I retire. Retirement is more fun at my age than it would be later."

"You've got a point. Also, you don't look married. Which makes it easier, huh?"

"Just one thing about you raises a question."

"Such as?"

"You have a sedentary job, Mary Alice, and from what you said, I guess you work at home too. But I know good conditioning when I see it. You walk around on springs."

She grinned, clenched her fist, and made a muscle. At her invitation I reached over and prodded it with a thumb.

"Very substantial," I said.

"I have to live with it, Trav, or give up. I'm big, and I've got good coordination. I ran with a pack of boys from the time I could run. I played all their games and all the girl-games too. I can win canes and boxes of taffy at those weight-guessing places. What would you guess me at? Don't try to flatter me."

"Hmmm. Between a hundred and thirty-five and a hundred and forty?"

"One fifty-six this morning, stripped, on my very good scales. I've got big heavy bones, and I grew a lot of muscle tissue at all the games. So I'm in training always, because if I let things go, they really go. The muscles turn to lard, and everything starts to sag and wobble around, very nasty. I do the Canadian thing. And I make all my points—men's points, by the way—every week of my life. I've done it so long, I *love* it."

"I dog it. I get soft enough so that it bothers me, and then I have to go to work on it."

"You look in real good shape, you know?"

"I've been working on it."

We looked at each other. The blue eyes seemed to get bigger, just big enough to let me in. I had the feeling I was reaching down into that blueness, to where something had gone click, startling both of us. I heard her breath catch, and then she took a deep deep breath, looking away as she did so, breaking the unexpected contact. I signaled the waiter, making a writing motion in the palm of my hand. He nodded and came toward the table, sorting through his checks.

We walked back side by side and about twenty inches apart.

"Thank you for a very nice lunch, Travis."

"You are most welcome, Mary Alice."

"Like Hirsh said, I want to help you any way I can."

"You've been a lot of help."

"Have I?"

"That estimate of the time it would take to change the items in the stock book was useful. It helps me see the whole picture."

"I'm glad."

"Perhaps when we get back to the store, you can let me inspect one of those books."

"Of course."

"My car is over there in that lot. Would you like to look at it?"

She stopped and frowned at me. "Why should I want to look at your car?"

"Maybe because it is older than you are."

"It is?"

"It's a pickup truck."

"Really?"

"Do you want to look at it?"

"Why not?"

As we neared it, I pointed it out. "Yecht," she said, "what a frightful shade of blue." And then she said, "But it's a home-made pickup truck!" And then she said, "My God, it's a Rolls-Royce." Then she braced herself against it and laughed. No silvery little tinkly giggle. Haw ho haw hah haw. Oh God. Oh ho haw! A bray. A contralto bugling.

"If you think this is funny, you should see my house boat, where I live."

"Whu-whu-whu-what's funny about *that*?"

"I can't explain it. I have to show you."

"Yuh-yuh-you *do* that. Oh dear." She found her kleenex and wiped her eyes and blew her nose. We headed for the office.

"Is it really *that* funny?"

"No. I hurt your feelings or something?"

"No."

"It . . . it was relief, kind of. When you said look at your car I thought, Oh God, another of *those*. You know. You'd have some kind of nasty little thing about two feet high and ten feet wide and twenty feet long, with fifty dials and a speedometer that goes up to two hundred. And I'd have to admire the ugly damn childish thing or even ride in it if you insisted. Then you'd show me your key that fits every Playboy Club in America and overseas, and then you'd try to do the old magic trick."

"What old magic trick."

"You know. All of a sudden you turn into a motel."

"And you laughed because none of that is going to happen?"

"And because that Miss Agnes is a very *dear* automobile," she said, pushing open the door to the shop.

Seven

On Friday morning I cleaned up after my breakfast, took a couple of overdue loads to the laundromat and sat and peaceably watched some women get their loads whiter than mine. I was not torn with jealousy. I wished them well. On the way back a fat man on a rackety little trail bike nearly ran me down, then yelled out his estimate of my ancestry and lineage. I smiled and nodded and wished him well. I remembered vaguely that the city fathers had put the roust on me. Move off your boat or leave town. I wished them well too. Nourish yourself well at that public trough, boys. Gobble any goodies which happen to float by.

Meyer was sitting on the dock, legs swinging, waiting for me. He came aboard. He stood behind me as I stowed the laundry.

"How did you make out?" he asked.

"Beautiful."

"What?"

"This is the best time of year. Right?"

"I stayed and talked to Hirsh for a while. By the time I got around to calling the shop, you were gone."

"We left early. Mary Alice and me."

"Turn around, Travis."

"What?"

"Turn around a minute and look at me."

"Sure."

He stared and nodded. "I see."

"What do you see?"

"That you're going to try to help Hirsh Fedderman."

"What? Oh, sure. That's right. As right as . . ."

"Rain?"

"Whatever you say, old buddy."

When my chores were done, we had a talk. I pulled my wandering attention in from somewhere out beyond left field and tried to settle down to the task at hand. I remembered what Mary Alice had said about how long the switch would take and how incredible it seemed to her, how she wondered if any switch had really taken place at all. I tried her approach on Meyer.

"I have to believe Hirsh," Meyer said. "If he saw it, he saw it. His mind is very quick and keen."

"She really knows all that stuff."

"What?"

"All that stamp stuff."

"I would think it would be more remarkable if, after five years, she didn't know all about it."

"What?"

"Never mind. Good God!"

"I wanted to give her a ride in Miss Agnes. It was a slow afternoon. Jane told us to take off. I followed Mary Alice to her place, in her old yellow Toyota. We had a drink in Homestead and dinner in Naples."

"Naples?!"

"I know. We were just drifting along, talking about this and that, and Naples seemed like the closest place. So we came back across Alligator Alley and came here, and I showed her the *Flush*. It knocked her out, like Agnes did. I like the way she laughs."

"You like the way she laughs."

"That's what I said. So then I drove her home and by then it was too late to even stop in for a nightcap."

"How late is too late?"

"Quarter past five."

"No wonder your face looks blurred."

"Meyer, the whole twelve hours seemed like twenty or thirty minutes. We just hit the edges of all the things there are to talk about."

"Are you going to be able to think about Hirsh Fedderman's problem?"

"Whose what?"

He went away, shaking his head, making big arm gestures at the empty space ahead of him. If he had come back, I would have told him that I had almost decided that there was no problem at all, that Fedderman had been mistaken. If there is no way at all for something to have happened, the best initial assumption is that it didn't happen.

On that Friday I arrived at the store at closing time and drove Jane Lawson back to her place, a so-called garden apartment in a huge development of yesteryear, about a half-hour bus ride from Fedderman's store.

She sat erect on the edge of the seat and said, "Our gal was pretty punchy all day, Trav."

"I haven't been exactly alert."

"Now turn left again and here we are. I hate that miserable bus, but it would be a worse bus ride for Linda." She had already told me that Linda was the elder of her two, a scholarship freshman at the University of Miami in Coral Gables. Judy was a junior in high school. Sixteen and eighteen. I had noticed she talked about Linda quite a lot and had very little to say about Judy.

She tried the door and then got out her keys and said, "Excuse the way the place will probably look. Working mother and two teen gals. I've tried. But they have a tendency to hang their clothes up in mid-air."

The living room was small and oven-hot. She hurried over to a great big window unit and turned it on high-high, and then raised her voice to carry over the thunder of compressor and fan. "The house rule is the last one out turns the beast off. It eats electricity. But it will chill this place fast, and then I can turn it down to where we can hear ourselves think. Isn't it terrible? Fix you a drink?"

"If there's a beer?"

"There could be. Let me look."

She came smiling back with a cold bottle of beer and a tall glass and excused herself to change out of her working clothes. There was too much furniture in the room. The fireplace was fake. There was a double frame on the mantel, and in one side of it was an incongruously young man with a nice grin, Air Force uniform, lieutenant bars, pilot wings. In the other half was a picture of the same lieutenant in civilian clothes, sports jacket and slacks. He was holding a baby and looking down into its invisible face while a Jane Lawson, eighteen years younger, stood by him, no higher than his shoulder, smiling up at him.

There was an alcove off the living room with some high-fidelity equipment, with racks of tapes in bright dog-eared boxes, with tilted stacks of records. The room was getting cool very quickly. I went over and checked the controls on the beast and cut it from high cool to cool, from max fan to medium. It shuddered and smoothed to about the sound of a good chain saw on idle. I was back looking at the pictures when she came out in an overblouse and faded blue shorts and sandals. She was a slight and pretty woman, with the residual marks of old tensions in her face, with a firmness to her mouth and corners of her jaw.

"That's Jerry," she said. "It seems incredible. He was stopped right there in time, just thirteen months after this picture. In another year Linda will be as old as I was when I met Jerry."

"Combat?"

"No. He was trade school. He wore the ring. They used to have more flameouts in fighter jets back then. He was on a night exercise, just two of them. That particular model, the way it worked, there was an interlock so that if you didn't jettison the canopy first, you couldn't eject, you couldn't make the charge go off to blow the seat out. It was supposed to be a safety thing, so a green pilot couldn't get nervous and blow himself through the canopy. But his canopy release jammed and all the way down he told his wingman exactly what he was doing to try to free it. No messages for anybody. Just technical information. A real pro."

"They must have to take a special course in cool."

"If I sound bitter, it's because they were already turning out a better canopy release thing and making the change in the field as the kits came in."

So I told her about the radio tape years ago, made in

Lauderdale, and broadcast only once before NASA came galloping in, all sweaty, and confiscated it. The interviewer had asked one of those good and tough-minded and free-thinking men of the early days of space orbiting how he felt as the rocket was taking off. Maybe it was because he had heard that question too many times. He answered it with a question. 'How would *you* feel, taking off, sitting up there on top of fifty thousand parts, knowing that every one had been let to the lowest bidder?' "

"Grissom?" she asked. I nodded. "I thought so. It sounds like Gus. I knew those guys. I came close to marrying one. The girls were little. They liked him. I was half in love and telling myself the girls needed a father. So maybe the new father was going to end up frozen hard as marble, circling us all forever, haunting us all forever. I dilly-dallied and I dithered and shilly-shallied and all those words. And the train left the station before I could make up my mind whether to buy a ticket. Maybe it's best. Who knows? Well, my troubles aren't what you came to talk about."

"This problem could give you trouble you don't need. If the investment items are gone, Hirsh is going to have to make it good with Sprenger. With a man like Sprenger, I don't think there'd be a choice, even if Hirsh did want to look for an out. It might clean him out. It might take the store and the stock to do it."

She was sitting in the corner of the couch. She pulled her legs up under her and made a face. "That would really be rotten. For him, I mean. He's been so good to me. I can't believe I've been there fifteen years. I answered a blind ad, and when I found out what it was, I didn't want it at all. He liked my letter. He begged me to try it. He offered me too much money. I couldn't even type. I thought somebody was going to take advantage of this crazy little man, so it might as well be me. I didn't find out until later he'd interviewed at least thirty-five girls before me without finding anybody he wanted. He was looking for a nut who'd go to a business school nights and learn to type just because it would make things easier for him. Trav, don't talk about the troubles I could have. I'll manage. With the pay and the pension and being able to use the PX at Homestead, I've stuck rainy-day money away. Jerry's folks have helped some, and they'd help more if I had to let them. The thing is to help Hirsh so he doesn't have to sell everything."

"That's what Mary Alice says too, but she can't really believe the good stuff isn't still in that book in the safety deposit box."

"Hirsh doesn't imagine things like that. Know what I keep thinking?"

"What?"

"Don't tell Hirsh. If one investment account could be cleaned out like that, so could the others, couldn't they? He hasn't had a chance to look at any one of the other five during the past two weeks."

"You certainly know how to relax a person, Jane."

"You thought of that already, huh?"

"They're all handled alike, pretty much, aren't they?"

"Yes and no. The oldest account is Mr. Riker Benedict, and that was started about the same time I came to work. In fact, it was the first account Hirsh set up that way, mostly because Mr. Benedict couldn't really believe that the things Hirsh wanted to buy for him would keep going up in value year after year. He's bought nineteen classic pieces in fifteen years, famous items. And he's looking for another one now. The collection is worth so much more than Mr. Benedict put into it, there's really no point in keeping on with it in the same way. But it's a ceremony, adding a new piece. The two of them will spend half a morning in the bank going over the great rarities, one by one, whether they are adding a new one or not. With the other accounts I would say that sometimes they go over the things previously purchased and sometimes they don't. The Sprenger account is the one where he never looks at the old purchases or the new ones either. He just sits there like so much dead meat. He nods, shrugs, grunts, and that's that."

"What would happen to those accounts if anything happened to Mr. Fedderman?"

"That's all worked out in the agreement. It's clear that he had no ownership interest in anything in the investment accounts, and his lawyer has a power of attorney in the event of Mr. Fedderman's death, and I think it's on file at the bank with a signature card. In the agreement the lawyer and the investor meet at the bank along with an appraiser certified by the APS, and the investment account is appraised, and if the current estimated resale value is higher than the breaking point in the agreement, the account is then accepted by the investor, and the agreement is surrendered. If the resale is less, the difference between it and the guaranteed price becomes a claim against the estate. But there would be no question of a claim of any kind on five of them. And on the stuff Hirsh has bought for Sprenger, I think Hirsh would come out a little bit ahead, actually, the way the market is going. You see, he hasn't really been taking any risk at all. This was just an easy way of easing the fears of people with risk capital. Sort of satisfaction-or-your-money-cheerfully-refunded. You can do that when the product is really tops."

"Unless the product mysteriously disappears."

"It's made him sick. It really has. Physically sick."

"I keep wondering how come Mary Alice keeps all the records and does all the work on the investment accounts?"

"Because I've been there longer? I used to do it, and then when Moosejaw retired and Mary Alice came on, I taught her the routines."

"Moosejaw?"

"Excuse me. Miss Moojah, a maiden lady with a very strong personality. A creature of legend. She didn't believe in the alarm system. There are eight buttons in handy, inconspicuous places. She kept a toy baseball bat under the cash register. Twice when she was alone, a would-be robber aimed a gun at her. Twice she picked up her bat and let him have it. One needed two lumps before he went down, and one collapsed on the first one. Then she'd push the button. It made Hirsh so mad he couldn't speak. He just made gobbling sounds. He was so afraid the next one would kill her. Anyway, I'm glad to have Mary Alice do the scut work. I'm sort of more into decision-making."

"Such as?"

"Well, the routine things, of course, that Hirsh hasn't time or patience for. When to reorder and how much. Albums and packets and mounts and so on. But the part I like best is watching the market and studying it and advising Hirsh. It's a lot of work, but he says I have a real talent for it. I study the changes in the catalog prices as they come out, Scott, Minkus, Stanley Gibbons, Sanabria.

Also, I get the list of prices realized from all the leading auction houses and find out what the lots are bringing in New York and on the West Coast and in London. It isn't all up, you know. I saw some little early warnings three years ago on Italian issues. They'd moved up or been pushed up too fast. So we had some pretty good things in counter stock, and some real good things in the investment accounts, and Hirsh moved everything out quickly. He lets me run a little risk account, like speculation in inventory. I saw that early Canada was looking active, so I put the money in those issues, and they've really moved. They were always good, but sort of stodgy. Now they're glamor. I think that—Do you *really* care about all this?"

"Would Mary Alice rather be making decisions?"

She pursed her lips. "N-No, I don't really think so. I'm more the cerebral type, and she's the manual type. That's oversimplifying. She loves to cut mounts and fix up pages. She loves to appraise estate stuff, item by item, and bring out the watermarks and count the perforations and check the color charts. She'd rather not have me handling any of the really good things. She got *furious* at me last year. When there is envelope paper stuck to the back of a stamp, you put it in a little wet box called a Stamp Lift, and after a while you can peel that paper right off the stamp. The old gum softens in the dampness. It was a pretty good Columbian, a four-dollar denomination with a light cancel. I took it out too soon, and I peeled part of the stamp right off. That's like making confetti out of a couple of hundred-dollar bills. She got so mad she wouldn't talk to me for hours."

"But usually she's easy to get along with?"

"A personal or official question, sir?"

I wondered if my ears looked as red as they felt. "It has to be personal, doesn't it?"

"Who should blame you? That is a pretty vivid hunk of lady. And you seem to have that old familiar look."

"Fox in the henhouse?"

She laughed. "More like a pro linebacker trying to line up on the wrong side. But on the personal side, I can't tell you much. She's fun to work with. The three of us make a good little team. I don't see her after work. Maybe there have been a lot of men trying to get close to that. If it works out the way it works out with the customers and the guys who work near the store, then they don't get anywhere either."

"How am I doing?"

"Who knows? It's early. I shouldn't give advice. I would go very very slow."

"What's her trouble?"

"I don't really know. I don't know a thing about her marriage. She won't talk about it at all. And as far as I can tell, she has absolutely no sex life at all, and that is a lot of big healthy girl with a lot of little motors running. From a couple of casual remarks I'd say that she certainly was turned on to it at one time. The only thing I can think of is that it was such a rotten, hideous marriage that it somehow turned her all the way off. And she keeps herself quieted down with all that exercise. The impression I get, the minute the man makes the first grab, she's off and running, and he never gets another chance. You spent a lot of hours with her. What did you really find out about her?"

I went back over it in my mind. "Not a hell of a lot. No family apparently. And she lived in Philadelphia when she was a kid."

"And also in Scranton. I've asked her direct questions. She says, 'Jane, someday when we have a lot of time, I'm going to tell you all about it.' But we haven't had enough time yet."

The door opened onto the shallow hallway, and a young girl came in. She was slender, taller than her mother, with brown hair darker than Jane's dark blond. Her hair was long and lifeless, half-hiding a sallow and strangely expressionless little face. She wore missionary barrel work pants, too heavy for September in Florida, a soiled body shirt. Her feet were bare. Her hands were as grimy as her feet. She carried a notebook and two schoolbooks in the crook of her arm.

She gave us one swift, opaque glance and headed past us toward the rear of the apartment.

"Judy!" her mother said. She stopped and turned slowly.

"You want something?"

"This is Mr. McGee. My daughter, Judy."

"Hello, Judy."

She gave me a briefer taste of that original look. She swept it across me. I was absolutely without meaning to her. She was something in a forest, aware only of other creatures like herself. I was a tree, and she did not give a damn what brand of tree. She half-nodded and made a small sound and turned back on her way. I sat down again.

"Judy?" her mother said.

She stopped in the doorway. "Now what?"

"I want to talk to you."

"So talk."

"Not this minute. I'm talking to Mr. McGee. I just don't

want to come looking for you and find you've gone out again."

"They're waiting on me."

"Go tell them to be patient then."

"Screw that. I don't want you hassling me. I told you that already."

"Go to your room and wait right there!"

"Is that an order?"

"What does it sound like?"

"Shove it, you silly old bitch. Phone the probation officer and tell him I've gone out. Okay?"

Jane Lawson started up when the girl left and then sat back down again. She put her fists on her bare knees and bent forward at the waist and rested her cheeks on her fists. In a little while she straightened, blinking, and gave me a frail smile. "Sorry."

"There's a lot of it going around."

"Judy . . . is at a difficult age. It's very difficult for young people these days."

"Don't you want to go talk to her?"

She gave me a grateful and appreciative look. "I'll just be a minute."

Very difficult for young people these days. Or any days. In what golden epoch was being a teenager a constant joy? There has always been a generation gap. It is called twenty years. Too much talk about unresponsive government, napalm, irrelevant education. Maybe the real point is that young lives have no accepted focal point. The tribe gives them no responsibilities, no earned privileges, no ceremonial place. In the family unit they do not fit into a gap between generations, because the generations are diffused.

Maybe that is why they are scurrying pell-mell back to improvised tribal conditions, to communes. The schools have tried, *in loco parentis,* to fill a vacuum, condition the young on a fun-reward system. It has been a rotten try. The same vacuum spawns the rigid social order of the Jesus freaks, another try at structure and meaning. The communes themselves are devices of the privileged, because if everybody went into communes, the communes would become impossible.

So the kids float. They ram around, amble around, talk and dream, and rediscover all the more simplistic philosophical paradoxes. And the ones in the majority who make it (as apparently Miss Linda Lawson was making it) find some bottom within themselves. A place to stand. A meaning derived from fractionated nonsense. They are not a brighter generation than ever before. They have been exposed to more input, so much they have been unable to appraise and assimilate it, but are able to turn it into immediate output, impressively glib, and commercially sincere.

And the few that can't make it, like the younger daughter, exude the ripe odor of the unwashed as opposed to the animal tang of healthy sweat. Their tangled and musty locks make the shining tresses of the others repugnant to all those Neanderthal spooks who would hate and resent youngness no matter how it might be packaged. The lost ones, like Judy, get so far into the uppers and the downers and the mind benders, hardly ever knowing what they are taking, seeking only something in the blood that will bring the big rush, and warp the world—that if told it would make a nice high, they would stuff a dead toad into their ear. The lost ones trade the clap germs back and forth until they cultivate strains as resistant to penicillin as were the Oriental brands of yore.

It is relaxing to climb down off the egomanic pedestal of guilt and blame and shame and responsibility and say, 'Who told me I have to understand the causes?' There are bad kids. There are bad trees in an orchard, bad apples on any tree, sick worms in any decaying apple. A world of perfection would be absurd. Even Doris Day couldn't sustain that kind of concept. Who needs it? We need the flawed ones, the lost ones, as a form of emotional and social triangulation, to tell us if we've gained an inch since Hammurabi. Rough rough rough on the people who love them, but by some useful design in the human fabric, the rejects manage to kill most of that love by the time they are grown. Think of it, dear Jane Lawson, as a trick of nature whereby some great smirking cowbird came long ago and laid its egg in your nest.

She came back in and said, "Thanks anyway."

"Something wrong?"

"She'd gone out the back way. I . . . had to check up on one of my sneaky spy tricks. That green rubber band around her books. I put a hair from my head under it the day before yesterday. It's still there. If she's not going to school, they're going to pick her up. They'll put her in a state school for girls."

"Probation for what?"

"I'd rather not say. She's in my custody, but I can't control her." The tears threatened to come again. "My lawyer said if we could find a place that would take her, we could jump the gun and go to the judge and get a transfer of custody. A private place. But either they won't take her, or the cost is so fantastic . . . He's still looking." She hit her knee with her fist. "What am I supposed to do? Chain her to the wall in her room? Beat her senseless?"

What do you say? My best guess would do Jane Lawson no good whatsoever. My best guess was that the girl was on the edge of leaving for good. And in some city as yet unknown, she would be studied with great care by experts. And if they were to decide it was merchandise worth salvage, she might indeed be beaten into total submission, cleaned up, dressed up, trained, and marketed for a few years. The merchandising experts cruise the bus terminals, and they watch the downtown streets for young girls carrying suitcases or packs. Impersonal appraisal. No uggos, no fatties, no gimps, no rich kids, nothing too too young.

"You didn't come here to get involved in a family problem," she said. She sighed. "Maybe in time she'll straighten out."

"Sure," I said. We smiled at each other. It was that special social smile people use when they don't believe anything they are saying.

Eight

When I phoned Mary Alice early on Saturday morning, she said that I'd caught her just before she went out the door. She said she was going to stop and see how Hirsh was and then do some shopping, and then she was going to her health club and work out, like she did every Saturday. What did I have in mind? Nothing special and nothing in particular. I had noticed the ocean was flat calm, and the weather people said the wind out of the west would hold all day, and I'd had a runabout tuned, and it was running well. So, running down outside, I could make it in very good time, and I knew a place that put up a good lunch, and I thought maybe we could run down the bay to a place I knew where we could have our own private patch of Atlantic beach for a swim and picnic. What she could do would be set the time when I could pick her up, say at the Royal Biscayne Yacht Club. She could leave her car there. I could drop her off there from the *Muñequita* later, or if she wanted, she could come back up to Lauderdale with me, and I'd get her back to Miami somehow.

She thought about it and decided that maybe the health club could be canceled out with no problems. That left the necessary shopping and seeing Hirsh and how about noon at that yacht club, okay? I told her twelve-thirty would be better for me, and she said fine.

I phoned the lunch order and told them when I would pick it up. I was unsnapping the big tarp cover off the *Muñequita* when somebody called my name. Two men stood on the dock, silhouetted against the glare of blue sky, looking down at me. I said I was indeed he. I freed the rest of the snaps, folded, and stowed the tarp, climbed up onto the side deck of the *Flush* and went aft, wanting a better look at them before deciding whether or not to ask them aboard.

"Permission to come aboard?" one of them said.

"Please do." They came onto the shallow aft deck. Solid handshakes. One was Davis and one was Harris. No first names volunteered. I have spent a lot of years making quick guesses, and at times my health has depended on accuracy as well as speed.

Both in their thirties, both of a size, six feet or a hair under, both somewhere shy of two hundred pounds, both softening in the middle and around the jaws, but not too much. The dark one had a Joe Namath hairdo and a villain's moustache. The other was red-brown and crinkly, with a swoop of sideburns.

The first impression was that they were used to working together. Men who do not know each other well express an awareness of each other in body movements and expressions. Familiar partners act more as if each were alone.

I couldn't put any geography together. The voices were Everywhere voices, like the men who do local news on television. Moustache was tanned, and Sideburns was permanently burned several shades of red, several degrees of peeling. Big hands. Old nicks on the knuckles. A very intent expression in the eyes, at odds with casual stance. I could read it very close to cop, but a few things canceled that out. The teeth were the persuasive, gleaming white you get from expensive show biz caps. Twenty-dollar haircuts. A drift of male cologne, leather and pine and fresh paper money. Summer weight knits, both slacks and shirts, and shoes so funny looking they had to be very in. Moustache had a fat gold seal ring on his pinky with a green stone in it.

In the back of my head all the troops hopped up out of the sack, grabbed weapons, and piled into the vehicles. They raced out to the edge of camp and set up a perimeter defense and then lay and waited, weapons off safety, loaded clips in place, grenades handy.

"Can we talk, Mr. McGee?"

"No reason why not," I said. I sat on the rail, one leg swinging free, the other foot braced, the knee locked.

Moustache was Davis. Memory trigger: Jeff Davis, dark hair, moustache. Harris: Harris tweed, tweedledee and dum. I didn't believe either name. I made no suggestions about where to sit. There was no awkward social hesitation. Davis folded himself into the deck chair, and Harris sat on the curve of railing six feet from me.

"We're representing somebody," Harris said. "He doesn't want his name brought into the deal yet."

"What deal?"

"There's a situation he wants you to look into," Davis said. "He thinks he's been had. He thinks he got tricked into the short end of a deal."

"You're confusing me, gentlemen."

"What's to confuse?" Harris asked, faking bewilderment. "He may want you to take a shot at salvaging the deal for him, getting back what he got conned out of. Isn't that what you do?"

"Do what?"

"*Salvage* work!"

"I don't do anything. I'm retired. Oh, sometimes I do a favor for a friend. I think the man you represent needs a licensed investigator."

"No, Mr. McGee," said Harris. "He needs you. He was very firm on that particular point. The way this thing is shaping up, he maybe might need you at a moment's notice. So he would be very grateful to you if you would just sit tight and wait to hear." He reached into his pants and took some bills folded once out of his side pocket. He pulled the bills out of a gold clip which said "After Tax" in block letters. He crackled and snapped five one hundreds, one five hundred free of the pack, reclipped the rest and put it away, folded the bills and took a long reach and shoved them into my shirt pocket. "Just to show he isn't kidding around."

"I couldn't help anybody I don't know."

"If he needs your help, you'll *get* to know him."

I pulled the money out and held it toward Harris. He pulled back. I tossed them into Davis' lap and said, "Sorry."

"You busy or something?" Harris asked with just a shade too much casual innocence.

"I'm doing a favor for a friend of a friend. Trying to, at least."

"What I think you should do is drop that one," Davis said.

"Should I?"

"The man we're talking about," he continued, "he heard about you someplace or other, and he got a good impression. He's not used to asking people for help, and they say they're busy or some damn thing."

"We all have these little disappointments in life."

"Is that smartass?" Harris asked.

"I didn't mean it that way. Think of it this way, gentlemen. If we all got exactly what we wanted all the time, wouldn't life get very dull?"

"This man gets what he wants," Davis said.

"Not this time."

"Suppose he wants to give you a choice, McGee," Harris said. "Suppose he keeps the deal open, and when you get out of the hospital and you can move around again pretty good, he sends somebody to ask you again."

I stared at him and then at his partner. "Now come *on!* What's your script anyway? Kick my spine loose and drive away in your 1928 LaSalle? You two looked and acted and talked like you know the names and numbers of all the players. All of a sudden, Harris, you open up with this hospital shit, and you sound like somebody got you from Central Casting."

Davis in the deck chair gave me the smile of a lazy hyena. "Every once in a while he does that," he said. "Remember that old movie, *The French Connection?* Want to know how many times this crazy turd went to see it?"

"Oh, come on, Dave," Harris said petulantly.

"The thing is," Davis said, "he gets hung up on some kind of image thing, and he likes to use it when he talks to civilians, because if they've been to all the same movies, they almost wet their pants when Harry comes on hard."

"You should learn to read people," I told Harry Harris.

Harry shrugged. "So it worked. That was one of the questions, right? To find out if McGee was—"

Davis cut him off. He evened the edges of the six pieces of money as he spoke and folded them once lengthwise. "Suppose you happened to be nibbling around the edge of something where this man we're talking about has an interest, and so he gets a reading on you, and he gets some kind of idea of what you do. So let's imagine that having you in the picture makes him back up and take another look at that particular deal. So not knowing how you fit, he thinks the easy way is to give you a retainer so you would come in on his side of it if things are getting fancy, if somebody has been stupid enough to play games with him, even though that somebody came highly recommended."

"How would this man think I'd fit?"

"What he said was you might even be trying to work out a way to give him the short end of that deal."

"I'm only interested in getting back something someone has lost. When there's no other way to get it back."

"The man could have thought you were trying some kind of Robin Hood bit. Or he might think you could be conned."

"Can we start using his name?" I asked.

"It's better we don't," Harris said. "Dave and me, we might not even know his name. Lots of things go through channels."

Davis said, "I can tell you one thing. The man would feel better about this trip we took if you would take this round one." He held the money out. "Kind of like a sign you're not trying to slip it to him. You don't have to back off from anything you have going on. It would make him keep on wondering about you if you don't take it."

I took a step and took the bills and put a haunch back onto the railing. They both looked relieved. The jargon changes constantly due to the telephone taps. Ten bills made a round one. Five round ones to a victor. When we first heard that, Meyer deduced that it came from V for Victor, V being the Roman five. Two victors make a spot. X marks the spot maybe? Ten spots make a big round one. Ten big round ones make a mil, and thus we are back into English.

I was not certain about my own judgment in taking it. It set up a dependency relationship. If you take the money of a man like Sprenger and then work against him, they can find you behind a shed in Tampa in the trunk of a stolen car, shotgunned and six days dead in the bake-oven heat, a silver coin in the rotting mouth.

We shook hands again. Away they went. Dave Davis. Harry Harris. I saw them stop and admire a big new Rybovitch fishing machine, looking like a pair of mod Indiana businessmen hunting for a charter. Dave Davis and Harry Harris?

I went below, went up to the bow and down through the service hatch into the bow bilge. I opened the false hull and stepped back from the slosh of seawater that spilled down and started the automatic bilge pump. I reached in and got my waterproof box, opened it, and put nine bills in with the dwindling reserve fund. It fattened it a little, but not enough.

I was beginning to run late. On the way over to pick up the picnic lunch, I wondered just what micro-percentage of the thousand dollars I had taken came from the pocket money and lunch money of Judy Lawson's high school class. I wondered what kind of little death they were peddling in the girls' rooms this week.

I buttoned up the *Flush,* tight and secure. I wanted to talk over the visit with Meyer and get his opinion, but there just wasn't time. All the required gear was in the *Muñequita.* She burbled her way past the moored fortune in transient and local cruisers and motor sailers and elegant houseboats. A few friends halooed. Teak baked in the sun, and brightwork shimmered, and toilet-paper danced in my wake in the bourbon-colored water of the boat basin. I went down past the gas docks, under the bridge, nudging the throttles up as I went through a little tide chop in the pass. I turned her south short of the sea buoy and angled out. The port engine coughed out at three thousand rpm, kept dropping below two thousand, building up to three, and coughing out again. I called Davey some unhappy names. He swore he had them both running perfectly. I pulled them both down to idle, waited a few minutes, and then popped them up to full throttle. Little doll came surging up onto her plane and scooted, with rpm moving up into the red.

I backed them off to thirty-eight hundred rpm, listened, made my apologies to Davey Hoople, master marine mechanic, age nineteen. A half millimeter nudge on the starboard throttle put them into final perfect sync. I was out far enough to make my straight shot to the Miami ship channel, so I held it on the heading and threw it into automatic pilot. I watched the needle as it searched. I had it about a degree too much west, so I took it out and tried again and hit it perfectly. I took a brew out of the cooler and stood on the pilot seat and sat on the backrest part, sea wind in my face, the horizon misty-pale and glassy, the *Muñequita* doing her thirty-eight knots without effort, the wake straight as a line on a chart.

I kept trying to sort out my guesses as to how and why Sprenger had sent a couple of members of the first team, but some bottomless blue eyes kept getting in the way. Fine day, fine boat, fine beer, and it had been a long long time since blue eyes. So I wrapped up the whole problem and shoved it into a cubicle over in a side corner of my mind and slapped the little door shut. A man should have his weekends, no matter what he does.

I tried to spot a yellow Toyota in the parking area as I came easing down the line of private markers into the protected basin of the Royal Biscayne Yacht Club. The small-boat area was off to the left beyond the rows of yachts and was built of those floating slabs of aluminum and floatation material which move up and down with the tide, simplifying access and mooring. A young Cuban, uniformed in the club colors, came running out, waving me off. "No, no, no!" he yelled. "Ess private! Ess cloob."

"Soy socio, hombre."

He looked startled and uncertain. He looked back over his shoulder for help. *"Eh? ¿Nuevo possible, señor?"*

"No. De muchos años."

"Pero—"

"Momentito. Ayúdame, por favor. Tengo mi tarjeta de socio."

He hesitated, then took the bow line and made it fast. I swung it in and cut the engines and jumped out with the stern line. After I made it fast I went back aboard and opened the shallow drawer under the chart bin and found my card. I handed it to him.

He frowned and then smiled. *"Ah. Especial. Bienvenido,* Meester McGee."

I read his name on the pocket. "Thank you, Julio." I dropped the card back in the drawer. I told him I was looking for a tall, dark-haired lady who was to meet me at twelve-thirty. It was now twelve-forty-five. No, he had not seen such. Would I please come to the small house of the dockmaster and sign the boat register? It would be my pleasure. He hoped he had not offended me. I said that it pleased me to see such care and diligence.

A few years back the cloob had a very ugly problem, and a member had asked me to help them deal with it. I posed as a guest and with a little good management and a lot of good luck, solved it without confrontations or publicity. The Board of Governors wanted to give me some special token of appreciation. They knew I had as much chance of slipping through their Membership Committee as a hog of entering heaven. So at the next meeting they amended the bylaws to permit one special membership, without initiation fees or dues, to be awarded by the board. I was nominated, seconded, and voted in, and then they voted to rescind the amendment to the bylaws. I seldom use it and knew it was childish to use that way of impressing, or trying to impress, Mary Alice McDermit.

I walked up the steps from the dock area to the edge of the lawns that slant down toward the water and the seawalls. A walkway and avenue of coconut palms led up to the main buildings of the club. The old Moorish portion has two new wings attached, wings as stark and modern as anything by I. M. Pei. So all of it together looks like a wedding cake for the Arabian bride of a suitor from Stonehenge. I could walk up there to the lofty paneled coolth of the men's bar and order one of the finest Planter's Punches known to man and sign for it. The bill would come in due course, on thirty-pound parchment with an engraved logo. I could stand and drink my drink, looking out through high windows at a dancing pool full of wives and children and daughters and grandchildren.

At least half the tennis courts were being used by hot-weather maniacs, out there going . . . pung . . . ponk . . . pung . . . ponk, yelling insincerities at each other and screaming of love.

The yellow Toyota came past floral plantings and parked in landscaped palm shade. Julio appeared beside me and said, "Ess your she?" When she got out and stood erect, dwindling her auto with a lot of female stature, I said, "Yes. Ess." And Julio went bounding toward the parking area to help with her gear. A very obliging young man. Very earnest. Very dedicated and doubtless very ambitious. He was bounding proof of the fact that the Cuban colony in Miami has the most upwardly mobile young people and the lowest crime rate of any ethnic colony in the U.S. east of San Francisco's Chinatown.

My she wore a big floppy fabric hat in a big white and yellow check. She wore a yellow top and a short white skirt so slit that her stride revealed the matching yellow shorts. She wore huge glasses with lavender lenses. She had a big yellow Ratsey bag and a big white shoulder bag. Julio took the beach bag from her and went on a dead run to stow it aboard the *Muñequita*.

"I'm so sorry I'm late, Trav. Traffic and bad planning. But, my God, this is some place to wait, if you have to wait. Wow! I got stopped at the gates, and I had to sign a guest thing and write in the name of the member I was meeting. I was positive you'd just picked this as a handy place. But he looked on a list. You *are* a member, huh? This is really some kind of incredible. There must be an army of guys just to keep the flowers looking so great."

Maybe it was better than a pretense of total cool, all this happy, awed enthusiasm. But I found myself wishing her approval wasn't quite as total and quite as genuine.

My twenty-two-foot runabout gave her some more pleasant astonishment. "I thought you had some kind of outboard thing. Hey, this is more like they race to the Bahamas."

"Same hull design they used a few years ago, but they had a lot more muscle than the pair of one-twenty-fives this one is wearing."

She hopped aboard, very lithe and springy for the size of her. She stooped and looked forward, under the bow deck. "Say, you've got mattress things and a toilet! It's all so neat!"

Julio nearly fell in while freeing my lines, because he couldn't take his eyes off Mary Alice. He radiated a worshipful approval. She had about seven inches and thirty-five pounds on him, and he was doubtless imagining walking her through his neighborhood on Sunday morning, dressed in their best, as if Snow White had finally made up her mind and decided on one of the dwarfs.

As I chugged, dead slow, past the yachts looking like ponderous caprisoned elephants in gleaming outdoor stalls, Mary Alice moved close to me and hooked her left hand over my near shoulder and made a laughing sound of delight. Her hip bumped me. I had the feeling that exact place where she put her hand would turn into a raised, radiant welt showing the precise shape of fingers and palm.

"You know what?" she said.

"What?"

"I shouldn't even tell you. I figured that this time of year, what happened was the owner hired you to stay aboard *The Busted Flush*. I mean, a lot of guys want a woman to believe things. You never really said it was yours. I mean, from the dock it looks kind of lumpy and funny. But that great kitchen and that huge living room and that tub and the shower big enough for four people, practically, and that crazy bed in the main bedroom, like one I saw in a magazine, you know, why should I believe it, Trav?"

"But now you do."

"You just don't look as if you belong to great clubs and own great boats is all. Or act like you do."

"What do I act like, Mary Alice?"

"I don't know. After I moved into the place I'm in now, a guy came around to hook up my phone. He got a thing about me, and when he has service calls in the neighborhood and he sees my car, he stops to find out if my phone is working. As if I wouldn't report it if it wasn't. He's almost as big as you are. A little younger. I mean, if he tried to make me think he owned *The Busted Flush* . . ."

"I won her in a poker game."

She hit me in the ribs with her elbow. "Oh sure. I *bet* you did. You're funny, you know. I can't tell what's a joke and what isn't. We can go fast now? How fast will this go anyway?"

"It's tuned right now, and the bottom is clean, and I put a new pair of wheels on her, so she should do very close to fifty, but I don't like to hold her there more than a few minutes because I don't like to buy new engines every year. Wait until we get past Dinner Key and I'll show you."

When I got past an area of prams and sailfish and little cats, I pushed it to full, with both mills yelling in full-throated unison. She stood tall above the top of the windshield, the wind snapping her black hair. She was laughing, but I couldn't hear her, and she had me just above the elbow in an impressive grasp. The reading was a full forty-four knots, which is a respectable fifty and a bit. I pulled it back down to cruising speed.

She roamed the walk-around and found the slalom ski stowed up under the gunwale overhang, zipcorded to bronze eyebolts. She wanted to know if we had far enough to go so she could ski. I said yes, if she didn't keep falling off, and she said she was the kind of freak who does all the physical things well after a few tries, and she'd had more than a few tries at the skiing. She went under the foredeck and pulled the privacy curtain, taking her beach bag with her, and in a little while she came out in a plain, business-like, off-white tank suit, her hair pulled tightly back and fixed there with a silver clamp. I had gotten the tow line out and clipped it to the ring bolt in the transom and held it clear of the slowly turning wheels.

She grinned, threw the ski over the side, and dived after it. When she had the ski and had worked her feet into the slots, I pulled the bar past her at dead slow, and she grabbed it and turned to the right angle and nodded. I pushed both throttles, and she popped up out of the water and the *Muñequita* jumped up onto the step in perfect unison. After she made a few swings, I knew she was not going to have any trouble. She gave me the pumping sign for more speed and then the circle of thumb and finger when it was where she wanted it. It translated to thirty-two miles an hour.

She was not tricky. There were no embellishments. All she did was get into the swooping rhythm of cutting back and forth across the almost-flat wake, far out there in the expanse of Biscayne Bay, far from land, far from any other water craft. She edged the slalom ski as deeply as the men do, laying herself back at a steep angle, almost flat against the water, throwing a broad, thin, curved curtain of water at least ten feet into the air at the maximum point of strain. At that point before she came around and then came hurtling back across, ski flat, to go out onto the other wing, the strain would sag her mouth, wipe her face clean of expression, and pull all the musculature and tendons and tissues of her body so taut she looked like a blackboard drawing in medical school.

She took it each time to the edge of what she could endure. It was hypnotic and so determined that it had a slightly unpleasant undertaste, like watching a circus girl high under the canvas, going over and over and over, dislocating her shoulders with each spin, while the drums roll and the people count.

I put it into autopilot so I could watch her. From time to time I glanced forward to make certain no other boat was angling toward us. I knew she would have to tire soon. I tried to calculate her speed. She was going perhaps twenty-five feet outside the wake on one side and then the other. Call it fifty feet. I timed her from her portside turn back to her portside turn. Ten seconds. For a hundred feet. Miles per hour equals roughly two thirds of the feet per second. Ten feet per second. Add seven miles an hour then to the boat speed. Very close to forty miles an hour. At that speed, if she fell, the first bounce would feel like hitting concrete. Water is not compressible.

I heard a thick, flapping sound over the boat noise and looked up and saw a Coast Guard chopper angling across at about a thousand feet.

I saw us for a moment the way the fellow up there saw us. Gleaming boat. Deeply browned fellow in blue swim trunks running it at speed, watching the graceful girl swinging back and forth, girl in a white suit, with a light, very golden tan.

For all he could tell, the girl was eighteen, and the man was twenty, and somebody's father had bought the boat.

Suddenly I felt bleak, oddly depressed. It took a moment for me to realize that one of Meyer's recent lectures on international standards of living was all too well remembered.

". . . so divide everything into two hundred million equal parts. Everything in this country that is fabricated. Steel mills, speedboats, cross-country power lines, scalpels, watch bands, fish rods, ski poles, plywood, storage batteries, everything. Break it down into basic raw materials and then compute the power requirements and the fossil fuels needed to make everybody's share in this country. Know what happens if you apply that formula to all the peoples of all the other nations of the world?

"You come up against a bleak fact, Travis. There is not enough material on and in the planet to ever give them what we're used to. The emerging nations are not going to emerge—not into our pattern at least. Not ever. We've hogged it all. Technology won't come up with a way to crowd the Yangtze River with *Muñequitas*.

"It was okay, Travis, when the world couldn't see us consuming and consuming. Or hear us. Or taste some of our wares. But communication by cinema, satellite, radio, television tape, these have been like a light coming on slowly, being turned up like on a rheostat control in a dark cellar where all of mankind used to live. Now it is blinding bright, cruelly bright. And they can all look over into our corner and see us gorging ourselves and playing with our bright pretty toys. And so they want theirs now. Just like ours, God help them. And what is the only thing we can say? 'Sorry. You're a little too late. We used it all up, all except what we need to keep our toys in repair and running and to replace them when they wear out. Sorry, but that's the way it is.' What comes after that? Barbarism, an interregnum, a new dark ages, and another start a thousand years from now with a few million people on the planet? Our myth has been that our standard of living would become available to all the peoples of the world. Myths wear thin. We have a visceral appreciation of the truth. That truth, which we don't dare announce to the world, is what gives us the guilt and the shame and the despair. Nobody in the world will ever live as well, materially, as we once did. And now, as our materialism begins to sicken us, it is precisely what the emerging nations want for themselves. And can never have. Brazil *might* manage it. But no one else."

Good old Meyer. He can put a fly into any kind of ointment, a mouse in every birthday cake, a cloud over every picnic. Not out of spite. Not out of contrition or messianic zeal. But out of a happy, single-minded pursuit of truth. He is not to blame that the truth seems to have the smell of decay and an acrid taste these days. He points out that forty thousand particles per cubic centimeter of air over Miami is now called a clear day. He is not complaining about particulate matter. He is merely bemused by the change in standards.

Now, as I watched the tireless lady zoom back and forth, he had made me feel like one of those regal jokers of olden times who could order up enough humming bird tongues for a banquet. What's your message, Meyer? Enjoy?

She slid back to a straight track behind the stern. She smiled and rolled her shoulders. She cocked her head and then tried some signals on me. First she held her left hand up, finger and thumb an inch apart. Then she pulled her hand across her throat, in the cut-power signal. Then as I started to turn toward the controls, she shook her head violently and held her hand out, palm toward me. I waited, puzzled, and she pointed toward the water off to the port side of the boat, and then she bent her knees and swung her fanny out to the right. So I had the message. I decided I'd better leave it on pilot but be close enough to take it out in a hurry.

She moved out to the side and gave me her signal and swung wider for speed. I pulled the throttles halfway back, and she tossed the line clear, into the wake, and came angling in too fast toward the port side, amidships. I moved quickly to grab her, but she yelled me off, turned parallel to the direction of the boat, slowing and just as the speeds were identical, she gave a little twisting hop which hoisted her rear onto the flat gunwale and would have been perfect except she was overbalanced. The slalom ski went up, and she fell over backward into the cockpit. I wasn't close enough to break her fall, and I heard the thump her head made against the deck and felt it through the soles of my bare feet. She scrambled up and went to the stern and brought the tow line in, and then I cut the power all the way back. In the semisilence I said, "You are totally mad. Miss the edge and you'd get swept right into the port wheel."

"That's how come I jumped too far."

"Did you ever try that before?"

"Onto docks. It's trickier because you have to get it just right, ending up at the dock just when you stop and start to sink. So this is easier. You can kind of adjust because it's like the dock is moving too."

"And that makes it easier?"

"You're cross because it scared you, Trav. Well, I'm a little scared too. I always get scared *after* I try things."

"You thumped your head pretty good."

"All this hair worked like a cushion. It's my elbow that hurts."

She showed me. She had knocked a flap of skin loose. I got out the kit and disinfected it and put a bandaid patch on it. She stretched and then squatted on her heels and bounced a few times and came up slowly. "You know, that's *really* a workout," she said. "I wish I could do that every day. I'd get hard as rocks. It would really firm me up."

"I didn't notice anything very loose."

"Then you weren't looking."

"I'm pretty sure I was looking."

She gave me a quick sidelong glance, not at all flirtatious. It backed me off from whatever was about to come into my mind. She said, "Pretty soon I am going to start eating those life jackets."

I looked ahead and picked out the familiar island shapes. I established my location and knew the water I could trust. I said, "You'll be eating in fifteen minutes, and you can start drinking right now, if you're up to it. Look in the ice chest over there. I laid aboard some of those cocktails in cans. Take your pick. Give me a vodka martini, please."

She picked a marguerita, pulled the tabs off the cans, and handed me mine, then clinked cans. I was glad to note I did not have to tell her why we don't throw the shiny tabs overboard.

"I feel great," she said over the engine noise. "Everything is pulled loose, sort of. All stretched. I want to have two drinks, eat myself blind, go to sleep in the sun, and then have a swim, and then ski all the way home."

"So be it," I said. "Won't you burn?"

She poked at her thigh. "My skin is thick and tough, like some kind of plastic. I don't burn at all. After I get pink about nine thousand times, then I gradually turn the color I am now, and then nothing else happens, no matter what."

I read the shallows ahead and slowed down and eased up to them and then along the edge until I found a notch deep enough to get me close to shore. I cut everything and put a couple of hooks over and slung the boarding ladder.

Then we offloaded everything and, in two trips, carried it up over the dune and down to the little cove on the Atlantic side, dispossessing a pale and malevolent crab, when we spread the two giant beach towels in the semi-shade of a pair of wind-torn old casuarinas. We had more of the extravagantly convenient drinks-in-a-can. (Were the emerging nations targeting on this delight in their misty futures?)

I went back and checked the hooks, reset one and trod it into better bottom, and brought back the battered and eroded old battery radio. It brought in the most useful Cuban station, playing, on this Saturday afternoon, a concert of symphonic pieces for Spanish guitar. With very few commercials.

We had a short swim before lunch. The drinks were making the bright day faintly, tantalizingly unreal. I caught her looking stealthily at my ugliest and most impressive souvenir of old trauma, the long deep one down the top of the thigh. I told her it was surgical. A wound had become infected, and they had chopped around in there three times, planning to take the leg off if they had to schedule the fourth. She asked if it was something that happened in some war, and I said that no, it had been a civilian difference of opinion. There were some less impressive marks from one of those wars, and the rest of them were either bad luck or good luck or bad judgment. She swallowed and said she couldn't stand the thought of being hurt. She simply couldn't stand it. Oh, not the little bang and bumps and sprains you get from athletics, or even a couple of busted ribs and a broken collarbone, which she got when she fell from the rings in a gym one time. She meant really really hurt, with stitches and drains and operations and needles and all that. She swallowed again. She said she had never even been really sick, not ever.

Having seen her eat and knowing that outdoors improves appetites, I had ordered enough for four. Hunks of sharp cheddar, cucumber salad, giant roast-beef sandwiches on dark bread, corned beef sandwiches, big crisp kosher dills, a big thermos of iced coffee, two big pieces of tart, deep-dish apple pie. It was successful. She kept making little humming sounds and small chuckling sounds. Through the dark curtain of hair I saw the solid jaw muscles bulging and sliding under that golden hide as she chomped away. I warned her about the horseradish but she slathered it on the roast beef anyway, yelped when she got into it, and then finished the sandwich, eyes tearing, snuffling as though with a head cold.

She yawned and lay back on the big towel I had provided her. She put a forearm across her eyes. In the middle of a sentence her voice dwindled and blurred and stopped. I saw the deep, slow, diaphragmatic breathing of heavy sleep, lips apart, edge of white teeth showing. Her upflung arm revealed the faint, sooty shadow of the shaven stubble. Her palm was turned to the sun, fingers curled. Her other hand, almost a fist, rested against the flattened, muscular belly. Tiny round beads of perspiration, the size of the heads of the pins they put in expensive shirts, clung to the pale fuzz of her upper lip.

I looked at the angle of the sun and got my watch out of the side pocket of the canvas bag I had brought from the boat. A straight shot to the Royal Biscayne would take forty minutes. And I wanted to be coming into Lauderdale past the sea buoy no later than eight-fifteen. So, to have some of the day left for more swimming, more skiing, I wouldn't want to sleep more than about a half-hour. I set the alarm. Meyer had given the watch to me because it amused him. It does not make a sound. At the specified time, a semisharp little metal nub starts popping out of a little hole in the underside of it, stabbing you in the wrist.

Nine

On Sunday morning after ten o'clock I got around to hosing down the *Muñequita* with fresh water from the dockside connection at Slip F-18. After I wiped the water-spots off the brightwork, I checked the batteries, oil level in the engines, used a dip stick to check the level in the two tanks against the fuel gauges, greased the linkage in the power lift, and carried the picnic items aboard *The Busted Flush.* By then the cockpit deck had dried, so I did a better job of making her white rubber fenders fast in the right places before I snapped the big custom cover in place all the way around. As I clambered up onto the *Flush,* I heard Meyer calling my name. He was coming along the dock at an unaccustomed briskness, and I went ashore and met him with a suggestion he buy me some coffee aboard his boat, mine having run out.

"And what was the big hurry?" I asked him.

As we strolled back toward his dumpy cruiser he said, "There's something I never thought of before. When you want to deliver surprising news, your first impulse is to do it in a hurry. If it's good news, the second decision is to slow down, take your time, savor the pleasure of delivering it. But with bad news, you keep hurrying. You want to get it off your hands. Share it."

"Which means yours is bad?"

"Bad. Sad. It's nothing I want to hang onto for the pure relish of it. Jane Lawson was killed yesterday."

I stopped. He kept going for three strides and turned and looked at me and said, "I know. She was more alive than most."

"Vehicle?"

"No. From what I understand from Hirsh, somebody trashed her house. The police think it was high school kids. The younger daughter runs with a batch of kids who have been feuding with other gangs of girls. They think it was revenge of some kind. The girl's possessions were pretty much destroyed, and it looks as if perhaps Jane came back while the damage was happening. She would have run into her place and tried to stop them, of course."

"If it was a gang of girls, yes. I'd buy that."

"It doesn't look intentional. It looks as if she could have been grappling with someone, trying to restrain them, and someone else grabbed her from behind by the hair to pull her away and broke her neck."

"Jesus God!"

"When she went down, they got out of there in a hurry. The other daughter came home and found her late yesterday afternoon. Hirsh woke me up at eleven-thirty last night, phoning me to tell me about it. For a while I could hardly understand him."

"Do they have a time of death?"

"They say between one-thirty and three, preliminary. The electric clock in the younger daughter's room stopped at two-fifteen when somebody threw it against the wall."

"Do they have the younger daughter, Judy, in custody?"

"Maybe. Hirsh said they were still looking for her at ten last night. Apparently neighbors are no help in that place. It's designed for a kind of privacy, so it is difficult to see people come and go. There are no community areas or activities. People are moving in and moving out frequently. With all the window airconditioners on and the televisions and radios and all the children in that development, nobody hears anything. And if there was some suspicion of something unpleasant going on, the neighborhood reaction would be to turn up the volume on the set and not check the time. Otherwise one might become involved. If you get involved, you can spend untold hours sitting around, waiting to be called into court."

"Meyer?" I said.

He gave a little start. "Sorry. I got sidetracked. Come along. I do have coffee made. I'll have to suggest a study of why people become involved and why they don't."

"Like the forward pass."

"You lost me, Travis."

"When you pass the ball, six possible things can happen, and five of them are bad."

He was silent until he handed me the mug of black coffee, reaching out over the stern quarter to hand it to me where I sat on the dock. "Five things can go wrong?" he asked.

"One, incomplete. Two, intercepted. Three, caught and fumbled. Four, penalized for offensive pass interference. Five, caught for no gain or for a loss."

"I forgot about the penalty."

"Also, they can smear your quarterback just as he unloads and put him out for the rest of the season. That makes six bad things out of seven chances. Why are we doing this, Meyer?"

"So as not to discuss Jane Lawson."

"Let's let her wait in the wings while I tell you about Dave Davis and Harry Harris."

He listened and had no comment until I requested one. And his comment was a pass. He said it needed thought. The alternate assumptions put it into the province of symbolic logic.

I said, "Jack does the family marketing whenever it rains in the afternoon, if it is not one of Jill's bridge days, provided it is not one of the Tuesdays or Fridays when Jack rides to work with Ben."

"Scoff, if it amuses you."

I gave him back his empty mug and stood up. "I have the feeling that nothing is going to be able to give me much amusement for quite a while."

When I was two steps away, he said, "You had your phone turned off last night?"

"I do believe I did."

I went back home and sat in the lounge and thought about Jane Lawson for a little while and looked at my watch. Twenty-five minutes before noon. I went to the master stateroom and opened the door. Mary Alice had shifted position since I had crept out. There was a faint breath of coolness in the airconditioning—she did not like it turned high—and she lay face down, diagonally asprawl across the big bed, sheet down to her bare waist, one hand under her cheek, the other fist clenched close under her chin. One tangle of black hair was sheafed across her sleeping eyes, and shining strands hung down over the side of the bed.

I eased myself stealthily onto the bed to sit and look down at her. There was her own mix of scents in the cabin air, a smell of sleep and girl and Mary Alice, a sort of smoky smell, pungently sweet, with an undertaste of tart, like a wine just turning.

I had not believed she would be in my bed. Not after I had defied Jane's warning about her. When the watch had stabbed me awake on the beach, I had leaned and propped my arms on either side of her and bent to her lips and kissed her awake. Her lips rolled softly open, and then she pushed me away and stared at me, pulled me back down very strongly for about a low four count, then shoved violently and rolled away, rolled up onto knuckles and haunches and stared at me through dark hair. I reached out and caught her arm and said, "What is it with you?"

She tossed her hair back, yanked her arm free. "I don't want to get into that anymore. I really don't."

"Never?"

"Never," she said and stood up.

I got up too and said, "It's . . . an unusual decision."

"Now you can tell me it's ruining my health. Anybody can look at me and see I'm a wreck."

"Mary Alice, it's your body and your decision to make. I'm not going to argue and pressure you. I didn't mean to upset you. I'm sorry."

"Why should you be sorry?" she said. "I'm . . . going for a walk, okay?"

She went down the little stretch of beach. She went as far as she could go without swimming, which was about a hundred feet. She picked up a handful of small shells from the tide line and stood plunking them out into the sea. I found a piece of driftwood, a flat board off somebody's dock or beach steps, and used it as a shovel and dug a hole deep enough to bury our debris above the tide line, with about eighteen inches of sand stomped down on top of it. When I looked at her again, she was sitting on the little slope of beach, arms around her legs, chin on a knee, staring toward Africa. I could tell that it was a time of thought for her, a time of decision. When at last she came back, she was determinedly merry and carefree. I could not read her at all.

There was time for another swim. We swam around to the bay side, and I got two sets of masks, snorkels, and swim fins out of the locker. We swam to a place where boats had anchored, and we found rare and unusual treasure on the bottom. Genesee and Blatz and Pauli Girl. Coors and Utica Club and Hockstein brewed in Rollie, Alabama. Vintage aluminum. Rare brands brought from afar.

Her forced jolliness seemed to become genuine later on. We frolicked and raced and startled some small fish. Then it was time to pack up and run for it, with no time for skiing on the way back to the Royal Biscayne.

Then she stopped me as I was slowing to make the turn between the club channel markers. She wanted me to wait a minute, right there. So I got myself opposite the tide and held it in place with just the port engine turning softly in gear. She stood in balance, her back to me, and then turned and came over and stood close in quarter profile.

"Would they mind my leaving my car there?" I had to lean close and make her repeat it.

"No. They wouldn't mind. Is it what you want?"

She turned her face further away. "I don't know what I

want. I'm stuck. Right in the middle. Dammit, when I *want* somebody to hustle me . . ."

I pulled her chin around and uptilted it, but she would not look at me. Her glance slid down and away, off to the side. I put the starboard engine in gear. I turned the boat until she was headed northeast, toward the channel. I took Mary Alice's hand and put it on the starboard throttle. I took hold of the port. I put the loop of line over the spoke to lock the wheel.

I said, "Okay. As I push this throttle, the port engine is going to pick up speed, heading for the channel, heading for home. Let's say that is my intention. But the wheel is locked, so if the starboard throttle stays right where it is, all I am going to do is make one hell of a big circle and end up aiming back into the yacht club."

She didn't say anything. Her hand was slack on the throttle. I slowly pushed mine up. We went almost straight and then began to turn more and more easterly. I could see I was going to have some problems with water traffic if I waited too long for her. She took her hand off, and as I was about to accept that as her decision, she hit the throttle with the heel of her hand, banging it all the way forward. She sat in the copilot's chair. The maneuver gave me a couple of very busy seconds flipping the loop off, yanking the throttle back, turning the wheel.

I said, "When you make up your mind, honey, you—"

"Shut up and drive," she said.

I went outside, got on my heading, and put it on pilot. She did not want a beer. She did not want a drink. She did not want any conversation, thanks. So I took a beer back and sat on the engine hatch as we roared through the calm sea, tipping and lifting a little in the swell that was just beginning to build. She stood up and leaned her folded arms on the top of the windshield, staring ahead for a long time, standing hipshot with ankles crossed. The light of the dying day was gold and orange. The shore was turning blue-gray, the sea to indigo.

I guessed that in another five minutes I would take it out of pilot and turn toward the sea buoy and the early lights of Lauderdale. She came striding back, losing her balance and catching it, looking angry, and said, "Can you turn everything off and sort of just float out here? Please?"

Done. A sudden silence until ears can find the smaller sounds. Dip and pitch and roll, water slapping the hull, something rolling and thumping in a gear locker, water sloshing the cooler.

She went back and sat on the broad transom which was also the engine hatch, swiveled to hang her legs over the stern. I sat beside her, facing inboard.

"I don't talk about my husband," she said.

"People have noticed."

So she talked about him. She hopped back and forth in time and space, with silences between. I didn't come in with questions. She had to set her own tempo of revelation. She had gone steady with a boy for several years. She'd caught the eye of an older man, one of the McDermit brothers who had a lot of food-service companies in Pennsylvania and New Jersey, catering airlines, operating coffee-break concessions and cafeterias in factories and offices, owning vending machines and warehousing facilities. He had big cars, phones in his cars, a duplex apartment with a staff, an executive jet.

She had played one against the other, in a girlish mischief. Then abruptly Tom, the boyfriend, had died in a one-car accident, lost control at high speed on the interstate. McDermit had been gentle, understanding, comforting. She had married him.

"Then it all turned so rotten," she said. "They owned race horses, those brothers. I was another thing, like a horse that costs so much to keep, you can do any damn thing you want with it. He liked to hit. He liked to hurt. He couldn't really make it any other way. He was trying to break me. We had a big fight, and I told him Tom had been a man, and he wasn't a man. He said he had a specialist put a gadget inside the wheel cap on Tom's right front wheel, set so that at seventy it would push a weight against a spring thing and blow the lugs off. He said Tom was dead meat. I said he was never going to touch me again, and I was getting a divorce. He said nobody was ever going to touch me again, so I didn't need a divorce. He said to get out if I wanted to, but if I let anybody have me, he'd have both of us killed."

She hadn't really believed him. She'd gone to a lawyer who accepted the divorce action eagerly, then suddenly cooled off. When she insisted on knowing why, he took her into a little conference room and closed the door. He was sweaty. He told her she should go back to her husband. He said the brothers were always involved in legal actions, and sometimes they were indicted, but nothing had ever gone any further than that. He told her he didn't want her business, she didn't owe him a dime, please leave.

She tried another town and another name, and McDermit had phoned her at work to say hello. He found her more quickly the second time. So she had come to Miami and gone back to her own name. "His people check on me. Somebody comes around every couple of months. You get used to it. Five years, practically. It isn't all that rough, getting along without. It isn't that big a part of life."

"Why now and why me, Mary Alice?"

She sighed. "I hope you can find your way in off this ocean in the dark."

"No problem."

"Look at all the stars! You can see them better out here."

"Evading the question?"

"No man in his right mind is going to take a chance on getting killed, just to get one specific piece of ass out of all the ass there is floating around. And besides, I'm not all that great in bed. I'm a big healthy girl, but I'm just sort of average sexy, like you'd find anywhere."

"Question still pending, lady."

"I'm saying it *isn't* now and it *isn't* you, because it could have been if I decided, but instead I've told you why it shouldn't happen. It would be stupid of you. And it would be stupid of me to let myself get into it. I've had it all pushed down out of sight, and I'm okay. I get along fine."

"Then let me ask it a different way. Why did you *almost* decide on now and on me?"

"Not because you are so absolutely irresistible, believe me. If I was inventing a guy to . . . break my fast with, he would sort of be like Michael Landon, only a foot taller."

"Like who?"

"If you don't know, never mind. I think that the way it started, I had the idea that if I ever got the nerve to take the risk, it should be with somebody who'd be awfully damned hard to kill, and then maybe he could keep me alive too. It was just . . . what is the word when you think of things you aren't going to do?"

"Conjecture?"

"Right! I conjectured about us. Then I woke up on the beach, and you were asleep, and I looked at you and kind of wanted you. Still conjecture. Then you kissed me, and I was having a dream it fitted into. Then I went down the beach and thought about it, and then I began playing some kind of fool game about it, but you have to come to the end of games, right? Something to get killed over? Who needs it? Come on, dear. You better start aiming me toward home. I'm sorry. I really am."

"And you don't play quicky games, do you?"

She snapped her head around. "You better not be asking me to."

"I'm not."

"If I wanted to sneak it, I could have had all a girl could need."

"I know."

"It would have to be something that starts and keeps going until somebody finally says whoa. Out in the open. People would know just by seeing me look at the guy."

And now, in the shadows of the curtained master stateroom, I wanted to see that look. I slowly ran the ball of my thumb down the crease of her back, from shoulder-blades to the little knobs in the small of her back. She sighed and moved slowly and made a small murmur of complaint. Then suddenly she stiffened, sprang up and back and away from me, eyes wide and blank in terror, as she grasped the sheet and pulled it up across her breasts.

She expelled the frightened in-suck of breath in a long grateful sigh, hooked her hair back out of the way with curled fingers, gave me a small and uncertain smile and said, "Talk about having a heart attack, darling."

"Bad dreams?"

"Mmmm. Hold me, huh?"

I stretched out beside her, atop the sheet, and put my arms around her. She put her face in my throat. She chuckled.

"What's funny?"

"A dirty joke a girl told me where I have lunch. It sort of fits. You know. I'll mess it up if I try to tell it."

"Try."

It was the one about the doctor with the gorgeous girl patient who comes in with a hangnail and has to strip for the complete physical, and it ends with the tag line, "Don't be silly, Miss Jones. I shouldn't even be doing *this!*"

And she didn't tell it very well.

"Darling?" she said.

"Wha'?"

"Tell me exactly what you promised and exactly what you are going to do."

"Hmm. Let's see. I am going to put extra drums of fuel aboard this here vessel. I am going to equip her and provision her for a voyage of uncertain duration. And at the first hint that your freak husband is after us, whenever you say go, we go, taking the *Muñequita* in tow. If the weather is good enough, we see if we have enough good luck and good management to get over to the islands. If not, we lay at anchor somewhere down Biscayne Bay or in Florida Bay until we get the right weather."

"When I say we're leaving, what do you do?"

"I do not argue. I do not discuss. I do not negotiate. I hang up the phone, start the engines, and wait for you."

She gave me a very strong hug. "That's our deal."

"That's our deal, M.A."

"Time is it?"

"Moving up onto noon."

"What! Good Lord!"

"Something must have relaxed you, honey."

"Sure didn't look like anything was going to at first. I was absolutely hopeless. I was just too tense and nervous and scared to be worth a damn. You are a very patient guy."

"In a self-serving kind of way."

There was a long silence and small motions finally, body language involved in question and answer, query and response, trick or treat. And off in the side of my mind was a fleeting recap of Meyer's insight, that we all tend to save good news as long as we can. But sometimes, with a little tickle of guilt, we find a compelling reason to save the bad for a little while too.

She was still taking her long sloshing steaming soapy noisy shower when I took her Bloody Mary into the head and yelled to her that she would find it on the counter beside the sink. She yelled her thanks.

Aboard the *Flush*, under a bunk, there is a big storage drawer full of lady items which have been left behind or bought for emergencies or donated to the cause. No point in even looking, because had there been a previous lady of these dimensions, I would remember. But her yellow top and shorts were still fresh enough.

The very best eggs and country ham and toasted English muffins with strawberry jam. We sat in the booth next to the stainless steel galley, and she was right about that blue-eyed look of hers. She looked at me often, during and between the forks of egg, the bites of muffin. Anybody intercepting that look would have wondered if it was melting the fillings in my teeth. Bloodhounds look at the moon that way, and kids look into candy stores that way, and barracuda look at bait fish that way.

We shared the cleaning up and took final cups of coffee into the lounge. So I took a deep breath and looked over her shoulder, out the port, at the sunny gleam of the row of boats and told her about Jane Lawson. Glassy shock. Exclamations of disbelief. Yawls and yawps of grief, pain, and anger. Reddened, streaming eyes, considerable nose-blowing, and then she wanted to be held, patted, comforted as the residual snuffles and snorts became less frequent.

She went and fixed her face and came back and phoned Hirsh Fedderman. He had to tell her all he knew about it. She made wordless sounds of shock and sympathy. The tears began running again, and she made frantic motions at me. I put the box of tissue within reach. She asked questions in a torn and tearful voice and honked into the wads of kleenex. After that was over, she had to have another session of holding, patting, comforting and then go fix her face again.

She came back and plumped herself down. "I'm exhausted," she said. "I felt so marvelous, and now I'm pooped. It makes my problems seem like nothing at all. Hirsh is really down. The poor old guy. The last straw, sort of. I don't know what he's going to do now. I know what I better do. I better go and be with him. He hasn't really got anybody else. Not near by."

She got her things. At the doorway from the lounge onto the aft deck, we kissed. For a casual kiss, she felt big and hearty, solid and tall, practically eye to eye with me on her tiptoes. For what she considered any important kissing, she had a strange knack of dwindling herself. She curved her shoulders forward, let herself cling, but without much tangible weight, delicately in fact.

She looked up at me. "We're some kind of special."

"That's what people keep saying about us, all over town."

"Can I be kind of a coward?"

"How?"

"Don't come to my place. That's asking for trouble. Don't phone me, there or at the store. Just to play safe. Okay?"

"Don't call us, we'll call you?"

"Constantly. You won't believe how often. I'm going to walk all tilted over from the weight of the dimes."

So I locked my floating house and went on ahead. I went and got Miss Agnes and came back around and picked up Mary Alice. She nipped in and slunched down, saying, "All of a sudden this is a pretty conspicuous car."

"And no matter what you ride in, you are a conspicuous lady."

"Isn't *that* the damned truth."

"Would you feel better if I wore a dress and a blond wig?"

She turned and stared at me. "You would make the most incredibly ugly woman in all Florida."

"Just stop being so edgy."

"I'll try. But he's a sick, murderous, tricky bastard."

Ten

I drove her to the club. The man at the gate remembered Miss Agnes far better than he remembered me. And as before, he looked as if it took a great effort of will for him to keep from asking to please never bring such an ugly old handmade pickup into paradise.

There was a slot where I could park near her Toyota. She got in her car, and I put her beach bag in. She gave me a shy, nervous, quick little smile and said she'd phone or maybe just drive up there, if that would be all right. I told her anything would be fine. She hit her brakes a foot shy of a lot of sedate gray Continental as she backed out and then thumped over some curbing as she made her turn. Goodbye, dear girl. And take care of yourself. And Hirsh.

I retraced the route I had used when driving Jane Lawson home. We had been talking. I had followed her instructions without paying too much attention to the turns. So I got partially lost at about the halfway point and nearly lost when I was almost there. When I came upon it, there were two cars in the drive with that vaguely official look. There was a rental Oldsmobile at the curb, and a burly brown man with a shaved head was leaning against the front fender with his arms folded, managing to look patient and impatient at the same time. He wore a white short-sleeved shirt and blue sailcloth Bermudas. His calves and forearms were thick, sinewy, and very hairy.

I parked twenty feet in front of the green Olds and came walking back. He said, "There is absolutely nothing to see here. Get back into that . . . vehicle and drag ass."

I took the final six slow strides that put me in front of him. He was fifty at a distance and early sixties close up. But he was fit. Very fit. He even seemed to have muscles on his forehead. I couldn't fit him into any part of the picture until I noticed the ring on his finger.

"Are you Jane's father-in-law, sir?"

"I'm General Lawson. Why? Who are you? If you are another goddamn newspaper—"

"My name is McGee. Travis McGee. I'm a salvage consultant. I drove Jane home Friday after work. She asked me in. While we were talking, Judy came in and left with some friends. I found out about this terrible thing this morning. I live in Fort Lauderdale. It is reasonable to assume that in the course of questioning Mr. Fedderman, her employer, and Mrs. McDermit, her co-worker, they would ask them when was the last time they saw Mrs. Lawson, and they would say when she left with me. So, in a spirit of cooperation, I thought it would be well to report to whoever is investigating the case. General, I am very sorry about this. I also wish to point out that all of this is none of your goddam business, and I am humoring you because I hear the habit of command is hard to shake."

He unfolded his arms, and his chin moved six inches toward me. "What's that? What did you say?"

"I said I gave you more answer than I had to."

"What were you to Jane?"

"I'll even answer that, sir. An acquaintance."

He closed his eyes for a moment. "They've been coming by. Creeps. Sickies." He tilted his head, frowning, staring at me. "They go by nine times at three miles an hour, or they stop and get out and stand and gawp at the door with no more expression on their face than a ball of suet. Families with little children, standing and staring, with God only knows what kind of dim thoughts moving around in their empty skulls. I've sent a lot of them on their way. The sun is hot, and I've got a cheap lunch sitting like a stone in my stomach, and the law is hunting down my granddaughter. In other words, I apologize."

He put his hand out. I took it without hesitation.

He opened the car door and sat sideways on the seat and looked up at me. "Pride is so goddamned wickedly expensive. I have been waiting here, thinking about pride."

"Sir?"

"Three sons. Jerry was the only one who went into the service and the only one who died. The other two are doing fine. I retired early. Heart murmur. The second star was a going-away present. Bought a little grove in California. Take care of the trees. Gardening. Golf. Bridge. Am I boring you?"

"No, sir."

"I'm boring myself. Somebody has to get stuck with listening. They paved a road near my place. I went and watched them every day. Isn't that fascinating? Old fart watching the big yellow machines. Made myself agreeable. Asked questions. Never saw such a crowd of fuckups, pouring money down the sewer. Found a couple of my retired NCOs and officers, as bored as I was. All put some money in the pot. Rented equipment after we bid low on a culvert. Made out. Ploughed it back in. Every one of those other six old farts have taken at least two million out of it. And I kept fifty percent of everything. Seven corporations. Factory structures in Taiwan. Flood control in Brazil. Bridges in Tanzania. Pipe lines in Louisiana. Shrewd old bastard, right? Wrong. Just bored doing nothing. Horse sense and energy and being fair. Nothing more. There's a Christ-awful shortage of horse sense in the world. Always has been. Ask me where the pride comes in. Go ahead. Ask me."

"Where does the pride come in, General?"

"Me beginning to make money hand over fist, and Jerry's widow with two little girls. I had to travel a lot, leaving Bess alone. Lots of room in that house, and if there wasn't, I could build more onto it. No, she was too proud. She wanted to make her own way. Raise Jerry's kids without help from anybody. Bess wanted to come down here and visit her and talk her into it and bring her back. She was sure she could. So my pride got in the way. If the damned girl wants to act like that, let her. Jane's pride and my pride. Send too big a check along with the Christmas stuff, and she'd send it right back. Oh shit, isn't pride wonderful? She stayed right here in this half-ass place leading a half-ass life, when if she'd wanted to spend a thousand dollars a day of my money, it would have tickled but not pinched. So she's gone down the drain after a lot of scruffy little years, and the youngest girl has gone sour. For what? There's no meaning to it at all. None." He put his elbows on his knees, his face in his hands.

I gave him ten seconds and then said, "Are you waiting for them in there?"

He looked at me as if he had forgotten who I was. "Oh, they're supposed to be finishing up. I can go in when they're through, they told me." He patted his shirt pocket. "Linda is over at the hotel with Bess. I've got a list of things. I don't want that little girl to have to come back here even one more time. She had one look. This was her home. She shouldn't remember it like the way it is now."

I excused myself and went up the steps and pushed the buzzer. I told my story to a fat young man with a guardsman moustache. He took me back through litter and ruin to a bedroom where two technicians were working in a perfume stink, patiently dusting the larger fragments of glass. A large man sat on the bed, murmuring into the bedside extension. He had a big head and golden locks and a great big face and jaw, with fleshy, regular features. He hung up and stared at me with a look of total, vapid stupidity. It did not change as I went through my little account for the third time.

He said, "My name is Goodbread, and so far I'm making the file on this one. What I hope, McGee, is that you are one of the kinks we get now and then, they kill somebody and come back and say they just happened to know that somebody and how are you boys making out catching the killer, heh?"

"Sorry I can't help you that way."

He favored me with a long, stupid stare. "I might anyway have Arn run you down and check you through everybody's computer file."

"There's somebody you could ask."

"The mayor?"

"Captain Matty Lamarr."

"Your first name again? Travis? Stand easy." He phoned again. He had a very soft telephone voice. He held the phone in such a way that half his big hand formed a cup around the mouthpiece. I guess he was getting the home number. The captain was a few years past pulling Sunday duty. He held the bar down, then dialed again. Big swift nimble fingers. He spoke, waited a time, then spoke again. Listened a long time. And another question. More listening. Expression of gratitude. Hung up.

"The captain didn't say you are his favorite people."

"He's not one of mine, but we got along all right one time."

"He says there's no use asking you what kind of an angle you are working."

"If any."

"He says he thinks you stay inside the law, just inside, most of the time."

"I try, Lieutenant."

"Sergeant. And he said you answer questions right, or you clam up, and you can be a help if you want to be."

"I liked the woman. I didn't know her well, but I liked her."

"The captain says that the only handle he could find to use on you was that you don't want your name in the paper."

"There's a point where that handle breaks right off, Sergeant."

His long stare was lethargic, his eyes sleepy. "So let me know if you feel anything starting to give, McGee."

"Can I suggest something to you?"

"You go ahead, and then I'll tell you if you should have."

"The woman's father-in-law is waiting out at the curb in a rented car. He wants to pick up some things for the older daughter."

"And?"

"If you know who you are keeping waiting, okay. But I read an article about him in a magazine a couple of months ago. That is Major General Samuel Horace Lawson, and Lawson International is listed on the big board, and in his line of work I would guess that he gives a bundle to both political parties, and if he gets annoyed enough, he is going to—"

"Arn!" Sergeant Goodbread roared. The fat young one with the guardsman moustache came in almost at a run, his eyes round.

"Arn, fill me on that guy you talked to out front."

"Uh . . . he's related. Lawson. Old folks. He just wants to get some stuff out of here when we're through. For the daughter. Why? He'll keep."

"Did he call himself General Lawson?"

"Sure. But you know how many old generals we've got around this state . . ."

Sergeant Goodbread went out and brought the general into the house, apologizing for the delay. He helped Lawson with the list of items and had Arn carry them out to the Olds. Goodbread talked for about ten minutes to Lawson in the living room. I could hear the voices but not the words. The airconditioner was too loud. I sat on the bed. The technicians kept going listlessly through the broken glass looking for clean fresh prints. Or even fresh smudges. Many many police officers have worked in criminal investigation until retirement without ever working on a case where a fingerprint made one damned bit of difference one way or the other. A skilled man knows a fresh print or smudge the instant he brings it out by the way the natural oil from the skin responds.

Lawson left. Goodbread came to the doorway and beckoned me into the living room. A chair and the end of the couch had been cleared off. A plastic tape box crunched under his heel and some brown stereo tape caught around his ankle. He motioned me toward the couch, and he bent and plucked the tape off his ankle before he sat in the chair. He took a stenopad out and opened it and put it on his heavy thigh and said, "Description of Judith Lawson, please."

I shut my eyes for a moment and rebuilt her, head to toe. I started to give it to him slowly, but I saw he was using some form of speedwriting or shorthand, so I delivered it more quickly. I gave him the conversation as I remembered it, not word for word, but reasonably close.

He closed the pad and said, "Thanks for your cooperation."

"Can I ask some questions?"

"What for?"

"I want to waste your time with my idle curiosity, Sergeant. Like I wasted your time telling you about General Lawson."

"He mentioned . . . Captain Lamarr mentioned you get kind of smartass."

"Is the reconstruction that she came home and found persons unknown busting up this place?"

"No way to check it, but she was wearing street clothes,

and her purse was found beside the body. Without a dime in it."

"And where was the body?"

He hesitated. "In that doorway there to that hall, legs in this room, head in the hall."

"Was the airconditioner on when the body was found?"

He looked at the ceiling, and for a moment that massive face firmed up, losing the practiced and deceptive look of the dullard. "On when I got here. Which seems several days ago and was yesterday. Linda Lawson said the only things she touched were the front door, which wasn't locked, and her mother and that telephone. Why?"

"When we got here Friday, the heat would knock you down. She apologized. The house rule was last one out turns it off, first one in turns it on. It made a hell of a noise on high, but cooled off the place fast."

He went over to the door and walked back into the room. He came back and sat down. "So the kids were busting up the back of the place when she came in, and this room was okay, and so she went over . . ."

He paused. I said, "If you hear a noise, you don't turn on something that makes it harder to hear."

He nodded. "And if you are going to sneak in and bust a place up, you don't turn on a lot of noise that would keep you from hearing if anybody is coming. And the daughter would have had to walk further to turn it on than to get to her mother."

We sat in silent contemplation. He tapped the stenopad and said, "Unless this little chickie was part of the group."

"For what reason?"

"Do they need reasons?"

"How did they get in?"

"Awning window in Judy's room was open wide, screen pushed into the room. A small person could wiggle through and go open the back door or the front."

I looked at the floor, at thin shards of picture glass and at a triangular piece of the face of the long-dead Jerry Lawson, a piece containing one eye looking up at me. Next to it was a tape cartridge, multitrack, plastic cracked, tape dangling from it. The color picture on the plastic housing was of a young girl, smiling mouth agape, eyes half-closed in song. The press-apply label on the tape box read $7.79. The broken box and label looked fresh and neat.

I picked it up. I handed it to Goodbread. He threw it on the floor and said, "I know, I know. Damnit. What kids wouldn't rip off new tapes? Take the money in the purse. Leave perfume. Smash everything in the kitchen, including bourbon, one bottle, seal intact. What kind of kids, everybody puts on gloves in the summertime before they touch anything? Something else too."

He got up and went into the next room and came back with a nine-by-twelve manila envelope. He undid the clasp and looked through glossies and selected one and handed it to me, saying, "You never saw this."

I studied it. At first it made no sense, and then I saw what he meant. It was a picture taken with a wide lens and flash, looking down at the doorway where the body had been. There was a ghost outline of a woman lying on her side, head tilted back.

He bent over me, pointed with a thick finger. "Along here some kind of bag or box of some kind of cake mix or cookie mix hit the wall and exploded and came sifting through the air. Then along here, where the side of this leg was, are pieces of a blue and white vase, very small pieces. When the examiner started to roll her over, I saw the clean floor underneath her, so I had them lift her off it very careful."

I looked up at him. "So what kind of glove-wearing kids, who wouldn't rip off tapes, perfume, or booze, broke her neck and went right on trashing the house?"

He sat down. "If you take total freaks, if they did not give one damn about anything, where do the gloves fit the pattern?"

"Where are the dirty words?"

"The what?"

"With paint, catsup, lipstick, anything. On the walls. Where's the big pie? Don't they always think of putting all the clothes in the middle of the kitchen floor or in the bathtub and pouring everything liquid on top of the mess?"

"I never thought of that," he said. "It's kind of orderly. Wrong word, I guess. Break everything breakable. Tip all the furniture over. Dump all the drawers. Slash the clothes and bedding." He tapped his notebook again. "Mama came home and had another fight with this kid. It got physical, and mama got killed. So the kid trashed the house to make it look as if she didn't do it. She trashed her own stuff."

"Or someone was in here looking for something to steal when she came home, Sergeant. Lost his nerve. Tried to grab her when she ran. Broke her neck. Then tried to make it look like kids."

"Except where is the girl? Why doesn't she show?"

"But if it was *your* way, she would have to show up to make it work, wouldn't she? Running would spoil her idea."

He wiped the lower half of his face with a big slow hand. He looked tired. "I've got more to think about than I need. I want to decide whether or not I want to stay on this. I can get off in thirty seconds, risking nothing."

"I don't understand."

"The general doesn't want publicity. The press hasn't made him yet. I told him I want to keep it that way as long as I can because without him, this one is low priority. Three column inches on page thirty-one. An indoor mugging of a middle-aged widow. If whoever killed her keeps on thinking it's handled on a routine basis—which means only so many man hours, lab hours, leg work, and then into the open file—maybe that person won't do such a good job of covering as they would if they knew all the pressure there is behind it. I can get departmental priority, quietly, on the basis of who he is, and it improves my chances of a wrapup on it. But if I tip the press, if I made a private call, say, to Gene Miller on the *Herald,* then it moves from page thirty-one to maybe a big story on the first page of the second section. It hits a lot of sensitive areas. It gets political. The person or persons we're looking for are alerted, and so they go back and put a lot more braces and rivets on the alibi. And as I told the general, they will cover Judy Lawson's trouble with the law, because when something gets big, on the days when there's nothing new, they go back and dig up the old and print it, because if it isn't known, it's new. And official sources get into the act."

"What do you mean?"

"Official sources revealed today that the persons who murdered Jane Lawson may have in fact been looking for her younger daughter Judy, arrested seven months ago by vice-squad undercover agents—"

"Vice squad!"

"She was fifteen then, working with two older boys. There was a rash of it at the time, kids working the parks and working over the tourists. The girl smiles and wags her little behind and tells the mark she'll give a ten-dollar treat over in the bushes or over in that camper or van. He goes for it, and the boys jump him and pick him clean. Maybe one mark in ten files a complaint. A lot of them are users. Maybe the others are behind in their car payments. They ran Judy through medical, and she wasn't using, and she wasn't dosed, and it was first time, so she got two years in the custody of her mother. The boys were already in the files and legally adults, so they didn't make out that well. Anyway, if it should break, they would take me off and give it to somebody with a lot more rank. The general has given me a deadline to come up with something promising, and if I don't, he's going to break it himself by coming up with such a reward for information it will clog the switchboards for a week."

"How much time?"

"Not enough."

"Where is he staying?"

"In a hotel."

"Thanks. Thanks very much."

"I've stopped being an information service. Where can I find you if I want you?" I told him, and he wrote it down.

"And if you think of anything, McGee, get in touch right away. Don't try to decide what is and what isn't worth telling me. Get in touch."

He stood up. I was dismissed. When I looked back, before closing the door, he was staring into space, big face slack, mouth sagging open, eyes sleepy and lifeless. It was a *shtick* I'd never seen before: Here is a cop so stupid you don't have to keep your guard quite so high. Here is a cop who needs help finding his way out of a phone booth. Somebody's dumb brother-in-law. Sure. I could see how that style would fit a lengthy interrogation. Long pauses. Simple questions. A lack of comprehension requiring endless repetition. "And what was it you said you did after that?" Then the eventual, inevitable, fatal contradiction, because the one thing successful lying requires is total recall of all the details of the structure of lies, and that is rare anywhere, even among men who face prison if they fumble just one critical question.

Eleven

I drove over to the beach and put old Ag into a private, fenced lot which bragged of its security measures. On the way I had stopped at a mainland shopping center and was now the owner of a red and white flight bag containing shorts, socks, shirt, and precuffed slacks which were going to be too short. I carried the cheap sport coat over my arm. The rest of the overnight essentials were in the new flight bag. Thai International.

The same cold-eyed man was on the desk. I told him to tell Mr. Nucci that Mr. McGee wanted to check in. He once again muttered on the phone, hung up, spun the visitab index, turned, and picked a key out of the mail rack.

He put a card in front of me and said, "Please."

I hesitated and could think of no reason why I shouldn't be exactly who I was and so signed in. A bellhop took me on a long easterly walk to far elevators. We rode up to eighteen and walked further east, to the end of the corridor. He turned on all the lights. It took some time. He had to work his way around a big room. He finally left, with tip, and I was alone with my big beds on a circular platform, with my electric drapes, my stack of six big bath towels, my balcony overlooking the sea, my icemaker, my sunken tub, my coral carpeting six inches deep.

I phoned Meyer aboard the Keynes. I told him that I was in 1802 at the Contessa, and it seemed a convenient, temporary refuge. I asked him what he did when he knew he had heard something that meant something, and he should be able to remember what it was, and he couldn't. He said he usually walked back and forth and then went to sleep. I asked him if that did any good, and he said practically never.

I tried Mary Alice and hung up after the tenth unanswered ring. There was a tapping at my door. A waiter brought in a tray with a sealed bottle of Plymouth gin, a double old-fashion glass, a large golden lemon, and a tricky knife with which to cut slices of rind. Willy Nucci followed the waiter in and waved him back out and closed the door.

Willy came over and shook my hand. He smiled at me. "How do you like this room? All right?"

"Willy!"

"Want me to fix you one of your crazy gin on the rocks, or do you want to do it?"

"Willy!"

"What I can do, pal, I can send up this Barbara I've got doing some PR for the place, living here in the house, little bit of a thing, she learned massage in Tokyo, and it's the damnedest thing, she uses her feet. She walks on your back. You wouldn't believe. Let me send her up, you'll never regret it. Pretty little thing."

"Sit the hell down!" I roared.

He backed up and sat down and wiped his mouth. "I was only—"

"Willy, the room, the bottle, a girl walking on me . . . What in God's name has gotten into you?"

"Anything you want in this hotel is yours. It is only to ask. Okay?"

"What makes me so important all of a sudden?"

"You've always been important to me, McGee."

Then light dawned. I stared at him. I laughed. He didn't. I said, "Willy, your grapevine works too fast."

"I hear what I have to know."

"Like I'm working for Frank Sprenger?"

"Remember one thing. This is the first time his name has ever been mentioned between us."

"Why should you and I have ever talked about Sprenger?"

Some of the tension went out of him, and his shoulders came down about an inch. "I'm not asking you what you're doing for him, am I?"

"I'm not doing anything for him, Willy."

The shoulders went up again. "You took his money. That I know."

"I took his money."

"Some of the things you've done haven't been all the way bright, McGee, but if you are saying what you seem to be saying, then you are being a hundred and ten percent stupid. If you take Sprenger's money, you do something he wants done. If you don't do it, you don't get to give the money back. You don't jerk around with any Frank Sprenger."

"We're involved here in semantics, Willy."

"You said you're not doing anything for him."

"I'm not doing anything against him."

Shoulders went all the way back to normal. "Oh! Then that's what you're doing for him. Not doing anything to screw him up. Which means he thinks you can or will be able to."

"One small item and not much money."

He nodded. "Like that thing we—" He stopped himself. "Like if he was involved in some kind of investment and didn't get what he thought he was buying, and somebody wanted you to help with the real stuff."

"Are these rooms bugged without you knowing for sure?" I asked him.

"People are in and out all day. I do the best I can for the owners. And the owners would want me to tell you this, Travis. And you tell Frank Sprenger for me. Any friend of his, any time, the best we got is what he gets. I personally guarantee it."

"I'll tell him what a damned good job Willy Nucci does for the owners. But I'd wager he knows that already."

"I try my best. What do you want? Just ask."

"I might want something later. Maybe later we could take a little walk together by the ocean and talk."

"I'll tell the switchboard, when you phone me it goes through right away."

"Thanks, Willy."

At the door he paused and turned. "Even if the only part you want is the massage, I'd recommend her. You'll sleep like a baby." I declined. He shrugged and left.

I tried Mary Alice for ten more rings. I tried Hirsh Federman. The woman said, "This here is Mrs. Franck speaking, a neighbor, I am sitting with Mr. Fedderman who is now sleeping at last, thank God."

"Was Mary Alice McDermit there? Or is she still there?"

"Here there is only me, Mrs. Franck, and there is Mr. Fedderman, like I said already, sound asleep. Who did you ask?"

"Mrs. McDermit. She was there today. When did she leave?"

"How should I know if I don't know her? I didn't meet everybody that comes here. This dear old man, he is blessed with friends. All day long too many people coming to see him, tiring him out, bringing enough food, we could feed Cuba maybe."

"Mary Alice works for him. She's a young woman with long black hair, six feet tall."

"Ah! Oh! You should say so. That one. Yes. Such a size person they are growing these days. It is something in the food. What time is it now? Nearly nine? So she left at four o'clock, five hours ago. You missed her by a little. If she ever comes back, who shall I say is calling?"

"Thank you, never mind. How is Hirsh?"

"How do you think he is? That nice woman being killed in her own home by wicked children, fifteen years she worked for him, a faithful loyal person. His heart is broken in two. That's all that is wrong."

"I know it would be wrong to wake him up, and you wouldn't even if I asked you. So would you happen to know if a woman who used to work for him is still alive. I think her name is Moojah."

"Of course Miss Moojah is alive! Wasn't she here

today, bringing a hot casserole? She's in the book. Why don't you look? How many Moojahs are there going to be? She lives in Harmony Towers, that has a three-year waiting list for senior singles. Miss Moojah will be alive when all of us have passed away, believe it."

After I hung up, I checked the directory. Yes indeed. A. A. Moojah. I wrote the number on the phone-side scratch pad, just as the phone rang.

"Hello?"

"Oh, great! Just dandy!"

"I called you twice. No answer. How did you find me?"

"Meyer told me."

"Meyer phoned you?"

"I didn't say that, sweetie. Meyer is sitting smiling at me like some kind of an owl."

"An owl. You mean he's here in . . . Oh."

"Yes indeed. Here I am in all my pretties, making my poor dear little yellow car go seventy-five on the turnpike."

"It always seems to me like downhill from there to Miami."

"If and when I feel like it, I'll check that out."

"When do you expect to feel like it? I have some things I want to talk to you about."

"Meyer is a wonderful conversationalist. I'm going to have another delicious drink, and then we're going to go eat somewhere nice. So don't wait up for me."

I started to explain that so many things were happening, it was too inefficient to try to commute, but I realized I was talking to an empty line.

I broke the seal on the bottle and was pleased to find that my personal icemaker made those nice little cubes the size of professional dice. After one sip I got out the card which one of my two visitors had given me—either Harry Harris or Dave Davis. The unlisted phone number was written on the back in red ballpoint.

When the phone was answered, I could hear music and laughter in the background. The girl said, "Whatever you were looking for, we got it."

"What I am looking for is Frank."

"We got . . . oops. Wrong way to go. Whom is speaking?"

"McGee. T. McGee."

"Just stand there," she said. She did not cover the mouthpiece perfectly, and I heard her bawling over the background noise, "Frank, somebody name McGee. You wannit?"

She came back on and said, "He'll come onto an extension in just a sec."

"Hello?" he said. "Let me hear you hang up, Sissie."

She let us both hear it, like a good rap on the ear with a tack hammer. "Sorry about that," he said. It was a deep, easy voice. "And sorry I couldn't come to see you the other day. I got tied up. I told them not to give out a name. Just the number where you could get in touch with either of them."

"They didn't give out any name, Mr. Sprenger. If it was in connection with something I was involved in, concerning a Mr. Fedderman, then I could add two and two, but I wasn't sure, of course. Then something made me sure."

"Such as?"

"I was over on the beach, and I stopped at the Americana for a drink, and somebody I know came over and said she understood I'm working for you now."

Five seconds of silence. "I find that *very* interesting. You wouldn't want to give me the name?"

"No, I wouldn't. But she doesn't work for you, as far as I know. I didn't appreciate it."

"How am I supposed to take that?"

"I don't know how you want to take it, Mr. Sprenger. I just don't want any confusion in anybody's mind about whose problems I'm supposed to be taking care of."

"Why don't you come to my office tomorrow, say about ten o'clock, and we can discuss your investment problems?"

"I found your Lincoln Road address in the book. About eleven would be better, I think."

"I'll see you whenever you arrive. Right now you and I are even with the board. I consider it full value received. Okay?"

I said everything was just fine. I hung up, smiling. It was worth a thousand dollars to him either way. If I was trying to con him into thinking there was a leak in his administrative apparatus, it was worth it to know I was dull enough to try to con him. On the other hand, if there was a leak, he was tough and smart enough to find it. I knew there was a leak. And I knew that if it was a plant, my friend Willy Nucci was too shrewd to set himself up by letting the plant know where the information was going. One thing seemed reasonably certain. Frank Sprenger would have it sorted out by the time I met with him on Monday. And be duly grateful. I could guess how his mind would work. Absolute loyalty, absolute silence, these are required, are so critical, they are seldom even mentioned. Any violation of this credo is a form of voluntary suicide. The reason is that if the unreliable one talks to someone who intends no harm, and if someone who *does* mean harm can learn of the defection, then the threat of exposure is deadly enough to extract the same information for other uses. There are two reasons why they use the same sort of cell structure as do intelligence apparatuses. It limits the availability and dissemination of potentially damaging information. And it makes it a lot easier to track down any leak.

I stretched out on a chaise, drink at hand, scratch pad at hand, and began working my way through a tangle of phone lines toward Sergeant Goodbread. I finally persuaded a communications person to patch me through to Goodbread's vehicle.

"McGee, I can't make any kind of statement. You know that."

"This is sort of personal. When you can get to a phone, call me. The sooner the better."

It took him six minutes to get to a phone. "It better be good," he said. "I still haven't been home yet. I'm dead on my feet."

"I want to give you some information, but I don't want to give you all of it."

"Have you lost your mind?"

"What I want to do is get you all the way off that idea of the daughter being involved or kids being involved."

"We've got Judy. She came home this morning and saw a police car and thought her old lady had turned her in, so she and her friends drove right on by. Friday night she and her friends drove up to Orlando to go to Disneyworld. They looked so scruffy they couldn't get in. So they drove over to Rocket Beach and spent the day, six of them, in an old VW camper and tried to stay over night, but the law took them in to see if they were on any wanted lists, then rousted them south out of the county. It looks as if it will check out all the way, if we have to. After they drove by the house, they went to a friend's place, whose parents are off at some kind of convention. Anyway, at about six this evening, some other friend called up that house to ask the girl if she'd heard about Mrs. Lawson getting killed and the cops looking for Judy. So the kid got smart and phoned in, and I had her brought in. It really shook her up. It's violation of probation, and nobody in custody of her. What would happen, she would go to the state school."

"If it weren't for the general?"

"He and his wife and the sister came in and talked to the girl. He wanted to bust her right out, right now, but the only way he could do it, it would turn into news. I want it to stay quiet. If the man who did it suddenly hears there is going to be every kind of heat and pressure he ever heard of, he could be long gone."

"The man?"

"She came home with him yesterday, say. She brought him to her place. They hassled. She started to try to run. He grabbed her by the hair to yank her back, not meaning to kill her, but he was too rough. Broke vertebrae. The spinal cord was pinched and lacerated. The time of death they say was maybe about two-thirty, but the injury could have happened then or earlier. There would be a lot of paralysis, but the heart and the breathing could have kept going an hour after the neck was snapped, maybe longer. She went down, and he probably started to get out of there, then decided to confuse everybody. I had a hell of a job convincing that old man to lay back. Judy's release can be arranged quietly tomorrow."

"Where are they staying?"

"Now it's your turn, McGee."

"I'm not pleading or begging. I'm just telling you that it would be a very nice gesture on your part, Sergeant, if you would accept what I want to tell you without going after what I really have to hold back."

"I'll decide after I hear the first part."

"There is a good chance that some person or persons unknown believed that Jane Lawson might have something very valuable hidden in her apartment."

"How valuable?"

"Four hundred thousand, maybe."

"Is there a chance they got it?"

"If there is a chance it was there, there is a chance they got it."

"Is it bigger than a breadbox?"

"That's as far as I want to go right now."

"The *hell* with that, McGee. Come in or get brought in. What are you trying to do to me, giving me such crap?"

"You are a good officer, I think. And if I get clumsy and walk in front of a city bus, I want you to have some kind of a starting place."

"Then *give* me one! The general is at the Doral."

"I did."

"Is it gold coins, McGee? Is it? Hey! McGee? Is it?"

Slowly, gently, I replaced the phone on the cradle, and its little night glow went on glowing.

I checked the time and wondered about the Doral. If one wanted to get anywhere at all with the general, it wouldn't be over the phone. Probably not in person either.

I wondered about breadboxes and gold. What were they getting for it lately? Sixty dollars an ounce? But not normal ounces. Troy weight. I scribbled some figures. A quarter ton of raw gold would be worth four hundred thousand maybe. Okay then. Smaller than your standard, everyday breadbox. But one hell of a lot more comprehensible than Fedderman's little squares and oblongs of paper.

He had showed me one in a catalog. British Guiana. Scott catalog number 13. One-cent magenta. Valued at $325,000. Unique, meaning there is only one in the world. Also, 1856. It is Stanley Gibbons catalog number 23, valued at £120,000. Crude printing in black on reddish purple paper and initialed in ink by a postmaster long dead.

So, to paraphrase Mary Alice, just what preoccupation of man *is* worth futzing with? Anything which relates to survival is acceptable on the basis that survival is both possible and laudable. Survival of self and species and environment.

Everything else then becomes a taste. Taste of the hummingbird tongues, taste of gold in the vault, taste of Barbara Barefoot, taste of uniqueness of oneself, because if there is only one British Guiana 13 in the world and you own it, you walk about with the knowledge of being the only man who owns it. You are unique. If you have the biggest pile of throwing-stones in the tribe . . . Whoa, that goes back to survival.

So what packrat preoccupation did I have? What special artifacts does McGee fondle?

As I was about to pronounce myself immune, I suddenly realized I am the worst possible kind. I collect moments of total subjective pleasure, box them up, and put them in a shed in the back of my head, never having to open them up again, but knowing they are there.

So what would be a gem in the collection?

A time when I am totally fit and I have just come wading through one of the fringes of hell, have been stressed right to my breaking point, have expected to be whisked out of life, but was not. I am out of it, and if there is any pain, it is too dwindled to notice. I am in some warm place where the air and sea are bright. There are chores to do when I feel like it, but nothing urgent. I am in some remote place where no one can find me and bother me. There is good music when and if I want it. There is a drink I have not yet tasted. There is a scent of some good thing a-cooking slowly. There is a lovely laughing lady, close enough to touch, and there are no tensions between us except the ones which come from need. There is no need to know the day, the month, or the year. We will stay until it is time to go, and we will not know when that time will come until we wake up one day and it is upon us.

And that is a McGee catalog 13, unique, shameful, and totally hedonistic. Misfit. An ant with a grasshopper syndrome. Rationale: One turn around the track.

I decided I had better take the whole thing and drop it in front of Meyer, like a crock of snakes, and let him do the sorting and prodding. Meaning, he says, is what somebody finds meaningful.

The phone rang, and she said, "Just to be sure you're alone in your broomcloset, luv."

"What else? You're downstairs? Go back through to the second batch of elevators."

"Just as soon as you take care of this man's problems."

"Bell captain here, sir."

"Mmm. Alfred?"

"Why, yes sir!"

"Any dear friend of mine is, by definition, a dear friend of Mr. Nucci's. Send Mrs. McDermit up, please. Cordially."

"Sir, I was only—"

"You were only trying to put a body block on any free-lance hooker trying to work your house, Alfred. And no one can tell by looking at them any more, can they?"

"Sir, I—"

"Find out what she would like to drink and have it sent up, please. And have the waiter bring a dinner menu, please."

"Right away, sir!"

Her little glass jug of marguerita, sitting imbedded in a bowl of shaved ice, reached 1802 about fifty seconds after she did, and just as I was explaining to her that any pretty lady coming alone into a Collins Avenue hotel after dark, carrying a purse as big as a bird cage, would be under suspicion of entrepreneurism.

We tried to be jolly and gay, but it kept fading off into a minor key and into silence. The conductor raps the stick on the podium and starts the music again.

Even the absolutely superb steaks did not get us back into our own places. An ugly death had bent our realities, and we were each on our separate journey to Ixtlan because it meant different things to each of us. We ate by the light of candles in hurricane globes, guttering and flickering in front of the open balcony doors, in the moist warm night wind that came off the sea. I wheeled the dinner equipment out into the hall and chained the door before we moved the candles to bedside, and even the strokes and promises, the rituals and releases of love did not pierce that curious, deadening barrier between us. We did what seemed expected and what seemed the momentary imperative, each living inside the ivory round of skull, looking out of it with night eyes at the shifts and shadows of conjoining.

Twelve

I awoke, and the candles had burned out. I could hear the sea and, approaching across the sea, a hard night rain, a bumble and thud of thunder. As I sat up, a vivid green-white flash filled the room, leaving me with the after-image of her pillowed head beside me, eyes awake and looking toward the dark ceiling.

I got out on my side and went around the bed to the big doors. The first driving rain came just as I was closing the second one, spattering and bouncing as high as my belly. The doors closed out the rush of wind, the storm sounds, and muted the thunder. I found the pulls and slid both sets of draperies across the doors. The storm was no longer something alive. It was on tape on a television set next door.

I put a breath of airconditioning back on to keep the air in the room from turning stale, and when she called me, I went to her side of the bed. She found my hand and tugged at me. When I bent to her, she pushed and said, "We didn't talk."

She hitched over, and I sat on the bed, against a solid warmth of hip under percale. She said, "Over the phone you said you wanted to talk. We didn't talk that kind of talk, did we?"

"No. We talked bad lines from old movies, I think."

She was in a total blackness. When I closed my eyes, nothing changed. She said, "It's funny. You know? They've all said so many things so many ways, there's nothing left for people to really say to each other. I mean I can say things, but behind it I can hear Cher saying it to Sonny." She changed to a thin, squeaky little voice. "I am Gabby Gabriele, your very own talking doll. Pull my string and I'll say anything you want."

I said, "Sometimes Jack Lemmon is speaking, sometimes Jack Lord, sometimes George Peppard, sometimes Archie Bunker."

I heard and felt the depth of her sigh. "That's it," she said. "Nothing is really real, and then Jane Lawson is dead, and that is very very real. She'd talk about her kids and the house, and she'd sound like Erma Bombeck, and that wasn't real. You wanted to talk about Jane, and then you did, and I didn't ask you."

"Sooner or later, Mary Alice, we have to talk about her, so I guess now is okay. I've got some facts. You have to help me put them together."

"Me help?"

"The damage to the house was done *after* somebody cracked her neck."

"After! But how—"

"Let me cover the ground first. It wasn't kids, because too many of the things kids take were still there. The trashing didn't have the usual pattern. It was imitation trashing, a diversion. The person involved wore gloves. There wasn't even a fresh oil-smudge on all the glass and pottery things that were broken. The trashing could have been a diversion for another reason too, to cover up evidence of careful search. Whoever did it came through the front door, I think, with Jane. Then later they blew more smoke by making it look as if some small person had wiggled through an awning window in the bedroom. Judy is in custody. She was a couple of hundred miles away."

She squeezed my hand in the darkness. "How could you get to *know* all these things, darling?"

"I took a deep breath and walked right into the middle of it, using the excuse I took her home Friday. If I'd found somebody too rigid and dumb running the show, I would have left it at that. There are only two kinds of people you can con. Greedy people and bright people. The greedy ones want to use you, and the bright ones want to see how far you'll take it."

"But what does it all *mean?*"

"Lots of guesses. Maybe it's as simple as it looks. Somebody came to the door. Pushed his way in. Killed her and took what she had in her purse and looked for more. Then take it through all the shades and gradations right up to the way way out, where she was the one who somehow got her hands on the rarities Hirsh bought for the Sprenger account, and maybe somebody in Sprenger's organization knew about it and went after her."

"But Mr. Sprenger doesn't even *know* anything is missing!"

I thought that over and decided not to go into it with her. Give Sprenger credit for a good intelligence system. When you put a lot of eggs into a lot of different baskets, you watch all the baskets. McGee starts hanging around Fedderman's shop. Let us say I do not look as if I collect stamps or coins. I am conspicuous. It is a handicap, professionally. So he gets a line on me through the plate on Miss Agnes. Or, an ugly concept to swallow, Jane Lawson tells him I am interested, having previously told him his expensive rarities have turned into junk. Or there is some kind of conspiracy involving Fedderman and Sprenger which I have not yet been able to figure out. I can start with the only point I am sure of—that Davis and Harris approached me with the idea that the man they represented had a hunch he had been taken but was not really sure.

Too many ifs and whereases to inflict upon the lady who lay close at hand, warm and invisible in the smaller hours of Monday, on one of the twenty-fifths of the many Septembers of my life. Should a man reach eighty, he has only had eighty Septembers. It does not seem like many, said that way. It seems as if there are so few each one should have been better used.

Meyer made one of his surveys of the elderly couples in the Fort Lauderdale area, the ones being squeezed between the cost of living and their Social Security. They were very bitter about it. They were very accusatory about it. Amurrica should give them the financial dignity they had earned. Meyer's survey was in depth, relating income over the working years to the pattern of spending. Meyer radiates compassion. He is easy to talk to. He ended his survey after forty couples chosen at random, because by then the pattern was all too clear.

He said, "I'll put it all into appropriate and acceptable jargon later, Travis, but the essence of it is that all too many of them were screwed by consumer advertising. Spend, spend, spend. Live for today. So they lived out their lives up to their glottis in time payments. They blew it all on boats and trailers and outboard motors, binoculars and hunting rifles and department store high fashion. They lived life to the hilt, like the ads suggest. Not to the hilt of pleasure, but to the hilt of spending. They had bureau drawers full of movie cameras, closets full of record players and slide projectors. Buy the wall-to-wall carpeting. Buy the great big screen. Visit all the national parks in America. Funny thing. They had all *started* to lay away some dollars for old-age income, but when the Social Security payments got bigger and the dollar started shrinking, they said the hell with it. Blow it all. Now their anger is directed outward, at society, because they don't dare look back and think of how pathetically vulnerable they were, how many thousands they blew on toys that broke before they were paid for, and how many thousands on the interest charges to buy those toys. They don't know who screwed them. They did what everybody else was doing. Look at the tabulation on my last question. 'If you had it to do over again, how much would you put aside each month, expressed as a percentage of income, and what would you give up?' Read the things they'd give up, my friend. It would break your heart."

I am no living endorsement for prudence and thrift. My grasshopper excesses are worse than theirs. Yet mine are deliberate. I do not expect to have the chance to become very old. And though my chance is perhaps less than theirs, to think that way is romanticism, like that of the seventeen-year old who vows no wish to live past thirty. I hobble down the raw streets of some unimaginable future, cackling, soiling my garments, trying to stop the busy people striding by so I can show them the dead bird I am wearing around my withered old neck. Not an awesome and magnificent albatross. A simple chicken.

"Where did you go, darling?" she asked.

I came back to the reality of my hand taken to her unseen lips, each knuckle slowly kissed. A coolness moved across my naked back, coming in silence from the unseen vent on high, drying the last of the sleep-sweat.

"I went roaming in my head. It isn't very orderly in there. A lot of brush and jungle trails and no signposts. So I get lost in there sometimes."

"I came after you, huh?"

"Thanks."

"That makes me feel spooky, thinking of the insides of heads like that. I don't go back into mine. It's full of dull junk. Old cardboard boxes from supermarkets, packed with old clothes and school books. It's full of things that are all over."

"Are you tidy? Is everything labeled?"

"No. Why should it be? I'm never going to go poking around in there. It's all throw-away. I ought to have a truck come and get it. I don't think back. Neither should you, dear. And there isn't any point in thinking ahead, because nothing ever comes out the way you think it will. So what I do is think of right now, and I do what I want to with it."

"I'm thinking of right now."

"Good. We weren't real good before, were we? Like yesterday, all except the first time yesterday. Jane dying made things strange. For us."

"She has to be involved with Hirsh's problem somehow, but certainly not out of any need for the money."

"Why do you say that? Why not any need for the money?"

"If she really had to have money, if she was desperate enough to try to steal from Hirsh, long before she got to that point, she would have asked her father-in-law for it."

"What if she needed a lot?"

"How much is a lot, Mary Alice? I would imagine he could have moved a million dollars into her name in that First Atlantic Bank and Trust within an hour of her phoning him."

Her breath whistled. The bed shifted, and the hip warmth pressure went away. Her grasp tightened on my hand, and I sensed, without seeing her, that she had hitched herself up to face me. I felt against my throat and chest a subtle radiation of the heat of her body, and the humid scents of her came clearer to my nostrils.

Her voice spoke from blackness at my throat level and not far away. "Are you sure? She never said *anything* like that!"

"I'm very sure. I met the man. I've read about him. He's very impressive."

"But I don't understand."

"Why she didn't tell you about it?"

"Not so much that. Why she lived so small and so shabby. Once Linda started going to college, Jane took that rotten bus every school day. I can't remember her going to a hairdresser. She was always letting her skirts out or taking them in. What kind of a weird kick was she on anyway?"

"Living her own life, maybe."

"If you want to call it living. I never knew she was such a freak."

"Apparently you and she didn't exchange life stories. You didn't tell her things either."

"That's sort of different. I could have gone back to McDermit, maybe. I don't know. I never asked. If I did, I'd have lived rich. If I could have stood it, I'd have stayed. But what kind of grief would she have had to take? Nothing at all. Just a nice life."

"Maybe she thought this was a better way to raise her kids."

"Do you mean that? Judy sings in the choir, maybe? And gathers wildflowers for mama dear?"

"She did all right with Linda."

"And she thought a five hundred average was okay? It seems to me that . . ."

After a long silence I said, "Seems what to you?"

"Forget it, huh?"

"Sure."

"Oh God, Trav, I don't want to talk about Jane or think about her or Hirsh or Frank or anybody. I just want to make love. Okay?"

"I can't think of any good reason why not, girl."

"You seem to be thinking clearly, dear."

It was better between us. The curious feeling of apartness was gone. She was not a strenuous partner. We slowly and gently and with mutual consideration sorted ourselves out so that there was no strain of support or numbing weight for either of us. In that perfect ease, that sleepy, lasting luxury, I drifted in and out of those fantasies which are neighbors of sleep. In one of the fantasies I was holding a gigantic and disembodied heart, holding it in that precise posture, moving against it in that precise rhythm which was the only way in the world it could be made to keep on beating with that small, deep, and solid rhythm, and could be kept alive.

Thirteen

She was all combed and showered and lipsticked and dressed when she woke me up and said that she was leaving to go back to her place and change and then go to the store.

My mind felt like glue, and I wondered if I was duplicating Sergeant Goodbread's habitual expression. "But Hirsh wouldn't want business as usual, would he?"

"Of *course* he wouldn't, silly man! But there's always the mail, and the things I haven't finished, and I want to see what Jane was doing that somebody else will have to finish. I won't open the place up. I'll print a sign and put it on the door. If there's anything Hirsh has to decide, I'll take it to his place and ask him. I hope there is. It will be the best thing in the world for him to start making decisions."

"Say hello to him for me."

"Get some more sleep, darling. I'd give odds you're going to need it."

She gave me a pat and went off to the door, springing along on those Olympic legs. She undid the chain and left, the latch clacking shut. I remembered how (only the day before yesterday) the webbed, interwoven muscles of her thighs had bulged when the full strain of the slalom cutback clenched her whole body. Visible at such times but never discernible to any loving touch, not on the shoulders or back, the arms, or legs. Firm, yes. But so sweetly sheathed by the resilient softness of the woman-padding of the little layer of subcutaneous fat. Grasp her more strongly, and the firm underlayer of muscle was then tangible, sliding and clenching and relaxing. And the tone and control of the athlete muscles was apparent whenever she moved, whenever she bent, flexed, twisted, lifted, and apparent in the tirelessness of her repetition of any stressing motion.

I bobbed across the surface of sleep, sinking and pulling myself away from it, and at last stood up and creaked a hundred muscles in gargantuan stretching, padded in and adjusted the four shower nozzles to soft thick spray for all the soaping and rinsing, and then to hard fine stinging spray for the cold that finally woke me up all the way. I brushed with the new brush, shaved with the new tools, put on my supermarket socks and shorts and slacks and shirt, my shoes from a previous life where I had lived aboard a houseboat somewhere, and went down to find a place in the hotel to have breakfast. The basement coffee shop had the windowless fluorescence of a bus station at midnight, so I went back up and was led across fifty feet of carpeting to a window table and handed a menu as big as a windshield—twice as big when opened. Three copywriters had swooned while trying to describe the taste of eggs scrambled with roe.

When I lowered the menu, Willy Nucci was sitting

across from me. It gave me a start, so visible, he said, "I could wear a bell, like a leper."

"I should have been able to hear your shirt."

"This was a gift, handwoven in Guatemala."

"By parrots?"

"You are very funny today. You are killing me."

The man came up and bowed and took my order. A large fresh orange juice. Blueberry waffle. Double on the Canadian bacon. Maybe some cinnamon toast. Pot of coffee. Willy ordered coffee. After the captain left, Willy said, "From what Alfred said, I guess you got to regain your strength."

"I thought he was wished on you. I didn't know he reported to you."

He glanced around nervously. "Why should I ever say he was wished on me? He's a good night man. When he isn't sure, he checks with me. I was making a joke."

"You were? Ho,ho,ho. What did he check with you?"

"If you were throwing my name around or you were okay and he should drop it right there. Drop it there, I told him."

"What if I was just using your name in vain?"

"He wouldn't have broke up any romancing, just had some hackie tail her to wherever when she came out, then depending if it was town or beach, a couple of friendlies would have picked her up for soliciting, and then it would have been put to her as either a hundred bucks and ninety days as a freelance, or case dismissed if she wanted to join up and pay her dues and learn the rules."

"How about a perfectly legitimate girlfriend?"

Willy almost smiled. "Unless a girl has very heavy connections, what difference does it make, after all? And if she's got the connections, she'll start naming them the minute she's picked up, and then it's a judgment call on the part of the friendlies."

"So he described her to you?"

"Long black hair, blue eyes, and tits that came up to his ears. She got a little pissed-off at how he acted and wouldn't give him a name, so he tried the description on me because he said he thought he'd seen her someplace."

"Where?"

"He couldn't put his mind to it. I told him to forget it, all and any part of it. He said she was built for heavy duty, for a man and a half. But a little too old to be a bonus item for anybody who turns her over to the union."

My juice came. I tasted it. I pushed it over to Willy to taste. He made a face and said, "Yeck. Know what does that?"

"What does that, Willy?"

"The oil in orange rind is practically the same molecular structure as castor oil. So whatever clown ground this fresh, ground right past the juice and pith into the rind. Be right back."

And that is why it is a good hotel. Willy knows everything. He checks every incoming purchase. He reaches up and runs his fingers along ledges. Fifty times a year he picks a room at random and sleeps in it and makes sure that every little thing he finds wrong is fixed.

He came back with fresh juice in a taller glass. He watched me taste it, relaxed when I pronounced it delicious. He said, "Who can knock the woman who did it wrong? A little round Cuban woman, she does the work of three people out there. God grant I shouldn't lose her and the union shouldn't slow her down."

"Before you sell the place."

"Sell! Why should I sell? Are you dealing off a short deck?"

"Sorry, Mr. Nucci."

"Here's your breakfast, McGee. Enjoy."

Sprenger Investment Associates was five blocks west of Collins on Lincoln Road, on the second floor in the middle of the block on the wide pedestrian mall. The big glass door hissed when I pushed it open. It was a combination reception room and bullpen, with a deep blue rug and gauze green draperies, big formica desks in kindergarten colors. A broad tape machine in a decorator housing was against the wall at the left, demonstrating its inhuman typing skill. A table contained stacks of literature about municipal bonds. One floor man was on the phone, another talking to an elderly couple, a third reading *The Wall Street Journal*. They were young men, expensively dressed and coiffed. Over on the right a computer printout station was making a subdued roar as the interleaf printout sheets came folding down into the bin. A girl who seemed to be fifty percent thighs stood at a waist-high counter deftly separating and binding a previous printout. Another girl was having a donut and coffee. The third girl stared at me from the reception desk, making her decision not to get up and come around the desk with welcome smile after she had given me a quick inventory, from shoes to sun-parched hair.

"May I help you?" she said in a voice which indicated she thought it was most unlikely that she could. It was cold in the room. She was pretty. There were goosepimples on her upper arms.

"Mr. Sprenger said he would see me whenever I got here."

"Are you sure he said that?"

"Why don't we try him on it, little chum?"

"I couldn't interrupt him, really."

"The name is McGee."

I saw at once that she had been instructed. But she had not been prepared for somebody who looked as if he had come to fix the wiring. Her eyes went round. "Oh, of course! I remember now. Mr. McGee." Her smile became very wide. Unreal, but wide.

"That's a dead tooth," I said. "Just beyond the canine on the upper left. A pretty girl should get that fixed."

Her smile shrunk enough to hide the gray tooth. She wanted to be offended but couldn't risk it. "I keep trying to get an appointment." She trotted back and through a door made of blond wood, her hair and her little rump bouncing.

She came out and very close behind her there was a tall frail old man, erect and handsomely dressed. Frank Sprenger, looking just as I expected him to look, had a big brown hand on the old man's arm just above the elbow. He took him over to one of the young men and got him seated and told the young man to brief Mr. Sumner on the new issues on the recommended list, nothing less than Standard and Poor double A. He came back and nodded to me and stood aside and let me go first. He was big and he was broad and he was brown. He had black, straight, coarse hair that looked as lifeless as hair on a museum Indian. His face was a chunk of bone with the skin taut over it. He had simian brows under an inch and a half of forehead. The skin folds around his eyes had a reverse slant from that of the Japanese, and imbedded in there were little bright intense blueberry eyes. He was dressed in a way that made him conspicuous in Miami in September—beautifully tailored banker's gray in summerweight weave, a white shirt custom made for what looked to me like a twenty-two neck and forty-inch sleeves, a blue silk tie, a gold stickpin, gold cufflinks.

His office was just as anachronistic. It was like a small library-study in an English manor house, and it looked out upon what seemed to be a ground-floor garden, surrounded by a stone wall. But as I sat in the leather chair he offered me, I saw that though the plantings were real, the turf was Astro, and the stone facing on the wall was by Armstrong.

His voice was a bit high for the size of him, and he projected it with very little lip movement and no animation on his face at all. It is characteristic of people who have either been in prison or who live in such a manner that their total environment becomes a prison of sorts, a place where communication can be a deadly risk.

"Thanks for seeing me," I said.

"Think nothing of it. You found a problem I didn't know I had. I appreciate it."

My chair was very carefully placed. Before him on the desk was one of those brass and mahogany gadgets which are supposed to tell you the time, temperature, humidity, and state of the world, as well as play music for you, FM, AM, or taped. I could not see the dials. His glance kept straying to it, and I realized I was probably being scanned. The world of electronic bugging has gotten so esoteric that the best defense is a receiver of great precision and limited range which constantly scans all frequencies on which a concealed mike could be broadcasting, and translates anything it picks up into a visual signal.

A quick run up and down the scale would not be enough, because the casual visitor might be set up to activate his sending equipment once things got interesting. Also there are some bugs, slightly more bulky, which can be activated and deactivated by an outside incoming signal. The best defense, of course, is to never say anything of use to anybody. The second best defense is the offensive technique of transmitting an overwhelming blast of white noise, a smothering hiss, on all frequencies, whenever you say anything you'd rather not hear played back some day.

I said, "A friend told me about a brand new development, a new way to bug a room, Sprenger."

He showed no surprise, only a mild interest. "Yes?"

"Everything is a sounding board. Every word we are saying moves the glass in that big window there. There is a transparent substance somebody can put on the outside of that glass that will reflect a certain kind of laser beam. The beam transmitter has to be in a very solid mount. It reflects back to a receptor, very sensitive, which translates the minute differences in the angle of the beam into fluctuating electrical impulses which can be translated into sound. They can do it from a half-mile away, and there isn't any device you can use which will detect it."

"Pick up the voices, the words?"

"A speaker is a diaphragm that moves back and forth like the head of a drum and changes electrical impulses into sound."

He got up and went over to his window, tested the yield in the center of it with big spatulate fingers.

"Could be," he said. "But nobody can see into this window from anywhere because of the wall. So they couldn't hit the window with one of those." He came back and sat at his desk.

"You live in this room? Or don't the other rooms you live in have windows?"

He rubbed his bumpy nose, closed his blueberry eyes for a few seconds, then said, "I'll check it out. You are doing me some good, maybe. You checked me out?"

"Enough for my purposes. I didn't know about this operation."

"It isn't a cover. It's a legitimate outlet for municipal bonds. Home base is in Memphis. We do three hundred million a year in face value right out of this office. We service the municipal bond portfolios of over forty smaller banks."

"But you're not regulated like regular brokers."

His deep tan turned to red tan, and his voice got louder, and he used more lip movement. "We have an association of municipal bond dealers pledged to clean our own house and eliminate the bad practices of the past and drive the shysters out of—What the hell are you laughing at?"

"I couldn't help it."

"What's so funny?"

"You're wired into every kind of hustling there is. Protection, franchises, smuggling, drugs, gambling, broads, unions, extortion, and you get all huffy about your clean bond business."

He thought about it. He tried a small smile which lasted almost a microsecond. "Maybe it's funny. It started as a cover. We bought somebody out. I got interested and built it up. Some of the skim goes away and comes right back into good bonds. I ask them, if the money comes back clean and it is supposed to go into legitimate investment, which would you rather have—a shopping center giving you a taxable ten percent return or bonds giving you five and a half tax free that you don't have to wake up in the night and wonder about?"

"You have a point."

"What bothers me about you, McGee, I can't read you getting into this strictly as a favor to Fedderman. Where's the connection?"

"I owed one to a friend, and he called me on it and said help Fedderman." I knew he would accept that kind of reasoning and thought I saw acceptance in those small eyes. "How did you make me?" I asked.

"In nineteen months I put a good piece of money into that little old man's action. He checked out as an okay old man. He's good for his guarantee. But I wouldn't want to find out some day—he's gone, and there's a jewelry store. Also there is another thing, I wouldn't want that little old man to have a big mouth and say Frank Sprenger is giving him bundles of cash, and having all of a sudden some kind of audit that spreads from his book to mine. I could give all the answers, but it still wouldn't look good. I'm supposed to keep my head down at all times. So I arranged to have people keep an eye on the little old man. Any change in his pattern. I heard over two weeks ago he was getting to work earlier, staying longer. Maybe he's packing? He starts to get appraisals on a lot he owns, on some securities, on the retail business. So when you came onto the scene, we were already at battle stations, so I got a fast reading on you, and it shaped up this way in my mind. The little old man is very nervous lately. You try to get things back when people lose them and the law can't help them. I'm not his only account, but maybe the stuff he bought for me is missing? If so, I am the injured party. Fedderman will have to make it good, if that's so, but I would rather have the items he bought."

"Why?"

"If I wanted money, I already had money. I wanted the stamps."

"That's what I mean? Why did you want the stamps."

"Personally? I didn't and I don't. A certain associate is under very close surveillance. He made a mistake and didn't cover it well, and he thinks they are maybe building a very tight case against him. He's old and he's tired and he won't last long locked up. Anything he tries to cash in, they'll know it. He has some action going down here, and so he asked me to put his end into something small you can carry in a pocket, as good as money. It used to be stones. They're too big a markup even wholesale and too big a discount elsewhere. I heard of Fedderman, so we had a nice talk, and I tried it to see if it would work."

"Tried it?"

"He sold me four stamps from Grenada. From the island. Two pairs they were. One-penny green. Fifteen hundred bucks. I had a courier going to West Berlin, so I told her to sell them there for whatever she could get, and she got forty-eight hundred West German marks, no questions asked, and about a five-minute wait for the money. It worked like he said it would, so I went his route. When that certain associate wants to make his move, he can slip away and get down here. I give him the merchandise and get him onto a freighter with new papers, and he can live nice in a warm climate until he is dead. As a matter of fact, it's too bad the stamp thing isn't a market that will absorb money faster and easier."

"What am I supposed to be doing for you?"

"Is my merchandise missing?"

"Out of a lock box in a bank?"

"I don't see how it could be. Maybe it didn't get into the box."

"I don't know for certain if it's missing. Fedderman thinks something is wrong. But he's old. He could be wrong."

"He'll have to make it good. That's the agreement."

"He intends to live up to it."

"So if the merchandise is missing, you're trying to find it for Fedderman? You can be trying to find it for me too."

"It would be the same thing. He'd turn it over to you. If it's missing."

"I don't know what he's been putting in the book. I get these lists. They don't mean a hell of a lot to anybody except somebody in the same line of work as Fedderman. If anything has happened, it's more inconvenience to me than anything else. You let me know how you're getting along."

He counted out some money and leaned and put it on the corner of the desk near me. I said, "I don't want to be on the payroll, Mr. Sprenger."

"I wouldn't put you on. That's expenses, nothing else. Expense money saves a man time and trouble and makes him more efficient. That's a policy of mine."

"Well . . . just for expenses then."

"You have anything, you use the number Dave gave you. There's always somebody at the place."

"I think Harry Harris gave me the number."

"Harry who?"

"Harris. Reddish brown kinky hair, sunburn, sideburns."

"I don't have anybody like that working for me."

"Oh."

"Nobody who does work for me would ever remember anybody who looks like that."

"Now that you mention it, Dave was alone when he came to see me."

"What if I got in touch with you about some other kind of a problem sometime?"

"I seldom take on any work."

"It wouldn't be often. You could be on a retainer."

"I travel a lot. I might not be where you could get in touch."

"For your information, maybe seventy-five percent of what I do is all legitimate business affairs and management problems."

"I didn't mean I was making moral judgments."

"Then what?"

"I'm no damned good at taking orders. You get that way, working for yourself long enough."

I saw his interest fade. "Suit yourself then. Thanks for stopping in."

I didn't stand up on cue. "Too bad about that other clerk in Fedderman's shop."

"I would have missed that entirely if the name Fedderman didn't catch my eye. It jumped out of the print at me. Lawlor? Lawrence?"

"Mrs. Lawson. Jane Lawson."

I was trying to watch him closely without being too obvious about it. He seemed awfully plausible. I picked the words with greatest care. "Frank, you bother me."

The blueberries turned to pebbles. "I *bother* you?"

"One little old man and two women in that shop. So they are involved, the women are, in all his accounts in some manner. So in effect they are handling four hundred thousand of money entrusted to you. You think there has been some hankypanky. The senior of the two clerks gets killed. Somebody got too rough. You read it, but you never stop to wonder if there is any connection at all. Is that logical? What's my other guess, Frank? What comes next?"

He frowned at me. "Now, come *on! I* sent somebody to shake the merchandise out of her if she had it? Why take a risk like that?"

"It turned into a risk when somebody got too rough."

He shook his head. "No, McGee. No, no, no. Your head is full of smoke. That was a nice little woman. You can smell the ones who will and the ones who won't."

"But you never went to the store?"

"She came to the bank once with Fedderman."

Suddenly that little itch in the back of my mind stopped itching, and I stopped finding some way to scratch it. I heard Jane Lawson's voice. "The Sprenger account is the one where he never looks at the old purchases or the new ones either. He just sits there like so much dead meat. He nods, shrugs, grunts and that's that."

"When did she come to the bank?"

He took an appointment book out of the middle drawer and leafed back through it. "May twenty-first. After lunch. The big girl came back from lunch and started throwing up. It was too late for Fedderman to reach me, so Mrs. Lawson came with him. I don't know why he apologized. What difference is it to me which woman puts the stamps in the book? Fedderman wants to make a big thing out of everything. Maybe you've got the same problem. Some freak got into the house and broke that little woman's neck."

I left with money in my pocket and vague unrest in the back of my mind. The pretty little receptionist was prodding at her dead tooth. She snatched her hand away, and gave me more smile on one side than on the other. I stopped and looked at the broad tape. Brownsville, Texas, was coming out with a twenty-million-dollar general obligation issue at five and a half percent to expand their sewage disposal system. Sharon, Pennsylvania, was assuming seven million dollars more of public debt for roads, bridges, and flood control. That was nice. I wondered how many Sprengers and friends of Sprengers had their hands cupped under the faucets, waiting for the honey.

I walked a block and took a beach cab over to the mainland. On the island of Miami Beach, all you can legally get is a beach cab. If he takes you to the mainland, he is supposed to come back empty. The mainland cabs taking fares from the airport to the hotels along Collins have some of the doormen well enough greased so they can beat the system. Sometimes I wondered how much Sprenger and his pals had to do with the weird cab system that was suddenly costing me about seven dollars. But Sprenger had covered expenses.

It was almost noon. I peered into the shop and saw Mary Alice and rapped on the glass. She stared toward the door and then smiled and came quickly and let me in, locked the door, gave me the close and hearty stance, the hearty jolly kiss.

"Did you sleep all this time?"

"Me? Heavens! I was up practically before you got the door shut."

"That isn't going to do either of us any good, buddy."

"I came to see about taking you to lunch and—"

"I'm *so* glad you came here, Trav, really. There's something that really bothers me. I just don't know what to think. It seems to . . . I don't want to say anything until you see it."

It was back in Hirsh's office, on his desk. I sat in his chair and examined it carefully. She stood beside me with her hand on my shoulder. It was a white cardboard box, about twelve inches long, eight inches wide, an inch and a half deep. There was wide brown mailing tape affixed to it, running around it the long way and then around the middle, overlapping. Where the tape crossed, there was a mailing label. "Mrs. Jerome Lawson." Correct address. It was stamped in big red rubberstamp letters, "Book Rate." The return address was "Helen's Book Nooke."

"The book store is two blocks from here," Mary Alice said.

There were three eight-cent stamps on the package, not canceled. There was heft to the package, as if it contained a book. When I shook it, the book slid back and forth. The box was a little too long for it.

I examined the ends with care. The tape seemed to be slit very inconspicuously at one end. I fiddled with it until I found that the end could be pushed inward. It folded down reluctantly against the resistance of some kind of very strong spring. Once it was folded down and the box tilted until the contents were beyond the edge of the folded-down part, the contents could be pulled out of the box.

The contents was an album or stock book just like the one I had been shown previously as being identical to Sprenger's. But this one was green. Mary Alice pulled it out of its fiber slip case and showed it to me. There was a name in gold on the bottom right corner. "J. David Balch."

"Who is J. David?" I asked.

"One of the investment accounts. See. There's nothing in here. This is a new stock book. I found this by accident. It's so weird. We each have a little space for personal stuff under the counter near the back. Like cupboards with doors. This was in a brown paper bag, and it was wrapped in a sweater of hers. But it was too heavy for just a sweater. So I started monkeying around with it, wondering if I could open it or maybe pry it open a little way to look in. Know what I thought? That maybe she hid it because it was a very dirty book. That Helen sells things that you wouldn't believe, if she knows you."

I looked at the box again. There seemed to be some reinforcing glued to the back of the flap and to the bottom of the box so that the springs would not push through the cardboard.

She said, "I feel like such a great big dummy. I just never thought of changing the whole damned book."

"You are not alone, M.A. This thing is a shoplifter's gaff. They usually make them in handier sizes, without such a strong spring. And usually they are tied with string. If you glue the string to the paper, you get a very convincing look. The professional shoplifter buys an item from a good store. She takes it home and doctors the box and then takes it to other stores. Put it down on a counter and you can shove things through the end flap very inconspicuously. They have purses that are gaffed. They can put them down on the counter on top of merchandise and reach down into the purse and pull stuff up into the purse from underneath, through the bottom. I guess this had strong springs because it had to go through the mail. We didn't think of changing the whole book because they are personalized and arranged in a certain order."

"I can figure that out too, Trav."

She went and got a three ring notebook and opened it up at the index tab which bore the initials F.A.S. "These are the inventory sheets for Mr. Sprenger's account. I haven't kept this in the safe or anything. Why should I? Now look at these little figures I wrote in. There are thirty-six double-sided pages, and seven transparent pockets across each page. I number the pages in ink up in the top corners. Okay. Take this stamp here." I read: US #122a* 90c car. & blk, w/o grill, VF $1500 ($1375) 28-6-4. The last three figures were written in.

I looked up over my shoulder at her. "Twenty-eighth page, sixth row down, fourth stamp over?"

"I don't want to seem like I'm accusing Jane."

"Build the case and I'll try to tear it down."

"Okay. When she was alone here, she could bring these pages back to this little duplicating thing and run off copies. They give her exactly what had been bought for the Sprenger account and the exact order in the book."

"And then she—"

"Let me do it. If I'm going to. Hirsh let her run that little speculative account, bid things in at the auctions, buy things from other dealers. It was like some kind of a joke between them. So she could have bought junk and put it into a duplicate stock book in the same order. And she always got the names put on the books."

"At a luggage store?"

"Luggage and leather goods. Cerrito's. We walked past it going to the bank."

"So she could get a second stock book labeled Frank A. Sprenger without you or Hirsh knowing?" She nodded. I said, "I wonder if they keep any record."

"Could you go find out? Please? Now? I have to be sure. I just can't stand . . . thinking about it and not knowing."

Fourteen

When I got back, I noticed her eyes were red. She snuffled and smiled and said, "I'm okay now. What did they say?"

I told her that they liked Jane Lawson at Cerrito's. Quite a few years ago, knowing that they were giving Hirsh a very special price on imprinting, she had asked if she could do it. The press was in the back room. She had become adept at locking the pieces of type into the press, aligning the album properly, and pulling the handle to give it the right pressure to impress the gold leaf letters into the leather. They were happy to have her do it. They enjoyed having her come in. They were shocked at her death and at the suddenness and the ugliness of it.

At M.A.'s suggestion, I took her into Hirsh's office and held her in my arms.

"Now I know the ugliest thing of all," she said. "The last and ugliest thing about it. She had to poison me."

"What!"

She pushed me away and stared at me. "You better believe it. We went to lunch together that day. That was because I was going to eat earlier so I could go to the bank at quarter to one. You know, I'd forgotten about it until today? That was back in May. I don't know the date. I could look it up. We had exactly the same thing. Exactly. That's what was so strange about it. I'm never sick. But coming back I told her I was feeling very very peculiar. By the time I got here, I was *really* sick. At the restaurant I went to the girls' room after our lunch came. That's when she must have put something in my coffee to make me toss up everything. You see, Trav, that's when she must have had the book full of junk all ready, in this box or one just like it, and she knew that Hirsh wouldn't go to the bank alone because he likes to make a little ceremony out of it. She had to know he'd take her. I didn't remember that one time because there are a lot of other times I went on the other accounts. And she went sometimes when I couldn't for one reason or another. You know what? I bet Mr. Sprenger would remember because that would have been the only time he saw her."

"But wasn't there another time you went to the bank to put things in Sprenger's book? July?"

"Right. But there was no reason to look at the old pages, like with the other investors. So nobody noticed. Trav, while you were gone, I've beat my brains out trying to remember if she had a box like this that day I was sick. I don't want to be unfair. I don't want to imagine anything that didn't really happen. But I keep thinking she had something she said she was going to mail. A package of some kind."

"How could she work the switch?"

"I'd guess maybe she'd go in there with the box empty and the duplicate stock book in her purse. She'd have a chance to slip the stock book full of junk from her purse to her lap, under the table. At the moment Hirsh would be showing Mr. Sprenger the first item, they would both be looking at it, and she could take the book out of her lap and open it on top of the good book and edge the book off into her lap. Probably with one hand she could shove it into the box, past the spring. I mean in *that* way, there would always be the book on top of the table. The table wouldn't ever be empty. Hirsh might remember if she mailed anything."

She sat on Hirsh's desk, and I stood frowning in front of her. "And I'm supposed to shoot it down?"

"I hope you can. I really hope you can. She . . . just wasn't that kind of a person."

"In May she scores. Big. In September she's still here?"

"I know. Mr. Balch's account must be worth at least two hundred thousand market value."

"Hirsh leafed through the book, and he guessed that the stuff that was substituted was worth about sixty-five thousand."

"What? Oh, no. You must have misunderstood. I think he included the good stuff we just added that day." She turned and indicated her notebook. "Jane was here a lot longer than me, but I bet I could take Sprenger's list and go up to New York with fifteen thousand dollars, and I could buy stuff that would look okay maybe to Mr. Sprenger or to you but not to a dealer. And . . . Hirsh sent Jane to New York in April to bid on some things when he couldn't make it."

"So where would she get fifteen thousand?"

"I don't *know*. I just don't *know*."

"Why do you say it that way?"

"Well . . . because we both do appraisals. You get so you know what to look for. It wouldn't be any big deal to see something really good and slip it out of the collection and put in something cheap that looks like it. They are estate things usually. The collector is dead. So it just looks like he made a mistake in identification. And it would be a hundred dollars here, fifty dollars there, two hundred in the next place."

"She'd have no trouble selling them?"

"Why should she? It's like they say, I guess. People start taking a little bit and then more and then a lot. Like a disease. If it was like that with her, Trav, then it wouldn't make any difference about her in-laws having money, would it?"

"Every big city has rich shoplifters. Kleptos. But the shrinks say they do it to get caught and punished."

"Don't you see? If something hadn't happened to her, she *would* have been caught. You would have found out."

"I would?"

"Hirsh said to me that Meyer told him that you have a kind of weird instinct for these things, that you have your own way of finding out who took what. I guess he's right. Look what's happened."

"Part of it has happened. Where did the Sprenger collection go? Who has it? Did somebody take it from her house or take the money she got for it? And are the other investment accounts okay?"

She stared and swallowed and put her hand to her throat. "Oh God, I hope so. I hope Mr. Benedict's collection is okay. If anything ever happened to those, it would kill both those old guys, I think." She hesitated, tilted her head. "No, maybe Jane was pretty shifty, but she wasn't stupid. You just couldn't sell those nineteen things anywhere. They're all famous. They've all been written up."

"If somebody wanted to get caught, though?"

"Maybe it wasn't like that with her."

"What do you mean?"

She got up from the edge of the desk and hung her arms around my neck. "I'm getting so I'm imagining things, maybe. I guess it could have been a year ago. Jane got real strange. Jumpy and nervous. She told me confidentially not to tell Hirsh, but she might quit and move away. She got some phone calls here she didn't want to talk about. They left her real quiet and shaky. And then after a couple of weeks she was herself again. But not really like before. She seemed . . . resigned and bitter. I was wondering . . ."

"Wondering what?"

"There are an awful lot of ways somebody could threaten a couple of young girls. She was always terribly concerned about them. If somebody wanted her to steal from the shop . . . I guess it's a dumb idea."

"We need all the ideas we can . . ."

Her fingers dug into my wrists. Her face changed. "Shh! Listen!" she whispered. She tiptoed to the doorway to Hirsh's cubicle office and looked stealthily around the door frame toward the front door.

"I thought I heard somebody," she said in a normal tone.

"Speak of being jumpy."

"Don't make fun, huh? I have this sixth sense pretty well developed after five years. I've had the idea the last few days that McDermit is having somebody make the usual check on me. It's about that time. Are you getting that boat ready like you promised?"

"Progress is being made."

"Like what?" she demanded, cool-eyed and skeptical.

"There are blocks that bolt to the deck just forward of the side deck, close to the pilot house. There are ring bolts outside, bolted through the pilot house bulkhead. Two fifty-five gallon—"

"I just wanted to make sure—"

"Two fifty-five gallon drums fit behind those blocks on the port and two on the starboard. A friend named Johnny Dow is bolting the blocks down where they belong. He'll put four clean empty drums in place—"

"Darling, please!"

"—clean empty drums in place and use braided steel cable with turnbuckles to make them secure, using the eye bolts. Meyer, who has the keys and knows the security systems aboard, will open up the *Flush* this afternoon, and Johnny will move it to the gas dock and get the drums filled with diesel fuel and get my tanks topped off and bring it back to the slip. Meyer has the list of provisions and maintenance supplies and will see that they are brought aboard and stowed today. I have a hand pump that starts a siphon action to transfer the fuel from the drums to the regular tanks."

"Please, dear."

"At the most economical speed, the additional two hundred and twenty gallons builds the maximum range, without safety factor, up to eleven hundred miles. I have not told Meyer why I wanted him to do me these favors, and I imagine he thinks it is busy work I have invented to keep him out of Miami."

"I'm sorry."

"I was damned reluctant to make that promise to you,

M.A. But you wanted it made, and I have made it. Having made it, I would not dog it."

"If I ever say 'Like what?' to you again, the way I said it that time, wash out my big mouth with yellow soap."

"I promise you that too."

"Brutal male chauvinist pig?"

"Well, if you put up a fight, I'm not sure I can manage the soap part."

She grinned, assumed the stance, jabbed with a long left, and then hooked off the jab, a respectable whistler missing by a calculated inch.

"My very best punch," she said.

"You keep impressing me in new ways, Mary Alice."

"Darling, what are you going to do? Stay in the same place again tonight?"

"Join me?"

"Too many eyes are watching me. At least, I have the feeling they are. I think somebody saw me get home this morning. I tried to be sly, but it turned out stupid. I left my car home and took a cab. And so, of course, arriving home at eight something in a cab looks worse than if I'd had my car. No, honey, much as I need you, I'd be too jumpy. Where are you going to be the rest of today?"

"Here and there."

"But what is there you can possibly do?"

"Once in Vegas I saw an old lady in the Golden Nugget, absolutely totally broke. The slots had cleaned her. So she was sidling around pulling at the handles on the off chance some idiot left a coin in one of them. I saw her find a handle that she could pull, and she hit three somethings and got about twelve dimes down the chute. She got a half hour out of those dimes before she was broke again and started to pull at the handles on the idle machines. That's my mysterious system, M.A. I go around pulling handles in case some idiot forgot he left a dime in the machinery."

"What if I have to get word to you?"

"Leave a message at the Contessa for room 1802. This shop is letter A. Your place is B. If you are coming to the Contessa, it is C. If you are going to Lauderdale to wait for me, it's D. Use a last name that fits. Miss Adams, Miss Brown, Miss Carter, Miss Dean. So I'll check in for messages now and then. 'Miss Carter called and will call again' means I'll head for the hotel and see you there. Clear?"

"Sure. You do that pretty damned fast, you know. You must have had a hell of a lot of messages from girls in your day."

"In my day? Thanks. I had the feeling these were my days, somehow."

"If I let you live through them, maybe. I've got more work to do here. What'll I do with this funny box?"

"Put it in the safe for now."

"Should I tell Hirsh? I don't want to."

"Save it for now."

"Okay, dear. Please take care of yourself."

"I came here to take you to lunch."

"I don't want to be seen with you. And I'm not hungry. And you don't know how unusual that is. I'm always hungry."

Harmony Towers had all the exterior charm of a women's prison. But inside the colors were bright and cheerful, and the people at the main desk were helpful. Miss Moojah was expecting me, and I could find her in Community Room 7, down that corridor to the end, through the fire door, and up the stairs one flight, and I couldn't miss it.

Fifteen old people were sitting in a circle in Community Room 7 and a swarthy young lady was saying, "Weeth the irregular verps, Mr. Lewis, you muss memorize, eh? Traer. To breeng. Breeng me a drink. Imperative. Traigame una copita. Eh?"

They all stared at me, and a woman hopped up, excused herself, and walked briskly to the doorway, motioning me back out into the hall. She was medium tall, erect, stick thin, with penciled brows and hair dyed mahogany pink. She had a massive, jutting, macrocephalic jaw. Out in the hall she looked me over with great care, and then said in a deep, metallic contralto, "Around here one gets so accustomed to seeing withered little crickety old men or fat wheezing sloppy old men, one tends to forget how they must have once appeared, Mr. McGee."

"I could have come later, after your class."

"I would rather you took me away from it. It is a matter of duty and conscience to attend. There are seven dolts holding the rest of us back. I have petitioned to have the class split in twain. I am so far ahead of the lesson schedule right now, it is pitiful. Come along. We can talk in here. A waiting room. There are dozens in the building. Waiting for what? An absolute waste. Please sit down. Hirsh told me you are a friend of Meyer, and you are trying to help him. He was reluctant to tell me why he needs help. But with a bit of urging he gave me the whole story."

"Did you really bash two holdup-people with a toy baseball bat?"

She looked astonished. "What's that got to do with anything? There were three. I didn't have to hit the third one. I told him that I would, and he believed me and left. Why do you ask?"

"I was curious. It seems to be just about the most stupid kind of behavior possible."

"You certainly say what you think."

"I'm trying to figure out how much weight I should give to anything you tell me."

"It was stupid behavior. The bat was a gift for my grand-nephew. Still wrapped. I snatched it up out of terror, certain the man was going to kill me. I hit him, and he fell down, and I became notorious. I was interviewed. My picture was in the paper. So I bought another bat for the little boy. When the second holdup attempt occurred, I felt I was in a dream. I had to retain my reputation as a character. I hit him in slow motion. His eyes rolled up out of sight, and he still stood there until I hit him again. More publicity. On the third attempt I told him I would hit him. He left. After he left, I looked for the bat. It was gone. Hirsh had disposed of it. I fainted dead away. Stupid, Mr. McGee? No. Not stupid. Silly. Very very silly."

"I had to know. Sorry."

"I understand. My mind is quite clear."

"Do you think Hirsh is right? Is the Sprenger stuff gone?"

"Yes."

"Have you wondered about how it could have been done?"

"Young man, we are all fascinated by larceny. Fortunately for civilization, most of us merely think about it. Obviously the entire album was taken and another substituted. It is equally obvious that Mr. Sprenger managed it by devising some diversion, some alternate focus of attention. Had I still been employed by Mr. Fedderman, he would never have taken on the Sprenger account."

"You made the decisions?"

"Of course not! I would have let Hirsh know I did not approve. Then he would know that if he went ahead with it, I would make his life totally miserable, and he would have decided it wasn't worth it. A man like Sprenger would find it amusing to steal his own property and then make Mr. Fedderman reimburse him for his investment."

"I see. Then there is no connection, you feel, between the theft and the death of Jane Lawson?"

"Did I say that? Did I even imply it? Then how do you infer I would believe that? Last Thursday morning those two young women learned what had happened. Jane Lawson had a lot of time to try to work out the puzzle. You were all trying, were you not? I imagine she devised a theory of how it was done and felt compelled to test it before reporting it. She had a very good mind, you know. Quite logical."

"Could she have been involved, on her own or as an accomplice?"

"Jane Lawson? The question is grotesque. It is . . . fifteen years ago he employed her. She seemed very pleasant and plausible. We had to teach her everything about the business. She learned quickly. A good memory. I am a very skeptical old woman. I set some traps which looked like the most innocent of accidents, where she could profit without any possibility of detection. She did not hesitate a moment. She is the sort of person who, if she were using a pay phone and found a quarter in the coin drop, would feel very uncomfortable about keeping it. With some people, with too many people, conscience is the still small voice that says maybe someone is looking."

"What if somebody put heavy pressure on her, like threatening her kids?"

"I think she'd pack them up and go to her in-laws and ask for help. And get it."

"She told you about the general?"

"Privately, in confidence. We worked together there for ten years, remember. I tend to pry a bit. Of course, I'm going to go back now and fill in until he can find someone. I let her know I did not think her decision was entirely rational, but I respected her for it. She should have married again, of course."

"Did you help train Mary Alice too?"

"Are you asking about her in the same way? Maybe not exactly in the same way? A personal relationship exists? I stayed on for two weeks after he hired her. She was, and is, a very troubled person, I think. She was quite depressed when she first came to work. She never discusses her background. I had thought her a fugitive in the legal sense. Now I think she is a fugitive from emotion. She has visited me here many many times. She brings little problems to me. Problems of identification. She hated to ask Jane or Mr. Fedderman to help her. She is not really highly intelligent. She has a high order of native animal shrewdness perhaps. In time she became fascinated by the high-value rarities. There is something touching and childish about her enthusiasms. I do not believe—in fact, I am quite positive—Mary Alice could not plan anything very complicated and carry it out."

I thanked her for her time. I said I would probably see her in the store. She said Hirsh was going to open up again on Wednesday, the day after tomorrow. She went back to her class, and I phoned the hotel from the downstairs lobby. I had checked at two-thirty. Now it was quarter to four.

A Miss Dunn had phoned at five after three and left word she would phone again. She did not leave a number.

I phoned Meyer, caught him aboard his boat. It was too soon for Mary Alice to arrive. I told Meyer she was on the way, ETA unknown. Keep an eye out for her. Put her aboard the *Flush.* Lock her in. Then wait for me aboard his boat. I taxied back to the hotel, packed in fifteen seconds, and tried to pay my bill. But it was courtesy of Mr. Nucci, who isn't in the house at the moment.

I walked to the lot, repurchased my old pickup and took the fastest route through a light rain toward the Sunshine Turnpike, swallowing the little bits of acid that kept collecting in the back of my throat.

Fifteen

I jumped down onto the cockpit deck of the *Keynes* and went below into the very cramped quarters where Meyer lived like a bear in a cave. A very clean bear in a very littered cave.

"She's aboard," he said. "With three suitcases, a hat box, and a train case. Your enchanted barge is all fueled, furbished, and provisioned, sir. May I offer my best wishes for a happy voya—"

"Knock it off!"

I do not talk to Meyer like that. It shocked and annoyed him. Then he got a closer look at my expression.

"She gave me the keys to her car," he said. "When she parked, she backed it in to hide the plate. She asked me to drive it away from here and leave it in an airport lot. Miami, if I want to be very obliging."

"Leave it right where it is for now."

"Okay."

"I want to ask you to do something without giving you any of the reasons or background. But there's a risk."

"A big risk?"

"I don't know how big. Maybe there's none at all. Tomorrow morning I want you to go to this address and see Frank Sprenger. Use my name to get to see him. Play it this way. You are very angry at me. I let you believe we were going to make a very nice score out of Fedderman's problems, share and share alike. In fact, I told you that we'd stay healthier if we got out of Sprenger's area until things quiet down, and at McGee's request you got *The Busted Flush* all ready for a long cruise, maybe over to the Islands, so bring your passport. So tonight McGee smuggled a woman aboard the *Flush.* You didn't see her. You don't know who she is. But from something I said while drunk, you think she came to the Contessa late last night and stayed with me in my room overnight. Tonight I told you your trip was off. I got ugly about it. I said I had better company. I said Frank Sprenger was almost as dumb as Hirsh Fedderman."

"Sprenger . . . and *Mary Alice!*"

"I don't know what he'll do. Maybe there'll be no reaction at all. Right now I'm . . . trying to work out a jigsaw puzzle where every piece is square, and when I get them in the right places, they make an abstract painting. But they also make an abstract painting any way I fit them together."

"If he's interested?"

"Remember No Name Island?"

"Of course."

"Find it by yourself?"

"No problem."

"You are going to tell him that my plan, when the two of us were going, was to take the *Flush* down into Florida Bay and lay behind No Name and wait for a good five-day forecast before running across to Nassau. You can take him to the place. For a fee. Just him. The two of you can drive down to the Keys and rent a skiff and go on out to No Name. Are you sure you can find it?"

"My God, Travis. It's—"

"All right. You can find it. It isn't on any chart, so he can't find it alone. Of all the ways I can read this puzzle, if I'm right at all, he'll be willing to come alone. If it's a mob scene, forget it. Be sure you aren't tailed by his people or anybody."

"How do I let you know if—"

"I'll listen to Miami Marine tomorrow afternoon from three-fifteen to three-thirty, four-fifteen to four-thirty, five-fifteen to five-thirty. If you don't come through with a call, I'll come in and come after you."

"But won't she be able to—"

"Once we're well out of here, I'll tell her I asked you to keep tabs on anybody who might come looking for me. If he doesn't bite, just tell me everything is quiet. If he reacts but the time isn't set yet, tell me you heard somebody was looking for me but you didn't get a chance to see them or talk to them. If you are set up with him and know about when he might come visiting, say a man with a beard came by and wouldn't give his name, but he's going to come by again at such and such a time."

"And come back at you the next day when it's definite?"

"I'll monitor at the same times. This is a big tricky bastard, Meyer. Don't listen to any lullaby from him. I think he might make you sit while he goes and gets a description from the night man at the Contessa, the night bell captain."

"Isn't that a little too tricky, the part about the hotel?"

"Suggestion?"

"I didn't see her, but I saw her car and went and wrote down the plate number, and I know where it's parked."

I thought it over. "I like it better. What I don't like is the way I keep thinking of reasons why, if I'm right, Sprenger would like to leave all three of us in deep blue water."

"If it works out and we drive down there, the two of us, and get the skiff from . . . what's that place by the draw bridge?"

"Regal Marine."

"On the way out I can mention I gave somebody a letter to mail for me if I don't reclaim it by such and such a day. Who would I be writing to, Travis?"

"Two letters. Our friend Captain Matty Lamarr, who has never been bought or scared, and to General Samuel Horace Lawson at the Doral." I thought about my luck. Our imminent eviction from what I had begun to feel was safe sanctuary had torn a hole in the bottom of the luck feeling. I sensed emptiness and a cool feeling at the nape of the neck. "Have you got paper and envelopes?"

"When this noble vessel, *The John Maynard Keynes,* sinks, it will be because of an overburden of paper bound and unbound. Here you are. May I read over your shoulder?"

"Meyer, will you accept the premise that the less you know, the more plausible Sprenger will find you?"

"A subjective judgment. But okay. Who will I leave these with?"

"Jenny Thurston. Allow room for delays."

Two short letters. All I had to give was my guess as to who and why. The combination of Matty's professionalism and the general's massive leverage would open up all the rest of it. I put them in the envelopes and handed them, unsealed, to Meyer. "You were reluctant," I said. "Chance to overrule."

He sighed and licked the flaps and sealed them tightly. He said, "Interesting analogy, about the jigsaw with square pieces and nonobjective art. So you put them together in a way, I suppose, that pleases you, and so you call it the only logical arrangement."

"That's what I seem to be doing."

"It is also an analogy for a madman's view of reality. No rules restrict his assemblage, because they're all square pieces. So he makes a pattern that pleases him, and then he tries to impose it on the world, and they lock him up."

"Thanks, Meyer."

He put his hand lightly on my arm, his wise eyes very sober and quiet. "Quixote, my friend. It has been too long for you, too long since there was a woman who moved you, who made magic. It started to be very good, and some automatic relays in that skeptical skull broke the connection. A sense of what-might-have-been can make a man very vulnerable. Suspicion can become one hell of a big windmill. And some kinds of windmills can break your ass."

"Contents noted," I said.

There was a pale pink scrap of day left when I unlocked the *Flush,* noting with approval that Meyer had unhooked the shoreside umbilical cords for phone, water, and electric and had taken off the spring lines and the heavy weather fenders. I didn't want to use any interior lights unless I was on engines or on the alternate one hundred and ten system off my generator.

In the gloom Mary Alice rose up from behind the far end of the big yellow couch and said, "Where the *hell* have you been?"

"Taking care of this and that."

"Don't you know you've got to get me *out* of here!"

I moved closer to her and checked on the validity of her anxiety by saying, "Settle down, honey. We'll be on our way in the morning."

Her voice got very thin. "In the *morning!* I can be *dead* by morning! Now. Please. Can't we just go a little way? Please."

I saw the dark shape in her right fist, pointed down at the deck. I took her arm and pulled it out of her hand. She resisted and then let go of it. I took it over to the light of a port. A little Colt .25 automatic, about as small as you can get and stay reasonably lethal.

"Where'd you get this?"

"Can we talk about where I got things when we're *moving?!*"

I handed it back to her. Maybe it would make her feel a little bit better. Her anxiety was genuine, or she was a great loss to the theater.

I went to the topside controls and cranked her up. When she settled down from the indigestion and flatulence that afflict her whenever I rouse her from indolence, I went down and cast off the lines, moved her ahead a bit, and left her teetering against a piling. I brought the *Muñequita* close with a boat hook, jumped onto her bow, took her lines off the dock, and scrabbled back aboard with her bow line, snubbed her close and bent the line around a stern cleat. I cut the timing very close. By the time I got back to the controls the bow was swinging very very near the bow of an old and very well maintained Consolidated in the next door slip. The unfriendly old man who owned her stood by his railing with a big fender, ready to lower it to where I might crunch into him.

"Watch it!" he bawled, just as I gave it hard right rudder and gave my port diesel a hard quick jolt of reverse. It held me against the piling and stopped the swing of the bow and started it moving out.

"Sorry," I called to him as I eased out of the slip. No point in trying to reply in kind. He had enough trouble in the form of a wide wife with a voice like a bearing about to go. He worked on the boat all week long with her telling him how to do what he was already doing. On Sundays they took a picnic cruise of three hours, and you could hear that voice of hers all the way out to the channel, telling him to watch out for the things he was already watching out for.

After I was under the bridge and past Port Everglades, heading south inside, in the Waterway channel with the running lights on, a healthy arm snaked around my waist, and the big lady pulled us close together and said, "Wow."

"I'll put it in the log. One heart-felt wow."

"You better believe it."

I showed her a distant marker to aim at and gave her the wheel and went aft and gave the *Muñequita* a little more line until she towed steadily without wallowing. Mary Alice was very anxious to give the wheel back to me.

"Makes me too nervous," she said. "Where are we going?"

"I know a good place about an hour and half down the line. We can anchor out. It's good water and out of the traffic."

"You tell me how I can help, huh?"

"You might be able to find your way below and come back with a pair of drinks."

It took a while. She had to hunt for things. She apologized. It was full dark. I was using the hand spot to pick up the reflectors on the unlighted markers. I was aware of her near me in darkness, sitting in the starboard chair, aware of how quiet she was.

"And about that automatic?" I said.

"Oh, a friend gave it to me. He was worried about me. He thought it would be a good thing for me to have."

"Ever fire it?"

"I drove way out into the country one time, to sort of ranch land. I found a beer can in the ditch and put it on a rock. I had a box of fifty shells. It didn't make as much noise as I thought it would, but I kept flinching. I had a newspaper in the car, and I stuck it onto a stub sticking out of a big pine tree. Then I could see where the bullets were going, and I figured out how to work it. If I didn't know when it was going to go bang, I flinched after it happened. Then they went where I was aiming. Then I could hit the can pretty good. Every other time at about twenty feet."

"That's pretty good."

"If I had to shoot somebody, I'd imagine his head is a big beer can."

"The torso is a bigger target."

She was quiet for about thirty seconds and finally said, "I'd shoot somebody who wanted to hurt me, right? So I think it would be better to shoot him in the part that does the thinking."

"I can't fault you for logic."

"What?"

"Do you think Jane Lawson switched the stamps in any of the other investment accounts?"

"Darling, can I make a new rule for us?"

"Such as?"

"You come to a point when . . . you want one life to end and another life to begin. I don't want to talk about any of that. It's all over now. I'm somebody else. So are you. We're both new people."

"What are these new people going to live on, M.A.?"

"I haven't seen you hurting for money. Not the way you live. You certainly had the sense to bring along a bundle, didn't you?"

"Even what they call a goodly sum runs out."

"In cash?"

"How else? And safely aboard."

"And we can get to the islands, can't we?"

"Slowly, in the very best weather. Sure."

"We can make the money last a long long time in the islands, living on this boat, can't we?"

"What islands did you have in mind?"

"You practically *have* to go to the Bahamas first, don't you?"

"Correct."

"Well then?"

"Well what?"

"We can just sort of poke along down the Islands to the end of them and then wait for good weather, like you say we need, and go across to the next batch. If we kept doing that, where would we end up some day?"

"Trinidad. Venezuela."

"Is there anything wrong with that?"

"These two new people are going to have a long and intimate relationship."

"From the samples, you haven't anything against that, have you? As any fool can plainly see, *I* like the idea. A crazy man has run my life for the past five years, and now he'll never find me again. He'll never have a chance to kill us, will he?"

"When we run out of funds, we'll seek honest work?"

"You're getting stuffy, you know that? What you should do now is just live. Right? It's a big adventure, and we're together, lover. We'll be in love and have fun and swim and eat and laugh and all that. You're the captain. You can marry us. Let's think up a new last name for the happy couple."

"McWorry?"

"Mister, I am *really* going to cure you of that."

I found my little parking lot, circled on three sides with mangrove. I checked the time and the tide chart and laid her just where I wanted her, cross-hooked so she would swing properly on the tide change. I pulled the *Muñequita* up onto the starboard quarter and made her fast there against fenders so she would not nudge us all night. I started the generator and checked the bilges and put Mary Alice in charge of the galley. I sat in the lounge with my drink, moving those square pieces around atop the game table in my mind, finding damned little to please me.

Sixteen

We got an early start in mist that soon cleared, and by eleven in the morning we were well down the length of Biscayne Bay in the most oppressive heat I could remember. We were making a stately six knots, but there was a steady six knot breeze from behind us, so we moved in a pocket of airlessness, in a reflected dazzle that stabbed up into the shade of the tarp I had rigged over the topside controls.

I kept it on automatic pilot most of the time, taking it out now and again to make a correction for tide drift. She sat in the white copilot seat in a salmon-colored bikini, slumped, with her heels propped atop the instrument panel, her legs apart, her fanny on the edge of the seat, the nape of her neck against the top of the back. She had piled her black hair into a half-knotted wad on the top of her head. Sweat trickled down between her breasts, down her belly, and into the top edge of the bikini bottom, darkening the fabric. She had exposed almost every optional inch of skin area to the breeze that never happened.

The heat made her cross. "Jesus, McGee, is it *always* like this?"

"This is very unusual weather we're having."

"Ha,ha,ha. Can we stop and swim or something?"

"Not through here. Have another cold beer."

"I don't want another cold beer. Heat makes me feel sick."

"When we change direction, we'll get some breeze."

"Like how soon?"

"Hour. Hour and a half."

"Dear Jesus. I just can't take much of this."

"Complain, complain, complain."

She snapped her head around and stared at me, her eyes narrow and furious. "Do you want me to make a list of *everything* I want to complain about?"

"If it would make you feel better, go ahead."

"Maybe my nerves are on edge for a lot of reasons."

"Could be," I said. No argument. I let the discussion die. It wasn't going to do either of us any good to talk about it.

Last night she had decided we would have a very busy bed, and she began to do a lot of flapping and roaming and rambling, changing from here to there, and changing back, apparently trying to express a special gratitude with a lot of extra-strenuous work. I stayed with her for a time, and suddenly it was all rubbery fakery, smack and slap, grunt and huff, like a pair of third-rate wrestlers in some lunch-bucket town practicing for the evening's performance for the nitwits who think it quite real.

As soon as I got that image of it, both the spirit and the flesh became weak. She settled down, still breathing hard.

"Did I do something wrong, darling?" she asked. "Did I move wrong and hurt you or anything?"

"No. No, it wasn't that."

"What then?"

"I don't know. It just happened."

"Does it happen often like this with you?"

"I wouldn't say so."

"You want I should help you? Here, let me help you."

"No, honey. Let's just wait."

"Wait for what? Violins?"

"Let's just take it easy. That's all."

"That's easy for you to say. What about me? You don't give a damn how I feel, do you?"

"Sorry about all this."

"It was going to be really great."

"Next time."

She made a sound of exasperation and moved away from all contact with me. From time to time she sighed. Then she got up and went across to the smaller stateroom and slammed the door, leaving behind a faint effluvium of perfume, exertion, and secretions, leaving behind some bedding for me to untangle, leaving behind that strange male guilt and shame impotence creates. The female and the male are both victims of the male sexual mythology. If I do not achieve, or if I prematurely lose that engorgement which creates the stiffness required for penetration, then my manhood is suspect. My virility is a fiction. I have been unable to give or receive satisfaction. The act has not been carried to its compulsory conclusion. Once any element of doubt enters the equation, then the male erection, that font of aggression and mastery, becomes as vulnerable, as delicate, as easily lost as a snowflake over a campfire.

She left me there alone, full of self-pity and yet with a sense of relief. There was just too damned bouncing rubbery much of her, and nothing anywhere that one mere hand could cup. I had all the self-derision of the suddenly gelded stud. I would auction off the *Flush* to some Burt Reynolds type and pursue the quiet life. Some gardening. Gourmet cooking. And a little philately. Or some numismatics, for a change of pace.

I thought of paying a call upon her, but instead I went to sleep. I was more apprehensive than curious.

Now, forced to recall how miserably I had disappointed the lady, I wondered if I might find a clue to a repetition of failure if I were to look upon her and try to summon erotic dreams of glory and see if I could detect the promise of some small physiological response.

Now, in the blazing shimmer and the white needles that came sparking up off every ripple, I looked sidelong and quickly at her sitting there and felt awe and a little stirring of alarm. There was so bloody much of her, all so firm and fit. A yard and a half of great legs, boobs like two halves of a prize honeydew, a mouth from here over to there, hands and feet almost as big as mine, a powerful-looking neck full of strings and cables and muscles which moved into a different and visible pattern each time she changed the position of her head. I was aware of all her hidden engines, all working away, from the slow hard kuh-dup of her heart to all the other hidden things, absorbing, nourishing, fractionating, eliminating.

"If you don't mind too much," she said. She made a nimble reaching flexing motion and dropped a damp wad of salmon-colored fabric onto the deck. "This is a monokini," she said. She stood up, eeled the rest of it down her hips and down her legs and stepped out of it. "And this is a nokini at all. And automatic pilot or no automatic pilot, this is not invitational. It's to keep from dying."

I pointed to the thunderhead building in the southeast, lifting into the sky. "With any luck," I said.

"Can you drive over that way and get under it?"

"If you look over in that direction, like two hundred yards, you will see some birds walking. Never drive the boat toward where the birds are walking. First rule of navigation."

"Oh, great!"

"Whether we get it or not, it'll change the wind."

"How soon?"

"Maybe an hour."

"Why do I bother to ask anything at all? *Why* can't you use the airconditioning while you're running?"

"It has to run off the generator. There's something wrong with the wiring. There's some kind of crossfeed somewhere. If I start the generator, everything will be fine until I cut in the airconditioning. Then it blows about seven fuses, and we're dead in the water until I replace them. On every boat everywhere, dear, something is always wrong with the wiring."

"Why does it have to be the airconditioning?"

"Because God hates us both."

"Don't say that!"

"Offends you?"

"Just don't say it. Okay? It isn't something to be funny about. That's all. It doesn't offend me. It just makes me feel strange. Crawly."

The *Flush* waddled along, the long V of her wash fading into the hot ripply dance of the big bay. The lady stood up between the pilot seats, brace legged, letting her black hair down and rewinding it to bind up the strands which had escaped. Sweat made oiled highlights on the long curves of her body.

My concealed amusement at myself had a very acid flavor. Here was the libertine's dream of glory, the realization of all the night thoughts of adolescence: a handsome, lithe, healthy superabundance of naked lady in her prime, alone with our hero aboard his crafty craft, stocked for weeks of cruising about, a lady as infinitely available as the very next breath or the very next cold beer or hot coffee, and our hero was wishing she had stood on the other side of her chair because he found her overheated towering closeness oppressive, yea even approaching the vulgar. It made me remember the time I went to the performance of a Spanish dance troupe, hoping there was a ticket left at the box office. There was, way way down front. It was so close I could smell the dust they banged up out of the stage. I could see soiled places on the costumes. I could smell the fresh sweat of effort mingled with the stale sweat of prior engagements, trapped in gaudy fabric, released by heat. I could hear the dancing girls grunt and pant. I could see dirty knuckles, grubby ankles, and soiled throats. They were very very good. Ten rows back the illusion must have been perfect. But I was too damned close to the machinery, and it killed the magic.

Okay, hero. You are a sentimentalist, a romanticist. A throwback. You want all those tricks of a bygone culture —the shy and flirtatious female, the obligation for pursuit, retreat, and ultimate capture. Pretty chauvinistic, buddy. This is the new casual world of equality. You are both made of the same order of meat. Should she have a yen for a beer, she can go get it and open it. Should she have a yen for an interlude of frictive pleasure, she can turn and swing astride you as you sit, and you can keep an eye on the channel ahead over her shoulder. Contact and excitation create a natural physical release. It is no big wondrous emotional complicated thing. The new message is that sexual mystery causes terrible hangups which create neuroses which destroy lives.

It all made me want to move to a small town in Indiana and start a little factory where I could make buggy whips, stereopticons, and hoop skirts, and sit in the glider on the porch on the summer evenings and hear the children at play and finally go inside and, by gas light, read that Admiral Dewey had been placed in command of the fleet.

A world I never knew. Maybe the worlds you never knew are always better than the ones you do.

She sat again and swung her feet up. "Won't this thing go any faster than this?"

"Not enough to matter. It's a displacement hull. It has to push the water out of the way. I could get three more knots out of her and use twice the fuel I'm using now."

"It's a real crock."

"But it's my real crock."

She shrugged and was silent. I tried to put my finger on what it was about her that was battling me and irritating me. It seemed excessively childish for her to complain so constantly about being mildly uncomfortable aboard a houseboat taking her away from something that really terrified her.

Children lack empathy about how the adults around them feel. Children have a tendency toward self-involvement which makes them give too much weight to trivia, too little weight to significant things. If the house burns down, the charred sister and the charred kitten are equally mourned.

I had believed her empathetic, sensitive, responsive. I had enjoyed being with her. This female person did not seem at all responsive in the same way. I went back over the relationship. A cartoon light bulb went on in the air over my head. At all prior times, up to last night and now, my involvement had been in exactly the same track as her self-involvement. So of course she had been responsive, in the way a mirror is responsive.

If you go to a play which is concerned with a dramatic relationship you have experienced, you are deeply moved. The actress will speak the lines in a way best designed to move you. But take the lovely, talented thing to dinner, and she will bury you in the debris of her tepid little mind, rotten reviews in London, the inferior dressing room on the Coast, the pansy hairdresser's revenge, her manager's idiot wife, the trouble with talk shows, and who has stopped or started, sleeping with whom or with what.

I had listened to drama and believed it. And now I could not believe that this was the actress.

I saw the squall riffle approaching way off the port bow, making a busier calligraphy on the water. It covered so large an area it could not miss us. I told her to prepare for sudden comfort. While she was looking at me with blank incomprehension, the rain breeze swept us, a coolness with a smell of rain and ozone. She made a glad cry and stood to face it, arms out in pleasurable crucifixion. It died away, and she said "Noooooo" in a long descending mournful minor.

"More on the way and rain behind it."

It was more than I expected. The strong gusts threatened to whip the tarp away, and I took it down, folding it with difficulty, stowing it under the instrument panel. Electricity winked and bammed around us as the rain came in silvery, wind-whipped sheets, heeling us to starboard, obscuring the far markers. The rain was unseasonably cold, and abruptly it turned to hail, the size of puffed rice, whipping and stinging us, so that she yelped with pain and surprise and ducked down below the rail on the port side, behind me, for shelter. Then more rain came, heavier but with less wind. I had backed the *Flush* off to almost dead slow, so that if we wandered from the channel we would nudge the shallows instead of sticking fast. Mary Alice gloried in the rain, upturning her face to it, laughing at the pleasure of it streaming down her body. Her hair was soaked and flattened. The deck ran with water. She picked up her bikini parts, wrung them momentarily dry and put them back on. But we had both started to shiver. I was going to switch to the pilot house controls when suddenly the rain ceased, and I could hear it steaming on across the bay toward the mainland. The depth finder was reading eleven feet, and I had to move easterly about fifty feet to get the distant markers lined up.

Cloud cover moved west, and soon we were in hot sunlight that made the deck steam as it dried.

She toweled her hair half-dry, flung it back, and said, "I'm *starving,* darling. I really am. After I eat, I'm going to chop my hair short."

"What?"

"It's too much of a damned nuisance on a boat ride. You could probably cut it better, huh? How about when we get to the place you said? Will you?"

"Reluctantly."

"Why reluctantly? Oh, could it help you turn on, if it's long?"

"I think long hair is becoming to the shape of your face."

She frowned. "I mean chop it off to only about here, not like when it was all shaved—"

"All shaved off? Why?"

"It was sort of like an initiation."

"Sounds like a very unusual club."

"I'll tell you all about it sometime, honey."

"We've got nothing else to do right now. Why not tell me?"

"Right now I've got to fix something to eat. You want to eat now too. Samwiches?"

After we ate, I said, "Okay. The story of the shaved head."

"I don't feel like telling it now."

"But I feel like listening to it now."

She stared at me. "Are you going to be like that? I don't *like* to be pushed around, Travis. I've had enough of it all my life. If you muscle me, I can't feel loving toward you. You understand what I'm saying?"

"I don't think I could ever adjust to a reward and punishment system of lovemaking."

"I have news for you. You're going to have to."

"Really?"

"When I'm happy, I'm the best thing that ever happened to you, and when you make me unhappy, I'm just no good at all. Sorry, but that's the way I am."

"I wasn't trying to muscle you."

"I accept your apology."

"I just wanted to know if you were in a home or a prison when they shaved your head."

"Oh, you are such a smart bastard! You just cut off the supply, friend."

"Prison then?"

"No, goddamn you to hell! It was a school for girls."

That was the forlorn tipoff. The ones which are attended voluntarily are called girls' schools. I asked no questions. I could feel the radiations of her anger. At last she sighed. "They caught me and a boyfriend with the whole trunk of the car full of radios he'd taken out of parked cars. We'd both been in trouble before. I was fourteen, and he was twenty. I was in a foster home, and those people didn't give a shit about anything except the sixty-two fifty a month they got for letting me sleep there. At the school we were in cottages. Twenty girls in a cottage. A matron was supposed to run the cottage, but ours was a wino, so two butch girls ran it. I wouldn't let them into my bed at night, so one of them stole a gold locket from one of the black girls and hid it on the underside of my bed with tape. They found it in a shakedown looking for some missing table forks, and so then they all jumped me and shaved my head. It took a lot of doing. I tore them up pretty good. Afterwards I used to jump the ones who did it, one at a time. They locked me up alone a few times, but I kept going until I got every last one. I guess I'll keep my hair long the way it is. It isn't all that much trouble."

"When did you get out?"

"This isn't the confession hour. Some day I'll tell you all that stuff. When I feel like it. Right now I'm going downstairs. You just drive the boat, huh?"

Her voice was weary rather than angry. It seemed quite pleasant being alone. I put the sun tarp back up. I took a beer out of the cooler. A ray leapt high and came down, slapping his wings hard against the water to stun enough minnows for an afternoon snack. Over to my right, in the shallows near a mangrove island, a mullet made three leaps. Mullet come out gracefully enough, then land flat out, on belly or side. They are vegetarians. They graze the undersea meadows where parasites fasten to their skins, and so the mullet leap and knock them loose and go back to grazing. Flying fish leap to glide away from the teeth of the predator fish. Dolphins leap for the pleasure of it. Sailfish leap to shake free of the steel hook.

So why, after the five quiet years in the depths, did my bikinied creature leap free? To knock away the parasites, to stun something she wanted to feed on. To escape the predator or the hook. Or for the pleasure of it.

I shuffled all the square pieces and put the puzzle together again. The trouble with square pieces is that there is no way to know if any are missing or how many are missing. Or how many pieces do not belong in the puzzle at all.

I checked the next marker number against my Waterway chart and found we were making better time than I had estimated. We would be there in time for me to monitor the Miami Marine Operator frequency for Meyer's call.

Seventeen

There are long expanses of tidewater flats north of the main channel through the eastern part of Florida Bay. Once long ago, when it had been imperative to find a safe place to stash *The Busted Flush,* a friend, now dead, had gone ahead in the dinghy, using a boat hook to take the soundings, while I followed at dead slow, taking bearings on other islands, marking down the coordinates. There were several false turns, but at last he found a way around an island about a hundred feet long, forty feet wide, shaped like a lima bean, where by great fortune there was good water close in to the muddy shore. Then he and Meyer and I worked like madmen, hacking mangrove branches and wateroak branches, trying to cover the bulk of the *Flush.* We were not more than half done when we heard the little red airplane coming and had to dive for cover. They should have seen it from the air, but they missed it.

I got out the chart to refresh my memory of the old channel. I had inked it in. It looked like a lumpy, runover snake. I had enough tide to make it, and the slant of the sunlight helped me read the water ahead. Even so I nudged the mud several times where the turns were sharp, where I had to back and fill, like a tractor trailer truck threading a Mexican alley.

I laid the Flush close in, close enough to spit into the mangroves, killed the engines, and threw over a bow hook and a stern hook, planning to go over the side and walk them into better position and make them firm, but something changed my mind quickly. Three somethings. A sky-darkening cloud of ravenous mosquitoes, sand flies and stinging gnats. As I bounded down the ladderway, Mary Alice came out onto the stern deck, knuckling a sleepy eye. Then suddenly she began dancing, hollering, flailing her arms and slapping herself heartily. We both tried to get through the doorway at once. We got in, and I slammed it and went looking for any open, unscreened port. They were coming into the galley. I slid that screening across and got out the bug spray and gave them a taste of civilization.

"*This* is your goddamn paradise?" Mary Alice yawped. "*This* is where we are supposed to wait for good weather?" She looked down and whacked herself on the thigh. "You are some kind of dummy, you know that?"

There were little ones coming through the screening. I told her to shut up and close all the ports while I started the airconditioning. Soon, after we had killed off the last of the invaders and the moving air began to feel cool, it began to seem better to her. I told her we were lucky there were no dive bombers, a kind of fly half as big as a mouse that folds its wings on high and comes arrowing down to take an actual piece of flesh out of your body, leaving a hole and a trickle of blood. He takes it away with him and sits in a tree and eats it like an apple. She wanted to believe I was kidding. I was, but only by about ten percent.

I explained to her that the wind had died, and when it came up again, it would be out of the north, and we could go out on deck without being dragged away and eaten. But for now I was going to assume the anchors did not need moving and the *Muñequita* did not need attention. I was not going out there. No.

Her disposition began to show considerable improvement, and suddenly it was time to gear up and listen for Meyer. She followed me into the pilot house, asking too many questions.

"Okay," she said, "so what good does it do if you know that somebody has come around looking for you?"

"Or you. Wouldn't you want to know who?"

"Knowing why is all I need to know. Anyway, what makes you think you can trust that hairy son of a bitch?"

"I don't think about it. I just trust him."

"If you've got somebody under the hammer, you can trust him. Otherwise, forget it."

"Another of Mary Alice McDermit's delicate aphorisms."

"Afor what?"

"Hush."

I tuned the channel another hair and got rid of some of the blur. We listened for the full fifteen minutes. There were calls for other boats and calls from other boats, but no traffic for us. She'd had a nap. She was getting hungry again. She was bored. She wanted a drink but didn't know what. There was a whiny sub-tone in her voice. I let her play with the radio, and she found some country music and turned it too high. It wasn't worth trying to get her to turn it down. She sat crosslegged on the floor, swaying back and forth, singing the lyrics she knew, scratching her bites.

He didn't phone on the second segment either. She was tired of the radio. She went in and changed her clothes and came back in a yellow terry thing like a body stocking that she said was too tight in the crotch. She kept tugging at it. It made her cross. She rummaged through the cabinet over the wall desk and found some cards. The only game we both knew was gin. She didn't give a damn what I might be holding and paid no attention to what I picked, so she constantly discarded right into my hand, and she constantly lost. She turned the radio on again and played solitaire on the floor in front of it. I don't know what her rules were, but she went out every time.

On the third and final fifteen minutes of monitoring, the marine operator came up with a call for "the motor yacht *Busty Flush.*" She had a short list, and I came in and identified and took the call. Meyer sounded as if he were calling from the bottom of a big laundry bag. As soon as he'd start to come in clear, they'd dump in more laundry. But I managed to extract from the blur that there had been a fellow looking for me. I felt my pulse give a hefty bump. I waited for the next part of our little code. Mary Alice stood at my elbow, listening to the insectile low fidelity of my tin speaker and, with her thumb, trying to relieve the undue stricture of the nether end of her yellow garment.

It was sick excitement to know that I had placed a bet on a three-legged horse and every other horse had fallen down on the clubhouse turn and my choice was lumping home at historic odds.

Yes, the fellow had a beard. "His name is George Sharsh. He said you know him. Do you know him?"

"George who?" This was beyond the limit of our code, and I was puzzled.

"Sharsh. S as in sniper. T as in telescope. A as in arson. R as in rage. C as in careful. H as in hide. Sharsh."

"Starch?"

"Right!"

"Sure, I know him."

"He said he'd be back tomorrow in the late afternoon or early evening."

"Tomorrow? Thursday?"

"Right. What will I tell him?"

"Stall him." I hesitated. That was wrong. Meyer might think I wanted him to try to delay Sprenger. "No. Just find out what he wants and see if you can take care of it."

Out of the depths of the laundry he said goodbye. I hung the Bakelite mike back on the hook and flipped the set off.

"Who is this George Starch guy?" Mary Alice asked.

"Oh, he comes around with a problem now and then."

"Like what?"

"Well . . . like a disposal problem."

"I don't get it."

She followed me back to the lounge. I had an urge to experiment. "George is sort of an agent. Somebody might be holding stock certificates that don't belong to them. George finds a way to unload them."

"He comes to you with stuff like that?"

"Once in a while."

I stretched out on the yellow couch. She leaned on the back of it, standing behind it, looking down at me. "I got this idea you were straight, sort of. What do you do, work both ends?"

"I do favors for friends."

"But Meyer wouldn't get involved in anything like that."

"Like what?"

"Fencing anything."

"Last night before I came aboard, I saw Meyer. He had a suggestion about your car. By now some friends of ours are baking a different color onto it, and they'll put Alabama tags on it and sell it right in Miami. Alabama tags make it easy. There's no title certificate. Meyer will probably clear three hundred."

"*He* suggested it? I'll be damned! Gee, you never know, do you? Whyn't this George Starch move things through . . . you know, regular channels?"

"That's like selling to a supermarket, M.A. They're so big they beat the price way down. I'm a corner grocery store, and I can make better deals."

"Unless they find out you're making better deals."

"I'm not a total damn fool, honey. If some hungry clown contacted me with a problem about a couple of barracks bags full of grass from Jamaica or Barbados, fresh off somebody's Piper Apache, I would route him to Frank."

She swallowed and licked her mouth and started to speak and had to speak again, the first attempt was so ragged.

"Frank? Frank who?"

"Frank Sprenger. What Frank do you think?"

"How would I know what Frank? How would I know?"

I reached up and patted her hand. It felt damp and cold. "Sorry. That's right. How would you know? He isn't in operations. He's just a guy who's acceptable to all parties at interest, and he works as a sort of traffic manager and resident auditor. I guess because you saw him all those times at the bank, I had the idea you would know what he did."

"Investments," she said in a small voice.

"All kinds, dear. All kinds. I never got to ask you this question. It's been in my mind. Frank is very very heavy with the ladies. You are far from being dog meat. I imagine he made his move. What happened?"

"He . . . isn't the sort of person who appeals to me."

I laughed. She asked me what was so humorous. I said it was like a deer in deer season refusing to be shot by a hunter in the wrong shade of red hat.

"Okay, so maybe he doesn't like girls as big as me. Some men are really turned off by tall girls."

"If everything else is in the right place, I think Frank might start to get turned off if a girl was fifteen feet tall and weighed four hundred lovely pounds."

"Well . . . he never tried anything. I had *no* idea you knew him at all. You never *said* anything about knowing him."

I stretched and yawned. "It was sort of a confidential relationship. He gave me a little fee to sort of represent him in the Fedderman problem. I wouldn't have fooled with it otherwise."

She gasped and stood erect. She ran around the end of

the couch and came thumping down onto her knees on the floor beside me, sat back on her heels, and stared at me. "He *paid* you!"

"A token. Two round ones for expenses. What's the matter with you anyway?"

She thumbed her hair back. "Exactly what did he tell you to do?"

"Why are you getting so churned up?"

"This could be very important. Please."

"He told me he heard that Meyer wanted me to help Fedderman, who thought that the properties in Sprenger's investment account had been switched. He said he heard that it didn't appeal to me. I told him that it didn't appeal because I thought he could handle his own problems better than I could. He asked me, as a favor to him, to check it out. To keep my eyes open and keep his name out of it, insofar as our private agreement was concerned. I'd say he took care of it himself without my help. You and I know who made the switch."

I waited for a reply, but I had lost her. She was still there, but her eyes were focused on something further than the horizon. She was chewing her underlip. Her eyebrows went up over the bridge of her nose, separated by two new deep wrinkles.

I wondered if I was wearing an identical pair of wrinkles. Good ol' Meyer had found a Meyer-like way of imparting ugly information. Frank Sprenger was enraged. And I had better be very careful and do an efficient job of hiding, because Sprenger was planning to take care of things with a rifle with telescopic sights and then burn my house to the ground. I could not imagine Sprenger, no matter how enraged he might be, confiding his battle plans to Meyer, no matter how much Meyer encourages confidences.

But I could imagine Sprenger asking specifics of the location of the *Flush,* the terrain, the cover, and asking details of her construction and fuel, enough to enable Meyer to make one of his intuitive yet logical series of guesses.

"So he knows you then," she asked. "He knows where you live and how you live?"

"Certainly. Dave Davis and Harry Harris have been aboard this houseboat. You wouldn't know them, I guess. They work for Frank."

"If he came looking for you or sent somebody, would they ask Meyer where you are and if anybody is with you?"

"I would imagine so. But Meyer would say he doesn't know."

"Would Frank know Meyer would probably know?"

"I guess so."

"Oh dear Jesus God."

"You better tell me your problem, girl."

"He can make Meyer tell him."

"If Meyer sees that Frank is serious about it, he'll tell him. He'll tell him the *Flush* is set for long cruising and you're aboard with me."

Her face crumpled. She toppled onto her side and wound her arms around her head. She began to sob.

I sat up and reached down and patted her. "Hey! Hey, what's wrong?"

She sat up, snuffling, eyes streaming. "Wrong! I'm dead, that's what's wrong. You killed me, you dumb son of a bitch!"

She scrambled up, stumbled and nearly fell, and ran back to the stateroom and slammed the door behind her.

I leaned back and closed my eyes. Now I could sit at the game table and take some of the square pieces and turn them the way they belonged and glue them to the table. Too few to be able, from them, to discern all of the pattern.

The brain is a random computer. Fragments of experience, sensation, distorted input, flicker across multiple screens.

. . . The last time I felt I had lost my luck, I made some bad moves which should have cost me more dearly than they did.

. . . None of Fedderman's older investment accounts would have been likely to know Sprenger or to put him in touch with Fedderman. Sprenger could have used a name given to him by someone else.

. . . Meyer's first instinct was that Frank Sprenger had been setting Fedderman up, using the inventory lists Fedderman gave him as a basis for buying substitute junk, using a double for Fedderman to make the switch easily.

. . . Willy Nucci had been very emphatic about how eager Sprenger would be to cover up any personal goof before it became public knowledge.

. . . When Meyer and I had talked about Sprenger at the steak house that night after I saw Willy, we had agreed that, on second thought, it did not seem to be Sprenger's style to try to go for a double by cheating Fedderman, when it would be easier to play the tricks and games he was used to. Easier and safer.

. . . "I like people. I really do." Mary Alice had said that as we walked to the bank. The people who really like people are so genuine about it they are unable to imagine how it would be *not* to like people. And so they don't go about proclaiming.

. . . Mary Alice had leafed back through the book, looking for the page which had Barbados stamps to see if there would be room for more from the same island on that page. She did not have her glasses. Hirsh often bragged about his vision. She knew he could see the pages. Hirsh was volatile. Was he expected to react, to reveal the discrepancy then and there, so that Sprenger could demand that Hirsh live up to his guarantee?

. . . In the store last Thursday, I had believed her declaration of honesty. But she had wept more readily than I would have guessed. Meyer had called her amiable and gentle. She had become just what I wanted her to be. For just long enough.

. . . Had her explanation at lunch that day, of how long it would take to switch the stamps from book to book, been designed to induce me to have the brilliant thought that maybe the whole book had been switched? If so, I struck out.

. . . My decision at lunch that day, to trust her and believe her, had been based upon my assumption that if she had the art, the guile, and the energy to project a false image so skilfully, she would not have spent five years in that little store.

. . . Had she sensed when I was vulnerable enough so that she could play that old game across the table, the blue eyes which become trapped in the silence of the stare of realization, widening in a kind of alarm, then, with obvious effort, breaking contact?

. . . Why would Jane Lawson wait fourteen years before

stealing anything? Why would she wonder about the authenticity of the items in the other investment accounts when Mary Alice didn't, not until much later? Jane Lawson was a very bright woman. If she had planned the action and made the switch the one and only time she filled in for Mary Alice, she would know that eventually I would find out about it. I would ask the right question of Hirsh or Mary Alice, and they would remember. So wouldn't she look a lot better if she casually volunteered the information? If she had done nothing wrong, she might not think of bringing it up.

. . . After five years of working with Mary Alice, it was Jane Lawson's diagnosis that Mary Alice would rather work with her hands than make decisions. They were close during working hours, but after working hours Jane never saw her. In the politest way possible, Jane had said she thought Mary Alice to be a little bit on the dumb side. Today I could agree. But not until today.

. . . Jane had called the device of putting a hair from her head under the rubber band around Judy's books one of her "sneaky spy tricks." It showed a certain talent for subterfuge. Would she mention the rubber band trick if she had used that same talent more profitably?

. . . Harris and Davis got to me much too fast, much too soon after I became involved. And their first objective was to sideline me, to pay me to back away from Fedderman's problems and wait for word from my anonymous employer.

. . . I remembered Harris being silenced by Davis. Harris had said, "That was one of the questions. To find out if McGee was—" Was what? Susceptible to being scared off? Too committed to the Fedderman problem already? Apparently if I couldn't be bought off or scared off, the third step was to clue me in by saying their boss was interested in the Fedderman situation—which was the same as naming him—and wanted to be certain I was not going to help somebody pull something dumb and fancy which would leave Sprenger on the short end. I could not have let them go back and report that I knew how to keep a good scorecard and I'd refused the money. To Sprenger that would have been tantamount to saying I was out to try to clip him.

. . . Mary Alice had reacted all too greedily to the ripe and pungent smell of money within the restricted tailored gardens of the Key Biscayne Yacht Club. She had almost visibly salivated. And when she got over believing I was probably the caretaker on the *Flush*, the touching began. Hand on my shoulder, hip bumping into me. People establish private space around them and do not move into yours or let you into theirs unless you establish intimacy or the promise of it. She had abruptly diminished the spaces we both maintained, moving into mine, letting me into hers. There must be a mutual willingness to reduce the space, or one person becomes uneasy and uncomfortable. Meyer uses that phenomenon to rid himself of the very infrequent person who bores him. He moves inside their space rather than trying to back away. When he stands with his nose five inches from theirs, they begin to falter and move back. Meyer keeps moving in, smiling. They see somebody across the room they want to talk to and excuse themselves. Or remember a phone call they have to make. With Meyer it is a deliberate kindness to do it that way.

. . . Out there afloat in the night off Lauderdale, she had told me that if she ever did want to take the risk, it would be with somebody so hard to kill that maybe he could keep her alive too. And after soliciting me, she tried to turn me off again, with both of us knowing it was too late at that particular time and place for any stopping.

. . . She had wept very quickly and abundantly when I had told her about Jane Lawson last Sunday. As she had wept easily in the store. As she had wept not long ago, right here, when she had toppled over. In the kind of early life she had, of foster homes and the school for girls, could the luxury of genuine tears be sustained, or would tears be one of the weapons of survival?

. . ."Don't come to my place. That's asking for trouble." I'd never been inside it. When I'd first seen it, she had answered my unspoken question, saying that there was a lot of difference in size and in rent between the big apartments on the top floors in front, and the little studio apartments on the lower floors in the rear. "Don't phone me there."

. . . Willy Nucci heard of my new relationship with Sprenger very quickly. But not too quickly for Willy. His network is all over the beach. Switchboards, housekeepers, doormen, car rental girls, apartment managers, bartenders. I'm only guessing. There is probably an unlisted number to call, an anonymous voice, and cash money in a plain envelope, enough to keep the flow coming in, as much cash as the information is worth. Willy wouldn't be so stupid as to be known as the destination of the flow. Then sharpsters would start feeding bad information, to con something out of Willy. Probably somebody close to Harry Harris told her hairdresser about the fabulous old houseboat some fellow in Lauderdale named McGee owns. Harry saw him on business. Which, to Willy, who might have heard it within twenty minutes, meant I was on Sprenger's team.

. . . In the thunderous night, in the darkness, she had lain naked under percale, squeezing my hand and saying ooo and ahh at my modest account of my deductive brilliance. She said she didn't want to go rummaging around inside her head. She said it was all junk, all throwaway. The news of Jane's in-law wealth had galvanized her, lifted her up out of the bed. In alarm? And she could not comprehend why Jane had never gone after that money. She thought it freak behavior. I thought it odd. But I could understand. The next morning she was up unexpectedly early and diligent and brisk.

. . . Alfred, the night bell captain, thought he had seen Mary Alice somewhere before. And she would not give him her name.

. . . When I had asked Sprenger, in his office, how he had gotten onto me so quickly, his explanation was detailed, garrulous, and unconvincing. So was his explanation about the source of the investment money. I think that what made both stories unconvincing was the ease with which he could have sidestepped my questions. How did you get onto me? I keep good track of things. Where did the money come from? An investor. Sprenger had not gotten where he was by saying one word more than required in any situation. And the explanation about the test with the courier in West Germany seemed more as if he was trying to sell me on how good an idea it was.

. . . I'd believed Sprenger when he said he had not gotten agitated when he learned Jane Lawson was dead. Yet he should have been. If he believed his investment account was intact, he might not have reacted at all. Yet he *knew* something was wrong. The only answer was that he knew Jane Lawson was not involved. That meant he had to know who was.

. . . I went to the shop from Sprenger's office where she had been working diligently all morning. And suddenly there were a lot of things pointing right at Jane Lawson. But when was the label on the gaffed box typed? And when and why were new albums imprinted in gold for Frank A. Sprenger and J. David Balch? Sprenger's, at least, had only a few pages left empty. "Jane, honey, while you're over there, whyn't you take these two and make me up the blue one for Sprenger and the green one for Balch, okay?" Had the figures written on the inventory sheets been for simplicity in finding a specific stamp or to make it easier to make up a whole duplicate book?

. . . Hirsh might remember if Jane Lawson had taken a package along that day and mailed it. She could have been given the package by a girl too sick to go to the bank that day. "Please mail it for me, Jane honey."

. . . The poisoning episode was increasingly hard to buy. She had to claim it happened, because that meant Jane Lawson had arranged it when she was ready to make the switch. How do you measure exactly how much emetic to give a big healthy girl, an amount that will render her too ill to go to the bank but not so ill as to have to be taken home? Banks have phones. Fedderman would have left a message for Sprenger. Sickness is easy to fake. A hunk of soap slides down easily. Send Jane off to the bank this time, and make the switch in July, at the next visit. Sprenger would probably call the signals. Easy for him to lean across the table and point down to one of the new purchases and ask Fedderman a question about it. Plenty of time for her to switch the books.

. . . Miss Moosejaw had said Jane Lawson would have added up how it was probably accomplished and had tried to test her theory. By asking a question? And the old lady had not thought Mary Alice morally incapable of robbery that devious, just mentally unable to plan and carry out something so complex. But with Sprenger to plan it, could she carry it out?

. . . If Sprenger was worried about somebody trying to get cute, was it hard to figure out who he had in mind?

I stood up. I wished I could somehow stand up and leave myself still stretched out on the couch. I wanted to shed myself, start brand new, do better.

Had I been spending the last many years selling real estate or building motels, I could not be expected to recognize that special kind of kink exemplified by our Mary Alice McDermit. There are a lot of them, and they come in all sizes, sexes, and ages. They are consistently attractive because they are role players. Whatever you want, they've got in stock. They are sly-smart and sly-stupid. They would much rather tell an interesting lie than tell the truth. Never having experienced a genuine human emotion, they truly believe that everybody else in the world fakes the emotions too, and that is all there is.

I once knew an otherwise sane man who became hopelessly infatuated with the peppy, zippy little lady with the bangs who used to do the Polaroid commercials on television. He bought every kind of camera they make. He took pictures of her picture on the tube. He cut her picture out of magazines. He wrote and wrote and wrote, trying to get a name and address. He went to New York and made an ass of himself visiting advertising agencies and model agencies. It took a long time to wear off. It was totally irrational.

I had seen somebody I had invented, not Mary Alice. I explained away her inconsistencies, overlooked her vulgarities, and believed her dramatics. And so it goes. It is humiliating, when you should know better, to become victim of the timeless story of the little brown dog running across the freight yard, crossing all the railroad tracks until a switch engine nipped off the end of his tail between wheel and rail. The little dog yelped, and he spun so quickly to check himself out that the next wheel chopped through his little brown neck. The moral is, of course, never lose your head over a piece of tail.

Goodbread merely pretended a vast stupidity. Mine, nourished by the blue eyes and the great body, had been genuine. But last night some strange kind of survival instinct had taken over. The body seems to have its own awareness of the realities. In the churny night, the tangly bed, abaft that resilient everlasting smorgasbord, body-knowledge said "Whoa!" And whoa it was, abruptly. One just doesn't do this sort of thing with monsters. Not with a big plastic monster which would kill you on any whim if it was certain it would never be caught, and if it anticipated being amused by the experience. Body-knowledge said she'd killed Jane Lawson. Not at the moment of Whoa. Afterward, in a growing visceral realization.

She had mousetrapped Sprenger somehow, and it was probably within her power to make him look like such a fool, the people he served would feel a lot better if he were on the bottom of the Miami River. Willy Nucci had explained the occupational hazards to me and to what lengths Sprenger would go to cover up any indiscretion, any violation of the code. The parties at interest had brought in the hard man from Phoenix to police one of their neutral areas, and after six years of service, he had gone sour. Over a woman. And that was his vulnerable area, right? Right.

I had set it in motion, knowing that if Sprenger ignored Meyer's information, all my guesses were wrong. So I could wait for him or run. I could bring Mary Alice into it all the way or use her as bait. I could try to negotiate with him or hit first.

I tried to guess what I would do if I were Frank Sprenger, but I found I did not know enough about the situation, the relationships, Mary Alice could tell me, but I did not like to think of the ways I might have to use to make sure she was telling me all of it. There was no way to appeal to her, except through her own self-interest. She was afraid of being hurt. She had said so after I had mended the flap of elbow skin. Not the casual bumps and bruises and abrasions. But really hurt, with infections and drains and IVs. And that I could not do.

Eighteen

I found her snapping the catches on her train case. She had changed to pale pink jeans and a light blue work shirt with long sleeves. She had tied her head up in a blue and white kerchief. She wore new white sneakers.

She straightened and looked at me almost expressionlessly. There was a little contempt there. Not much else.

"I'm splitting," she said.

"You've thought it all over, eh?"

"You blew it, baby. You really blew it. It could have been okay for us. Frank will have guys watching every place for five hundred miles where you could dock this boat. I don't give a damn *what* you do."

"Where are you going?"

"You know something? That's dumb. That's really dumb. All you are going to know is that you put me ashore back by that bridge where the cars were. When Frank wraps wire around your dingus and plugs it in and starts pushing the button, you're going to wish to God you had something you could tell him about where I went."

"Why should he care where you go?"

"Oh boy. He can talk his way out of how I could run

when he wasn't looking and how he'll find me and so forth. But he can't risk what I'll say to the McDermits about him. How long before it gets dark here?"

I looked at my watch. "Little over an hour."

"How long would it take the little boat to get back to that place where the bridge is?"

"Fifteen minutes."

"I'm taking the train case and this suitcase and leaving this other junk. I want it to be a little after dark when you let me off. You better put on better clothes for the bugs out there. You got some kind of repellent to put on?"

"What's he got to do with the McDermits?"

"Huh? Oh, I'm married to Ray. He's the middle brother. They got him on tax fraud and conspiracy and a couple of other things over five years ago, and he's in Lewisburg. He's doing easy time. Except he can't do any balling in there, and he's as spaced out on it as old Frank is. Ray was going to get out last year on parole. But the silly jackass got into some kind of mess, and it will be at least another year. Maybe two. Are you going to change?"

"This is probably as true as the last version you told me."

"So forget the rest of it. All right?"

"And forget the boat ride, M.A."

She had the little automatic tucked into the waist band of her jeans on the left. It was not an especially deft draw, that cross-draw recommended to the FBI agents, but it was fast enough for somebody six feet away too stupid to anticipate it.

"We will definitely not forget the boat ride, friend," she said. She backed away, aiming more carefully. "I can't run the damned thing, and I am definitely not going to ruin you so bad you can't run it. Unless you get cute and I make a mistake, and then I'll try to run it. It can't be a lot different than a car. I'd rather you run it. What's the best place? Right up there over your collarbone, maybe. Through that big muscle that comes down from the side of your neck? You want to hurt while you run the boat, or do you want to be okay and feel good and say goodbye nicely?"

"You read me wrong," I said. "I said forget the boat ride, because according to the tide tables, there shouldn't be anything out there now except mud flats and sand flats and a trickle of water here and there. Can't you feel how solid the deck feels under your feet. And the little list? We're aground, and so is the *Muñequita.*"

I watched her expression and her eyes. She glanced toward the port. She couldn't see from that angle. She sidled to her left, and the instant her eyes swiveled away from me, I took the long step, the long reach, caught her by the wrist and by the elbow and gave the funny bone a powerful tweak. She yelped as her hand went dead and the gun fell. I yanked my eyes and face back just in time, and her hooking slash with her left hand left four bleeding lines high on my chest and packed her fingernails with tissue. I shoved her onto the bed so hard her legs rolled high and she almost went over the other side. I picked up her automatic and swiveled the little safety up into the notch on the slide and put it into my pocket.

She sat on the side of the bed, and the tears rolled as she looked dolefully at me. "I'm sorry. I'm so s-scared, honest, I don't know what I'm doing. I'm sorry, darling."

"That doesn't work either."

"What?"

"Sprenger wants you. So if I want to maintain good relations with him, the easiest thing to do is wrap you up and hand you to him. I'll say, 'Frank, old buddy, she conned both of us, but here she is.' "

The tears had dried and stopped in moments. She sat scowling in thought, nibbling her thumb knuckle. "No. I'm trying to give it to you absolutely straight. It would finish the both of us, not just me, because he couldn't be sure of how much I told you. He can't afford any part of it getting out."

"So the more you tell me, M.A., the more dangerous I am to Frank, and the more chance I might want to play it your way."

She studied me and then gave a little nod as something seemed to go click way back in those blue eyes.

After Ray was sentenced, she said, it became obvious that there were some people in Philadelphia who believed he had done some talking to make his sentence lighter, and they were willing to get back at Ray McDermit through his young wife. Ray didn't want her visiting him. He said it drove him up the walls. Sprenger kept an eye on the McDermit interests in the Miami area. He was new then, about a year in the area. He flew up and brought Mary Alice back down. She was to find a job where she would stay out of trouble. The McDermits provided rent on a handsome apartment and the utilities, a car, but no cash in hand. Ray had said it was his wish that if he wasn't getting any, he wanted to be certain Mary Alice wasn't giving it to anybody else. She said he was called "the crazy brother." He wasn't crazy, but it was hard to guess what he would do. From inside prison he exercised a lot of power with the threat of revealing the damaging information he had in his head.

"I thought I could cut it," she said. "Besides, Sprenger wasn't about to get careless about keeping an eye on me. And if I goofed, I had no idea what Crazy Ray would want done to me. But I knew it would get reported back and whatever he wanted done would get done. I got to like the store and the stamps and all, sort of. And I practically killed myself at the Health Club, but I got awful restless. I really did."

She had figured out, finally, that Sprenger was the key to her personal freedom. She worked on him for a long time. He was very cool and cautious. Finally desire was stronger than circumspection.

"Those cats that have the choice of a couple hundred girls, the one they want the worst is the one they shouldn't have," she said. "I knew the leverage it gave me once we started, and so did he. What I was afraid of, he'd have me killed and have it look as if I just packed and left. He couldn't be expected to be able to keep me from splitting. He set up our dates, you'd think it was a CIA operation. If it ever got back to the McDermit brothers, you can imagine. A man who'll rip off your wife when he's supposed to be keeping her on ice will cut a piece of your money too. I was afraid once he had all he wanted, I was going into a canal, car, clothes, and everything. So I told him I had confided in a certain person, who would never never tell, unless, of course, I disappeared or something. And then I had him between a rock and a hard place. If he hurt me to make me tell who, I'd make a phone call to Philadelphia, and he was dead. He was right on the hook, and he knew it, and he had no way of stopping anything I wanted to do. And what I wanted was money of my own, and I told him if he'd become a client of Fedderman, between us we could take him for what he was worth, which I figured at four hundred thousand, from things he had said. He explained to me he was supposed to have good judgment, and I wanted him to make a stupid, dangerous, amateur investment in postage stamps, for God's sake. He said Fedderman would go to the law if he got swindled, and the name of Frank Sprenger would come into it, and some people would come and take him swimming. I made him talk to Fedderman. I made him check it out that there's a steady market for rarities. He found out there's no duty hardly anywhere in the world on importing or exporting rare stamps. I had the leverage, and I kept at him. He had to use his own money. He went over just how I wanted to do it, and he figured out better ways. After we started, I found out Ray wasn't getting out and might even have to go the whole ten years. Which would make me an old bag, thirty-three damn years old, and the hell with *that* noise. So it made it more important to me to take Fedderman."

I could see how neatly she had trapped Sprenger. But I wondered that he had not arranged a fatal accident or a fatal illness so plausible the confidant would have felt no need to make a report.

I could guess at his dismay in investing a fortune in little colored bits of paper.

She got up and went and looked out the port. "There's enough water out there to run the little boat, right?"

"Right."

"You're pretty tricky."

"Keep talking."

She sat on the bed again, choosing her words carefully, explaining to me that it was her guess that by now Frank

Sprenger had reported her missing, and with whom and how, to the McDermits. He would have to do that to take the edge of plausibility off any report the confidant might make. There wasn't one, but he had no way of knowing. Or maybe now there was one. Me. The only way Sprenger could feel completely safe would be to arrange the private, efficient, anonymous deaths of Mary Alice McDermit and Travis McGee, and recover the fortune in rarities with which Mrs. McDermit had fled.

"They're aboard?" She nodded. "Show me."

She snapped the train case open. I went over and stood over her, tensed for any unpleasant surprise she might bring out of the dark blue case. She took out the top tray, and under it were three six-by-nine manila clasp envelopes, with cardboard stiffening, each filled to about a half-inch thickness. She opened one and eased some pliofilm envelopes out and spread them on the bed. I saw blocks of four and six stamps, still in Hawid and Showgard mounts, showing old dirigibles, old airplanes, black cattle in a snowstorm, portraits of Chris Columbus, with and without Isabella.

"All here," she said. "Years and years of the good life. It will last forever in the right places. I cleaned some goodies out of the safe too, stuff he has for stock.

"Where'd you get the junk you substituted?"

"Indirectly, by Frank, through an independent agent-buyer in New York. I made new inventory lists without any description of quality. He bought junk. Stained, torn, thinned, repaired, regummed, faded, rejoined, even forgeries. They cost a little over twelve thousand, I think. I took them to my apartment and mounted them and put them into the duplicate book. Then when we were close enough to all the traffic could stand, Frank distracted Hirsh, and I switched books and shoved the good one into that box Frank got me that I showed you. We went out together, and I mailed it. Frank thought it was coming to him, but I'd changed the label. God, was he ever irritated! But what could he do?"

"What could he do?" I wanted to go further with it, but sensed that this was not the time to push. I picked one of the transparent envelopes up and looked at a block of six showing a mob scene around Columbus in chains.

"Careful!" she said. "That's thirty-five hundred at least."

"Anywhere?"

"Practically." She gathered the stuff up and put it back into the envelope. She closed it, hesitated, put the other two back into the train case, and handed me the one she had just closed.

"What's this?"

"It's worth about forty percent of the whole thing, that envelope. I think we should be entirely honest with each other. You've got to forgive me for trying to do a stupid thing. I need your help. Do you have a passport?"

"Yes. Aboard."

"And some money?"

"Yes."

"I can really be a very loving person, dear. That's at least a hundred and sixty thousand dollars in that envelope in your hand."

"You mean, leave us flee together, Mrs. McDermit?"

She looked annoyed. "Well, why the hell not? What else have you got working for you? It's what we were going to do anyway."

"Only at some port of call with an airstrip, I was suddenly going to find you missing."

"I thought of it. I thought I might, after a long long time alone with you."

"With me, the great lover?"

"That would probably never never happen again, and if it does, you shouldn't be so silly about letting a person help."

"But now we start going by air right away?"

"What's the best way to do it?"

"Oh, probably take the *Muñequita* right across the stream to Bimini. It might jar your teeth and kidneys loose. Top off the tanks and run to Nassau. Tie up at Yacht Haven and take a cab into town and get a visa for London or Rome or Madrid and go out to the airport and wait for something going our way."

"That easy?"

"The first part of anything is usually easy."

"I always wanted to see the Islands. I really did. I just hate missing the Islands. Maybe we can come back some day."

Yes indeed. I would have truly enjoyed showing her the islands. How the big aluminum plant and the oil refinery of Amerada Hess blacken the stinking skies over St. Croix. Maybe she'd like the San Juan Guayama and Ybucoa areas of Puerto Rico where Commonwealth Oil, Union Carbide, Phillips Petroleum, and Sun Oil have created another new industrial wasteland where the toxic wastes have killed the vegetation, where hot oil effluents are discharged into the sea and flow westward along the shoreline in a black roiling stench, killing all sea life.

She might be impressed were I to cruise into Tallabea

Bay and describe to her the one and a half billion tons of untreated wastes from Commonwealth-Union Carbide which put a two-foot coat on the bottom of the bay. Or we could take a tour up into the mountains to watch how the trade winds carry the bourbon-colored stink of petrochemical stacks through the passes all the way to Mayaguez, ninety miles from the refineries. While in the hills, we could check and see if Kennecott Copper and American Metal Climax have started to strip-mine the seven square green tropic miles of high land which they covet.

It might have made quite an impression.

"Can we start now? Can we?"

"It's full dark on an outgoing tide. The morning is good enough. In the morning I can take the *Flush* back out the way we came and leave her in storage at Regal Marine. Abandon her and it attracts too much attention. The Coast Guard would get in the act and Civil Air Patrol and guide boats and so on. Then we can go on from there."

"Okay. I feel so much better. I'm so glad we had this frank talk, darling.

"I guess we accomplished a lot."

"Oh, we did!" She lifted the train case back out of the way and hitched over to me and put a shy kiss near my mouth. I held her and looked past her hair at the manila envelope I still held in my right hand.

Pore helpless little critter. Sharing her wealth, but only on a temporary basis. Only until she could find the right time and place to slip an icepick into my brain through whatever orifice seemed handiest.

"Shouldn't we have a drink to celebrate?" she asked.

Of course, of course. She trotted to the galley to make the drinks. I changed into khakis and a white T-shirt and went to the lounge. As she came smiling in with the drinks, I said, "If Frank were to come here tonight . . ."

She jerked and lost some of my drink on the back of her hand and on the carpeting as she was handing it to me. "Jesus! Don't come on like that, will you?"

"Hypothetical question. Would he come alone?"

She sat opposite me and pondered it. "I don't know. It depends. He's the kind of guy who likes all the odds his way. I'd say this. If he didn't come here alone, he'd leave alone. There isn't any such thing as trusting people, not when it's worth money to them to put a knife in your back. What he'd probably do, he'd fake one of his slobs into thinking it was some other kind of deal, and when it was done, he'd drop the slob right beside us."

"Is he really as rough as you seem to think?"

"You've got me nervous. Is it okay to pull those curtains across? I don't like all that black looking in at us."

"Go ahead."

She pulled all the heavy curtaining and turned off two of the four lights. She sat beside me and said, "That's a lot better." She touched my glass with hers. "Happy days," she said.

"Happy days, Mrs. McDermit."

"Is it like a joke, the way you keep calling me that?"

"I guess it's like a joke."

"The best thing would be if Frank *did* come here and we were ready and waiting and we took him."

"Would he be hard to take?"

"You better believe it. He's a freak. He knows it all—judo, knives, guns, everything. Like a hobby. And he is fabulously strong. Not just ordinary strong, but special, the way some people are. He can hold his hand out like this, all his fingers spread, and put four bottle caps between his knuckles, here, here, and here, and the last one between his thumb and the side of this finger. Then he can slowly make a fist and bend every cap double. Don't look at me like that. It isn't a trick. He has to be careful to place them right, or they can cut into his flesh. There's another thing he does. You know the kid game, you put both hands out palm up and the other person puts their hands palm down on top of yours and tries to yank them out of the way before you can turn your hands over and slap the backs of their hands? I've never seen anybody fast enough to slap him or fast enough to get out of his way. And, wow, does he ever slap! He told me once that when he was fifteen years old, he was a bouncer. He never had to hit anybody, he said. He just took hold of them above the elbow and walked them out, and they always went. They couldn't use that arm for a few days either."

"Good with guns?"

"Not fast-draw stuff. Not like that. He has these custom guns, like he had one in the car he showed me once, like a rifle, with a place for his hand to fit perfectly, carved out to fit his hand. And a telescope fastened to it, with a lot of straps and gadgets. He said he makes his own loads. He belongs to clubs where they shoot at targets, and he wins cups and medals. Do you know what he told me? He said he could put a ten-penny nail into a tree, hammer it in and leave a half-inch sticking out, and he could stretch out on the ground a hundred yards away and drive it in with his first shot every time. I said I didn't believe it. He said he'd show me, but he never did."

"He may yet."

"Will you please *stop* that! It makes my skin crawl.

And it's getting too cold in here. Can you do something about it before my teeth start chattering?"

I went over and turned the thermostat down. The deeper voice of the compressor stopped. The generator chugged on. I heard a wind sound and a faint shift of the bulk of the *Flush*. I took Mary Alice out onto the deck to prove to her the bugs had been blown away. We went up onto the sun deck. There were ragged clouds obscuring and revealing a third of a moon. I could see a considerable distance by moonlight. The flats stretched out in every direction, mud flats, sand flats, grass flats, dotted with the mystery shapes of mangrove islands, from handkerchief size on up to fifty acres.

It was not a reassuring vista. It was not terrain I could protect easily. The obvious way to get at me would be to keep in direct line with the nearer islands, pick a close one, come up behind it, wade out the flats to the edge of the mangrove and then settle down and wait, with a clear field of fire through the shiny green leaves and the gnarled branches and roots.

I would be able to tell better by daylight, but the nearest one big enough to use as a screen for a long approach seemed to be at just about nail-driving distance.

"I don't like places like this," said the lady.

"You won't be here long."

"Hurray."

I went back down the ladderway and out to the aft deck. I stripped down to my boat shoes and went over on the shallow side and walked the bow anchor and stern anchor out to a better angle. I climbed aboard the *Muñequi-*

ta and unsnapped part of her cover, enough to get a small hook out and make it fast to a stern cleat before I walked it back to where she would ride quietly.

I got back aboard the *Flush* by getting up onto the diving shelf permanently affixed to the transom just above water level, then climbing up the two folding metal steps, and swinging over the rail. She watched me dry myself on my T-shirt and said, "How can you stand to go down into all that black guck? There could be stuff down in there that bites?"

I pulled the T-shirt back on and picked up the pants. They had lost some weight. I spun her and got her throat into the crook of my arm and felt around until I came upon the outline of the little automatic, pouched down into her groin. She stabbed back at my eyes, and I tightened up on her breathing until she was pulling at my arm with both hands. I slid my free hand down inside the jeans and found the gun and pulled it out. I spun her back away from me. She thumped into the bulkhead, coughed until she gagged, and said, "I'll feel better if I've got it. Please?"

"Sorry."

"You creaked my neck. You know that?"

"Sorry."

"I wouldn't shoot you with it. You know better than that."

I went in. She followed me, complaining. Now her throat felt sore. I didn't have to be so rough. Some kind of bug had bitten her on the forehead out there. See the lump it made? Why are you carrying your pants? Put them on. You look ridiculous. I went to the head to get away from her, picking up my manila envelope en route. It was the same heft, but I looked inside, just in case. All apparently in order. All yours, Hirsh, Deo volente.

Ever since one Boo Waxwell nearly brought me and friends to an untimely end aboard this same *Flush,* Meyer and I have improved many an idle hour trying to add surprises to the furnishings. They have to be unexpected and not complicated. Meyer is very good at it. I opened one of his. It is quick and easy. You open the medicine cabinet. It is set into a double bulkhead. The bottom shelf seems to be a part of the outer frame of the cabinet itself. But if you take the stuff off it and push it up against the pull of a friction catch, it opens like the lid of a box. I reached down in there and took out the oily Colt Diamondback, checked the load, put it back, and put its far smaller and weaker cousin beside it. The recess was deep enough to stand the envelope on end where it would not touch the weapons. I slapped the lid down, put toilet articles back on it, and shut the cabinet. Invisible hinges, a very sturdy catch, a nice deep dry hole. One of the better efforts.

I had to do some thinking before I got back out in range of Mary Alice's noisy petulance.

I knew she had no idea of where we had come from, what our direction had been coming in. So if I headed in the wrong direction, she would not object. I wanted more open space than I had. If I could go gently aground, or appear to be aground, with a half mile of open flats on every side, I might lure the marksman close enough to equalize our skills. Like within ten feet? Topsides, in the bin, on its brackets, was the old Springfield shark rifle with the four-power scope, but the barrel was slightly keyholed and the slugs had a tendency to tumble.

She made him sound like he kept popping out of a phone booth in a funny cape and zooming into the sky. I had seem him. All right, so he looked very impressive. Our very short acquaintanceship had been interesting so far. Especially the way I had kept taking his money. And his girl.

He could use an island for a screen, and he could use Meyer, just to see if he could verify Meyer's ill will toward me. He might bring Davis along, the one with the dark moustache. Expendable? Who knows? Murder and arson. Boats burn hot. Four can fry as cheaply as three. One good thrust with a gun butt or a solid smash with a piece of pipe and you can forget about using the family dentist to identify his work.

No, stasis was not my style. The more I thought of ways and means, the less I liked it. Running is no good either, unless it is the kind of running where you circle back and come out on the trail right behind the hunter. So tomorrow I take the *Muñequita,* and I wait just as close to Regal Marine as I can get. Hello there, Frank. Looking for anybody in particular?

She rattled the latch on the door to the head. "What are you doing in there anyway?"

"Thinking."

I heard her mumble as she walked away. I came out and made another drink and fixed us something to eat. She had stopped complaining. She looked thoughtful. No thanks, she did not want to play any music. No, no gin rummy, thanks.

"Trav?"

"Yes, honey."

"You don't want to ask me anything else about anything?"

"I don't think so."

"It's all cleared up in your mind?"

"I think so."

"Well . . . okay."

She began yawning. She came over and wanted to be taken off to bed. I told her to take herself off. She went pouting away to her own bed. I stayed up a little while trying to tell myself that everything was going to work out just right, like everything always had, almost.

But I could not get into it. I am apart. Always I have seen around me all the games and parades of life and have always envied the players and the marchers. I watch the cards they play and feel in my belly the hollowness as the big drums go by, and I smile and shrug and say, Who needs games? Who wants parades. The world seems to be masses of smiling people who hug each other and sway back and forth in front of a fire and sing old songs and laugh into each others faces, all truth and trust. And I kneel at the edge of the woods, too far to feel the heat of the fire. Everything seems to come to me in some kind of secondhand way which I cannot describe. Am I not meat and tears, bone and fears, just as they? Yet when most deeply touched, I seem, too often, to respond with smirk or sneer, another page in my immense catalog of remorses. I seem forever on the edge of expressing the inexpressible, touching what has never been touched, but I cannot reach through the veil of apartness. I am living without being truly alive. I can love without loving. When I am in the midst of friends, when there is laughter, closeness, empathy, warmth, sometimes I can look at myself from a little way off and think that they do not really know who is with them there, what strangeness is there beside them, trying to be something else.

Once, just deep enough into the cup to be articulate about subjective things, I tried to tell Meyer all this. I shall never forget the strange expression on his face. "But we are *all* like that!" he said. "That's the way it *is*. For everyone in the world. Didn't you know?"

I tried to believe him. But belief is a very difficult feat when you crouch out here in the night, too far from the fire to feel its heat, too far from the people to hear the words of their songs.

Nineteen

Something woke me, and I rolled out of the bed and stood half-crouched in darkness, head cocked, listening. There was a whisper and slap of very small waves against the hull, and a softer and equally regular sound of the waves slipping up into the mangrove roots and sliding back. Nothing else. I had turned the generator off before midnight.

I have learned to trust my undefined anxieties. They are sentinels standing guard. I must find out if they are being alerted by shadows or by reality. If they cry wolf nineteen times and on the twentieth time it is a real wolf, it is better to check every time than roll over and go back to sleep and lose your throat.

I moved naked through the familiar degrees of darkness of the known spaces of my home-place. The door to the other stateroom stood open. I moved two steps into the room and listened and heard a small snorting sound at the end of each inhalation and a long flaccid rattle of the soft palate during exhalation. She was in sleep. A man will sometimes imitate snoring to feign sleep, a woman never. My eyes were used to the darkness by then, and in the faint starlight of the port I could make out the dark blur of her hair on the pillow, then a suggestion of profile. She was sleeping on her back.

Before going to bed, I had checked all the locks, all the security devices. There was no way to deactivate them without starting up a klaxon that would whoop the birds awake three islands away. I wondered if someone had come aboard over a side rail and the shift of weight had turned on my silent, subjective alarm system.

In retrospect, Frank Sprenger seemed strangely more impressive. The blueberry eyes stared out from the sun-browned folds of skin. His neck seemed broader than his skull. I went back to my stateroom and pulled a pair of shorts on. It is strange how a man, totally naked, feels a little more vulnerable. It seems to be a distraction, an extra area to guard. Cloth is not armor, yet that symbolic protection makes one feel at once a litttle more logical and competent. Doubtless the hermit crab is filled with strange anxieties during those few moments when, having outgrown one borrowed shell, he locates another and, having sized it carefully with his claws, extracts himself from the old home and inserts himself into the new. The very first evidence of clothing in prehistory is the breechclout for the male.

When I had rolled from the bed, I had plucked the Airweight from its handy bedside holster without conscious thought. I put it back where it belonged and got the M35 Browning out of the locker. It is a 9mm automatic pistol with a staggered box magazine, so that it has a fourteen-round capacity. It fits my hand, and I like it. It goes where I point. The way to get that instinctive relationship with a handgun is to tape a pencil flashlight with a very narrow beam to the barrel, exactly in line with it, and rig it so that you can comfortably turn the beam on for an instant with thumb or finger. Then stand in a room in the dusk, turn and fire, spin and fire, fall and fire, at the lamp, the corner of the picture, the book on the table, a magazine on the floor. Point naturally as if pointing the forefinger, arm in a comfortable position, never bringing it up to the eye to aim. An hour of practice can develop an astonishing accuracy. After that you practice in a secluded place with live rounds.

I am being turned off handguns. Meyer did it. He made three casual statements, apropos of gun legislation. He said, "The only two things you can kill with a handgun are tin cans and people." And he said, "Way over half the murders committed in this country are by close friends or relatives of the deceased. A gun makes a loud and satisfying noise in a moment of passion and requires no agility and very little strength. How many murders wouldn't happen, if they all had to use hammers or knives?" And he said, "Studies have shown that if a person is not a psychopath, not a soldier, not a cop, there is only a one in ten chance they can bring themselves to fire a gun directly at a robber."

So there has been a diminishing pleasure in the look and the feel of handguns and in the ability to use them. I am even beginning to dislike the shape and feel and smell of them. But as long as I pursue a career in my version of the salvage business, I am going to affront people who yearn to read my obituary. So the weapons are tools of a precarious trade. Just as, I suppose, a carnival fire-swallower might find it useful to keep some fire extinguishers handy. He might even hate fire extinguishers because they are reminders that something might go wrong, but unless he is an idiot, he will keep them within reach, fully charged, and know how to use each one.

Out on the deck I was in a brighter world. I kept to the heavier patches of shadow. I made two circuits, stopping, listening, waiting. The damp wind was out of the north, warm and steady. A nightbird went by, shouting of doom in a hoarse, hopeless voice, even laughing about it.

I eased back into the lounge and reset the master switch and listened again. It was almost four in the morning. I tucked the pistol into the belly band of the shorts, the metal slightly cooler than the night air. I knew I had taken on a load of adrenalin that would take an hour to be so totally absorbed I could sleep. As I neared my bed, I heard her speak in her sleep. "Marf? Shugunnawg. Whassawhummer?"

I went in. She whined, rolled her head back and forth, whined again, and turned onto her side. So one of those words had probably alerted the sentinels and turned on the alarms. She was down inside her head, asking questions.

I sat on the bed, put my hand on her shoulder, and shook her. She came fumbling up the dark ladder. "Whashawanname, Frank? Crissake. Oh. Whassamarra?"

"You were having a nightmare."

"Come *on*, McGee. I never even dream."

"Everybody dreams, M.A. Some people remember more than others. You were talking, You woke me up."

"Talking? The *hell* you say. What about?"

"Asking questions. But not in any language the world has ever known."

"How do you know they were questions?"

"Rising inflection. Marf? Whassawhummer?"

"Oh boy. Marf. Where are you? Oh. Well, anyway, I asked questions. You certainly didn't ask many."

"What do you mean?"

"You're looking down at me from somewhere, and I can't see you. Come down here some." She pulled at me. I stretched out and put my feet up. She put her head on my shoulder and rested a fist on my chest. "You know what I mean about questions," she said.

"Do I?"

"You're so tricky. You know? You left me waiting for the other shoe to drop. Like anybody would think you would ask about how come Jane got the other stockbook printed with Frank's name."

"I assumed you asked her, saying you'd run out soon."

"Sort of like that. I asked for spares for all the investment accounts, because Lighthouse stopped making that kind, and if they had names on, we wouldn't make a mistake and sell them out of stock. Well . . . what about me telling you she poisoned me?"

"Window dressing. You were sick one day. And remembered it later, when you needed more window dressing. And those numbers on the sheets to indicate arrangement were for your own benefit in making up the junk book. And you invented that bit about how upset she was long ago and about her talking about going away. You can't check anything out with a dead lady. She can't verify conversations. And people *have* smashed up a house to conceal a search."

"Okay. You're so smart about everything, aren't you? You didn't even have to ask me about how much more I knew about the whole thing, did you?"

I stopped breathing for about two seconds and hoped that it had not been noticed and interpreted. If I were to ever be certain, I had to make the whole thing seem casual, unremarkable. I had to make my indifference persuasive. So I yawned widely and noisily and turned toward her, stripping the coverlet down below her hips, the better to hold and stroke and caress her.

"Hey, no problems, huh?" she said.

I slipped the pistol under the pillow. I yawned again. "No more questions about old Jane, honey. I know you killed her."

She turned her mouth away from me, stiffened, caught my moving wrist, held me still. "You are so damned sure," she whispered.

"Forget it," I said. I worked on her, trying to bring her along, trying to soften her tensions.

She pulled back again, "Why are you so sure?"

"I told you all the reasons it wasn't kids."

"But if it was a person trying to make it look as if kids had done it, why me?"

"Does it matter one way or the other? Forget it, honey."

She tried to forget it. I could feel her trying to let go, trying to let her body take over. She pushed me away. "Wait a second. Please. Look. Is there any proof?"

"When Fedderman finds out the good stuff is missing out of stock and finds out you are gone without saying goodbye, what do you think it's going to look like?"

She tried to shake me in her exasperation. "But proof, damn you!"

"Relax. Nobody saw you coming or going. You didn't

leave anything behind. They are even buying your version of when it happened."

"*My* version?"

"You set the electric clock in the bedroom ahead to two-fifteen, then you yanked it out and heaved it at the wall." I wanted to hold my breath again. Instead, I gathered her close, kissed her throat. She sighed. "The thing about it, darling," she said. "I *really* liked her. I really did." She sighed. Her breath had a trace of the staleness of sleep. "What do people expect a person to do when they don't leave you any kind of option at all? Know what she was going to do?"

"No. Who cares?"

"Stop a minute. Put yourself in my place. I didn't go to her house on my own. She asked me to come there. To talk. Or else. The way she sounded, I parked a ways off. She got hold of me at Hirsh's. Okay, so I cut that sort of short and went to her place. She was waiting for me, very cold and unfriendly, all dressed to go out. Know where she was going? To tell Hirsh and make him phone the police. Oh, she'd figured it all out that it had to be me. She knew how. Not exactly, but too close. Stop a minute. I made some offers. I begged her. I pleaded. I turned on enough tears for a fountain. And then she saw what was going to come next, so she ran, and I caught her and grabbed her, and we both fell down in the doorway. I was very mad at her. She was underneath, on her face, and I got up and pushed her back down and kneeled on her back and got hold of her hair and yanked up and back. It made kind of a crunchy little sound, and she went soft as butter. Yeck. All loose, sort of. I thought she was dead then, but I guess she lived a while. I sat down and thought it all out, and then I found red rubber gloves under her sink. I took the money out of her purse and wrecked the whole house and left."

"How did you keep from getting all spattered with all the stuff you broke?"

"I didn't. What I did first was take everything off and put a shower cap on my hair. I just wore that and the gloves, and took them with me when I left. I got splattered. After I was through, I took a shower and got dressed. I tried not to look at her at all the times I went past her. I *really* was awfully fond of Jane. Do you forgive me?"

"Do I *forgive* you?"

"Oh, I knew you'd understand, my darling. You scared me, being so sure. I tried to think of everything, even that back window to make it look as if a small person had gotten in that way. There was so much to do and to think about, that's why I was late getting to your yacht club. I was late and very nervous and scared."

"Nobody would have known it."

"Remember when you kissed me for the first time and I went off down the little beach to think?"

"I remember."

"Right up until then I was going to keep on with Frank. Then I realized that I had really bitched him up, the way that trouble with Jane came out. What I should have done was tell Frank right away and let him handle her. Being so very cautious about things, the way Frank is, I knew just what he would do to keep from being linked up in any way with Jane's death. I knew the son of a bitch was going to try to make me switch back, put the good book back, and sneak the junk out of the bank. Then he would cancel the deal, take the good stuff and arrange to have it sold, and try to come out practically even. Where would that leave me? I decided it better be you from then on, not Frank. It was the only way I could keep the whole thing. Poor Frank. By now, from the way I ran, he's figured out that I killed Jane and I've got the goodies. He knows that Fedderman will probably yell swindle and report me missing. And there is no way in the world Frank can keep from being brought into it. Even if he keeps it quiet that he even knew me outside the bank, he is going to have to explain where all that cash came from. I guess he can, but he's going to look like a very dumb person. I don't think Hirsh is going to have to pay him back. I don't think Frank will live that long. I guess I love you, McGee. Do you love Mary Alice?"

"Immeasurably."

"Well . . . now you can prove it. With—Oh, goddamnit, you're gone again. What the hell is the matter with you?"

"I think I know what woke me up."

"I can tell you something that didn't."

"You can't set a trap to catch a trap."

"What is that supposed to mean?"

"I can't very well surprise your chum by getting to him a lot earlier than scheduled, because that is exactly what he is doing. This is important to him. Why should he give a stranger a schedule and stay with it? Besides, if he is a marksman, why should he come in at dusk, with night coming on? Dawn is better. And not far away. Welcome, Frank boy." I was thinking aloud.

She was gone, abruptly. She knocked the shade off the fixed lamp, found the switch, ran around the foot of the bed to my side, made some small gobbling sounds and ran back to her side.

"Frank?" she said. "Here? Soon?"

"Settle down. We'll play it as if he were going to show up about dawn. Today. Every day. You cooked him. You cooked him as many ways as there are."

"What have you got there?"

"What does it look like?"

"It's a gun, damnit. I meant, where did it come from?"

"Put some clothes on."

"What am I going to do in them? Are we leaving? Or what?"

"Put on the pants and the long-sleeved shirt again."

"If you think I'm going out into those bugs, you're—"

"Shut up, will you? Just get dressed and shut up."

"You can't tell me what to—"

"I can take you out onto the bow, with a deck chair, and tie your arms to the arms and your feet to the footrest, and your neck to the backrest and leave you there and see how good a shot he is."

"Now come *on!* I don't mind jokes, but when you—"

I stood up. "No joke. The more I think about it, the better I like it."

She let her mouth sag open as she looked at me. And then she swallowed without closing her lips, an effort that made her throat bulge and convinced me she was taking me seriously.

"You *mean* it!"

"Just shut up and get your clothes on."

She did. It did not take her long. She went into the head and came out with her hair brushed glossy and a new mouth in place.

"Can I ask you something, Trav?"

"Like?"

"What makes you think he's coming here?"

"It's too long a story."

"Okay."

I put on khakis, and a dark green knit shirt with short sleeves, and old deck shoes. She followed me up to the sundeck. I went forward and stepped up onto the rail and hooked an arm around a stanchion for balance. I looked south through the nine-power Japanese glasses. Though there was a line of gray in the east and the glasses had good light-gathering qualities, it was like looking into a smudge pot. I couldn't even find a horizon line.

I dropped back to the deck, looked around, trying to organize something. Running would indicate to him that I'd guessed right. He would have to assume Mary Alice had told me everything useful. *Not* running would indicate innocence or stupidity or some of both. It might be the best answer. I discovered that I was trying not to think of Meyer. If my guess about Sprenger's actual schedule was right, Meyer could have been subjected to some sudden and very ugly persuasion. Stubborn old bear. Weird old economist.

Think, damnit! Like the little signs IBM used to distribute before they suddenly realized that if it were ever obeyed, if men everywhere really began to Think, the first thing they would do would be to take a sledge and open up the computers. A few are doing it already, sly seers, operating in sly ways. They have to guard the computer rooms these days. A little alnico magnet, stuck in exactly the right place with a wad of chewing gum, can erase a hundred thousand units of information before they find it.

Think! But the *Flush* felt like a ponderous toy, something in a foolish game for over-aged children. Meyer and I had been using it as a treehouse, hiding the secret words, the pacts, the membership list, the slingshots, and the Daisy Air Rifle. Now a real live man was going to come across the flats and blow the treehouse out of the water. Maybe I could get out the old bubble pipe and waft some soap into his eyes.

Prediction. He would have to have Meyer with him, because though Meyer could find No Name from the remembered shape of it, he certainly could not describe to anyone else how to find it.

Prediction. He would have someone with him. He would not want to rent a skiff with an outboard himself or send Meyer to rent it. The safe play would be to send a third man, with instructions to come back in the skiff from Regal Marine and pick them up.

So then, three of them. If he brought "Dave Davis," which seemed possible, it would make a goodly weight of meat in the rented boat. He would want a good boat, for capacity and for speed. Regal Marine certainly catered to some very early-bird fish freaks. Predawn rentals, so you can get out to the feeding grounds by dawn, aching to hook into the King of All of Them.

Once he had found us and identified us, Meyer's function would be ended. Once Sprenger had killed us and located the investment account items aboard the *Flush,* the third man's portion of the job would be finished. I did not care to use up any mental energy speculating about how he would handle everything from then on. I would not be able to care.

The band in the east widened until it began to shine gray upon the world. The islands began to show, in a thin milky mist. So this one, No Name, was too close to the *Flush,* and we stood too tall beside it, to make it good cover for a boat moving toward us. It would have to be the island in front of us, over a hundred yards away.

It was light enough, or would be by the time I got the hooks in and the *Flush* cranked up, to retrace the winding, unmarked channel back south to good water. Live to fight another day or run again. Or meet up with Sprenger and company under the worst possible conditions. If there is anything more vulnerable to sniper fire than a pleasure boat in shallow waters, I would like to hear about it. Maybe those Texas sportsmen who used to shoot the sand hill cranes from cover as the big ungainly birds came gliding in for a landing had found something easier to kill. Suppose I did manage to disappear? What would then happen to Meyer? He could wear a sickly smile and say, "Mr. Sprenger, they were *supposed* to be here!"

So whether he came at dawn or at dusk, the problem was the same. Instead of having all day to think about it, I had a fraction of an hour.

Go wait for him in the mangroves? Set the scene here so he would . . . A rusty gear in the back of my mind groaned and turned. The dry bearings squealed.

"What's with you?" she said.

"Always try on the Indian's moccasins," I said.

"What?"

"You'll see what I mean when I get through. If I have time to finish. Here. Take these. Use this to focus. You keep sweeping that area over there. If you see any kind of a boat coming toward us or moving across that area, sing out."

"Where'll you be?"

"Busy."

Twenty

It didn't take too long to prepare the major elements of the scene. I warned Mary Alice to hang on when I backed the *Flush* off and then rammed her up into the mangroves, with a great crunching, crackling, settling, listing. I took the *Muñequita* away from the island over to water the right depth, and pulled her plug. She had enough floatation so she would stay up completely awash, but I didn't want her drifting, so I put her on the edge of a sand bar. She ended up with water almost covering the pilot seat, the other seat canted up and out of the water. I smashed her windshields with a wrench. I had taken the Winslow life raft out of the hatch. I fitted the paddle together, popped the yellow raft as fat as the air from the cartridge would inflate it. I had to be very careful walking on the bar. It was love time for the sting rays, and they were thick, almost buried in the sand and matching it in color. They averaged eighteen inches across. There is never a bit of trouble if you scuff your feet. They shake themselves out of the sand and go skimming off, underwater fliers with leathery wings.

Halfway back to the *Flush*, I stopped paddling and

looked at the *Muñequita*. Her plight touched my heart. She was abandoned, a derelict. The sun had changed from deep red to orange to a blazing white just above the horizon, promising a blistering day.

When I climbed aboard, she looked down at me from the sun deck and said, "What the *hell* are you doing?"

"You're supposed to be watching."

"Okay, okay. I'm watching."

"Have you got with you any kind of hat that Frank Sprenger would know and remember?"

"He isn't much for noticing clothes. Unless he's bought them for you. I like big floppy cloth hats with big brims. I've got a red one that's *really* red, and he kidded me about it."

I swarmed up and took the glasses and got up on the rail and searched. I saw a dot moving across the glassy sea a long long way off. I hustled her below, and she got the hat out of one of the suitcases she had planned to leave behind. It was more than red. It was a vivid scarlet. I dug around in a forward gear locker and found the old fenders I should have thrown away, but was saving in case I had to use them in a lock somewhere, with the sides of the lock black with oil. They were of ancient gray canvas, stained and worn, and filled with matted kapok. They were cylindrical, about thirty inches long and as big around as her head.

I tried the hat on one and it fitted.

"You have fallen out of your tree," she proclaimed.

"You are going to be hiding, minus the long black hair, and this is going to be your body, floating in that two-man raft."

Once she got the idea, she helped. She did give a small cry of desolation when I gathered all that hair into my left fist and then gnawed through it with the kitchen shears between hand and skull. She fastened it into a long fall with rubber bands. I taped it to the fender. I wanted a lot of weight in the raft. I checked on the distant boat and found it closer each time. I used a spare anchor, wired to all the fenders, and a lot of canned goods to overload the rubber raft. I threw a blanket over all the junk, tucked it down, shifted the stuff around to look like a woman shape under the blanket. The fender with hat and hair was at one corner of the raft, shining black hair spilling out from under the scarlet brim to lay in sharp contrast against the yellow rubber.

I took it out quickly, wading, swimming, pushing it, and used a small mushroom anchor to hold it into a very gentle tide current so that the red hat end was toward the island I thought he would use as cover when approaching.

When I climbed up onto the *Flush,* she was standing there, looking quite changed with her hair gnawed off ragged and short. She was staring out at the raft and held her clasped hands close to her throat. When I turned and looked, I saw what caused the curious expression on her face. It was better than I hoped. It was spooking her. She floated out there, dead in a raft. I wondered if she had ever really been able to comprehend the fact of her own eventual and inevitable death. Today, my friends, we each have one day less, every one of us. And joy is the only thing that slows the clock.

When I got the glasses on the boat, they brought it so close I had the startled feeling they could see me as clearly as I could see them. Three of them, in a pale blue boat, proceeding very slowly, angling from my left to my right. From there I knew they could see the white of the superstructure of the *Flush* through the trees on No Name. I estimated they were a little bit less than one mile away, and they were moving very slowly because they were crossing the shallows. The direction indicated they were moving over to where they could turn toward No Name in the concealment of the island a little over a hundred yards west of me. Yet I could not be certain they were not merely early morning fishermen.

I went below and got back in a hurry, carrying the spotting scope. I turned the eyepiece to the sixty-power click and used the angle between the rail and stanchion as a rest. Sixty power makes an object at six thousand feet look one hundred feet away. The narrow field made it very difficult to track a moving object. They were coming into deeper water and picking up speed. I caught them in quick and momentary glimpses. It was one of the countless imitations of the Boston Whaler, with the central console where the operator can stand and run the big outboard by the remote controls. I could not catch the man running it. He seemed big enough to be Davis. The time I got him in focus long enough, he was looking south. I saw a planter's hat with bright band tipped forward, jammed down on his head to keep the wind from whipping it off. Yellow shirt.

Meyer sat on the stowage box in front of the console, leaning back against it, arms folded. Or tied? Folded. He wore his old souvenir hat from Lion Country. The white hunter variety, with a plastic band stamped to imitate leopard. Frank Sprenger was in the bow, sitting on the casting platform. He wore a black T-shirt, white shorts and a bright orange baseball cap with a long bill, and big dark sunglasses. He held a fishrod in his hand, pointed straight up. He wore binoculars around his neck.

When I saw those, I backed down and away. She was waiting for me on the side deck, swallowing frequently.

"On their way," I said, answering the question before she could ask it.

"What do we—"

"Now listen. Carefully. We've got ten minutes, probably more, before Sprenger gets in position. He'll leave his friend in the boat, and he'll wade to that end of that island, where the sand bar is. The other end is in water too deep, and this end is closer to us. Okay now, what he would want to do would be get comfortable, get a nice clear field of fire through an opening in the mangroves where they begin to thin out, and then wait until we were both on deck and then drop me first and then you. I think he would want information to keep from wasting time in search, so he would drop me with a head shot or a heart shot and get you through the legs."

"It makes me sick even to listen to—"

"So he is going to look and find the kind of ruin he might have caused himself. Both boats disabled and your body in that raft. Somebody got here first. That thing about moccasins, I was trying to say that it is the kind of thing he would accept, would believe had happened. His little world is falling apart anyway, and so this is one more rotten disaster he hadn't counted on. But it isn't going to make him reckless and impatient. He's a careful man. He'll wait quite a while, I think. He'll watch for some movement by that dummy in the raft. Sooner or later he'll have to satisfy himself. I think what he'll do is sink the raft. Then wait a while longer and finally come aboard, maybe alone, more probably with friend."

"Where will we *be!*" she demanded, her voice stretched thin.

I took her below. It was beginning to heat up below and would get considerably worse. I warned her to expect it and endure it. Silently. She wanted her little weapon, so I traded it for the other two manila envelopes and put them in the same hiding place as the one she had given me. No point in having Sprenger find her two and decide that was the batch and leave.

I took her down into the forward bilge and through the crawlway and up into the rope locker. Even though she was a big big girl, there was room for her and a lot of anchor line, and there was ventilation of sorts. I told her she could sit with her feet dangling, but when she heard anybody, or *if* she heard anybody coming through the crawlway, to pull her legs up inside and pull the door shut and slide the little bolt over to lock it from the inside. I made it emphatic. "Stay right here no matter what you hear, what you imagine, what you think. Don't try to think. Just stay until I come after you. Get cute and we're both dead."

"Where will you be? What are you going to do?"

"Take care of you. Shut up and wait. Not a sound. I've got a good place. I'll get the jump."

I left her there and went and opened up my good place, stocked it with what I thought I'd need, left it open and ready. I went to the galley and knelt and looked cautiously out of the lower right corner of the fixed glass opening by the booth that adjoins the galley.

I had thought it would give me a view of everything. The angle was slightly wrong. I could see the yellow raft and the wreck of the *Muñequita* and most of the nearby island, but I couldn't see the sandbar end of it. I could see to within ten feet of where I guessed he would take up his position. Now be as patient as he.

I could not have told Mary Alice the truth about what I wanted to do. I wanted the ruse of the raft, the red hat, the silence, the disabled boats, to lure them aboard, Sprenger and friend. I had the idea they would save Meyer for some conversations once they saw my stage setting. Tie him to the mangroves while they came aboard the *Flush.* And then, when I had my opportunity, I would merely pop out of my secret place, sap the nearest one behind the ear with a delicate twist of the wrist, hold the other one under the gun and yell boo. Turn him around and darken his world too, then truss them both with utmost care and diligence. Go get the lady with the unusual haircut and add her to the stack. Go get Meyer and the boat and bring the boat around. Use the big anchor and the power takeoff winch to pull the *Flush* out of the mangroves. Cork up the *Muñequita* and rig a pump and float her. Take both small boats in short tow and retrace the winding channel back to the main channel, and put Meyer, with a cold brew in hand, at the wheel, while I make a call through the Miami Marine Operator to one Sergeant Goodbread. Sergeant? This is McGee. I've got something for you.

No problems. Virtue prevails. A brisk encounter, made successful by the element of surprise.

Every ten minutes I looked at my watch and found that one more minute had gone by. I could hear a distant hysterical laughter of terns scooping up bait fish. I heard a jet go over, very high. I heard a drop of my sweat splat onto the vinyl floor.

My pants were dry, salt crusty, and now beginning to darken with sweat around the waist. The boat shoes were still damp. The wind was slacking off. I could see the water turning glassier. The bugs should come up out of the mangrove and grass marsh and shorten Sprenger's iron patience.

He would not be emotional now. Now it was a chore. He had been brought in from Phoenix six years ago on more of a basis than his pretty face. If punishment for trying cute tricks is quick, merciless, and permanent, fewer attempts are made, and the whole interweave of cooperation and concession runs more smoothly. If unaffiliated strangers come to the city to undercut the going street prices, and they are found long dead in an elegant apartment beside their long dead girls, fewer strangers come to town to go into business. If a man testifies before the grand jury and they find his head in a hat box in a coin locker at the airport, all grand juries accomplish less.

I changed position. My legs were cramped. Come *on*, Frank! I happened to be looking at the raft when I saw the scarlet hat leap into the air all by itself, along with the flat echoless smack of high velocity across water. The hat jumped up about a foot, leaping toward the middle of the raft. The impact knocked the fender forward, so that it slipped down below the round yellow bulge of rubberized fabric. It pulled the hair with it, so that only a small fringe still hung over the round of the life raft, visible from the island. I could not have hoped for a more realistic effect.

The raft began to sink at the foot end. There were three more shots, spaced one second apart. The raft settled more quickly and almost level. It disappeared. Air bubbles belched up. Then there was just the red hat, floating high on the water, but beginning slowly to settle as the salt water soaked into the fabric.

There was a silence of perhaps five minutes, and then the spaced shots began again. Six of them. I saw where they were going when the second one sent red dust into the air from the lens of the port bow running light of the *Muñequita.* He shot her lights off and the little chrome knob off the top of the ensign staff and the little elbow off the top of the windshield wiper.

He certainly wasn't using any target rifle, not at that rate of aimed fire. The sound had a vicious, stinging quality about it. Six shots gave me a vague clue. It was probably a bolt action, small-caliber, high-velocity load job, like that .243 Winchester Special, which dropped about a half inch in the first hundred yards, firing a seventy- to eighty-grain slug at a muzzle velocity of around thirty-six hundred feet per second.

Boats have a personality, a presence, a responsiveness. Little Doll had done her damned well best at all times for me, and I had sunk her onto a sand bar so somebody could shoot her bangles off. It had to be confusing her.

There was a shorter wait, and this time the six shots came smacking at *The Busted Flush.* I heard the ship's bell ring and the dying scree of ricochet off brass. Crash and tinkle and zing. Thud and whine and whizz of splinters.

Just about enough time for a reload and it began again. One got into the galley and clanked around among the pots. Then a lengthening silence. My cue to disappear. Tall white rabbit hops back into top hat.

I had bet Meyer that I could go aboard the *Flush* and hide and he could not find me in a two-hour search. He knew the old houseboat well. We bet one hundred dollars, plus welching privileges, which means that if you lose, you can buy the winner a very good dinner and try to renegotiate your loss.

He did not know that while he was up in Montreal for a week, listening to people read papers on international currency and exchange, I had found an exiled master carpenter from Cuba. When you open the door to the head, you are in a short corridor with the master stateroom at your right, the guest stateroom at your left. Affixed to the bulkhead straight ahead is a full-length mirror, already installed when I had won the houseboat in a poker game. I had done some measuring. The little Cuban was amused. He said it was possible. He moved the interior bulkhead out a few inches. He went around into the galley and made a tall provision locker a few inches shallower. He removed the mirror, cut a hole just a hair smaller than the mirror, put a brass piano-hinge down one side of the tall mirror and reinstalled it. I tried it for size in there. If a man does not have a swollen gut, even a large man takes up surprisingly little space if you measure him back to front. Less than twelve inches. But it was too dark in there. I located a good piece of two-way glass at an exorbitant price, and he installed it in the mirror frame. It was much better that way.

The Cuban removed every trace of his highly skilled labor. He devised a simple but solid catch which would hold the mirror-door closed and could be released by inserting a long wire brad into an almost invisible hole on the right side of the mirror, in the bulkhead next to the frame. For the occupant there was a simple turn block on the inside. He did a lot of winking, because he thought it was where I planned to tuck the errant lady when the husband came storming aboard. I did not advise him that I had never gone in for the middle-America hobby of scragging the random wife at any opportunity. But there had been a lot of times when people had come aboard looking for other people, when it had been unfortunate all the way around to have no good stowage area for people who would rather not be found. And as long as I had it, I thought I would make Meyer pay for it. He lost the bet. He marveled at the ingenuity, the craftsmanship. He bought me a legendary steak, a great wine, and wheedled me down to ten percent of the original bet.

They would come aboard. They would search the *Flush.* And sooner or later, they would both be in the short corridor between the staterooms at the same time. At which time I would pop out, the Browning automatic in my right hand, the woven leather sap in my left, all ready and eager to thump their skulls with ten ounces of padded lead at the end of a spring.

I moved toward the lounge, staying back out of sight, listening. I had the shirts memorized. White shirt on Meyer. In case of bad trouble, fire at yellow shirt or black shirt. Soon, a little sooner than I expected, I heard the unmistakable sound of more than one man walking through thigh-deep water. I couldn't tell if it was two or three, only that it was more than one.

So I nipped back to my safe and secret place. I'd left the mirror-door standing open. It was still open. The mirror lay on the corridor floor, and the biggest piece was smaller than a dinner plate. One of those twelve shots had come angling down the corridor or had spun off something or . . .

What now, big white rabbit?

Terror is absolutely nonproductive. It is not worth a thing. So if it is new to you, you don't know how to handle it, and it can freeze you. But if you have felt it before, many times in many places, you know that if you can start moving, it will go away. You can't spend time thinking, or you will freeze up again. You have to move without thought. It can be like shifting into some rare and special gear, some kind of overdrive seldom needed and seldom available. I dipped down and picked the pistol and sap off the floor of the useless refuge. They were going to come into the lounge from the aft deck. It was the logical approach for them. And it was the only below-decks space that was large enough to improve my chances. I got there as fast as I could and as silently as I could. There was only one place in the room where I could not be seen from the doorway or from the ports. I crawled to it, to the shelter of the long curved yellow couch, and flattened out. I could look under it and see the sill of the open door. I could hunch forward a foot and a half and be able to see the whole doorway.

All right now, McGee. Forget the childhood dreams of glory. Have no scruples about firing from ambush and firing to kill. No Queensbury rules, fellow.

I heard the diving platform creak. Water dripped. There was a grunt of effort, slap of wet palm against railing, thud of rubber soles on the decking. Then the sequence was repeated.

"Goddamn the bugs!"

"Shut up!"

"There's nobody on—"

"Shut up!"

There was ten seconds of silence. And suddenly something came bounding into the lounge. I had the impression of some animal, some vast, vital, rubbery strength that covered fifteen feet and landed lightly, poised, every sense alert. Next, a pair of big wet tennis shoes stopped by the sill, just inside the room.

The voice by the door said, "There's nobody on this—"

I was going to have to get rid of that voice by the door to give all my attention to the animal presence over beyond the couch. I wormed forward and saw all of him, Davis, soaked to the waist, revolver in the left hand, the hand nearest me, the hand now sagging down to his side. I told the gun to go where I pointed it, as it always had, forgetting the first one was double action, missing the hand, putting the second one into the hand. He screamed and pounced for the dropped weapon, trying to grab it up with the other hand, and I hit that hand, and he went diving, tumbling out the doorway onto the deck as I spun, hitched back, looked up, and waited for the round target of the head to appear over the back of the couch. The three shots had been very close together, a huge wham-bamming sound far different than the whippy lick of the rifle, and leaving a sharp stink of propellant in the hot air.

The rifle cracked like a huge whip and laid its lash across the edge of my thigh. I suddenly had the wit to flatten out again and look under the couch. He wore white boat shoes. I had to turn the automatic onto its side to aim. I couldn't point it naturally. I had to aim it. The shoes moved closer. I had to aim again. The side of the shoe burst into wet red, and he made not a sound. I took my chance on bounding up rather than trying for the other white shoe and bringing him down. But as I swung the pistol, he fired without aiming, a snap shot, doubtless hoping to hit me, but it worked like one of those impossible trick shots out of a bad Western. It slammed the gun out of my hand and spun it into the far corner, leaving my hand and arm numb to the elbow.

Sprenger worked the bolt quickly and aimed at the middle of my forehead and then slowly lowered it.

"You're a damned idiot, McGee. And a damned nuisance."

"You haven't got a lot of options."

He tested the foot, taking a short step on it. He did not wince, limp, change expression. But pain drained the blood out of his face and made his tan look saffron. He had shed his sunglasses.

"Meaning I need you?" He waved me back and took another step and propped a hip on the corner of the back of the couch.

"Is Meyer all right?"

It took several moments for the implications of my question to get through to him. "You are some kind of people, you two. He's a bright man. He knows a lot about the tax future of municipals. We had a nice talk. I'm losing my touch. I can't read people anymore. That damned McDermit woman is insane. Was insane. Once she got leverage, it was like all she wanted was to get us both killed. I read you wrong. I read Meyer wrong."

"Is he all right?"

"So far. He probably isn't comfortable, but he's all right. Thanks for letting me know he's trading material."

"If you could get back there to the boat."

He looked at his bleeding foot. "Blow it off at the knee and I could get back there." I believed him. He shook his big head. There was a glint of rue in the little blueberry eyes. "I had nearly five hundred round ones stashed, in case I ever had to run and had a chance to run. *Postage* stamps! Dear Jesus Lord!"

"A sterling investment, Mr. Fedderman says."

"What could I do? She would have screamed to the McDermit brothers I was laying her."

"There wasn't any dear friend primed to make a report."

He thought that over. "I couldn't take a chance. You can see that. That woman would *rather* lie than tell it straight." He leaned back and looked out the doorway. He lifted the rifle slightly and said, "Something you should know. At this range, anyplace I hit you—"

"I'm dead from hydrostatic shock. It hits fluid, transmits the shock wave up veins and arteries, and explodes the heart valves. You came close. You put a skin burn on my thigh."

"You know a lot of things. Walk way around me slowly and take a look at Davis, from the doorway."

I followed directions. Davis was out. He was on his face, legs spraddled, one smashed hand under his belly, the other over his head. I could see little arterial spurtings from the torn wrist, a small pulsing fountain that was as big around as a soda straw and jetted about three inches.

Blood ran into the scuppers and drained into the sea. His head was turned so I could see his face. His closed lids looked blue. His moustache was glued to white papery flesh. He had dwindled inside his clothes, but his big straw planter hat was still firmly in place. The small jet dwindled quickly. Two inches, one inch, nothing.

I turned around slowly and took a slow step back into the lounge. "He just bled to death."

He looked puzzled. "I thought you hit him in the hand."

"Both hands. He couldn't stop the bleeding, using the one that wasn't so bad."

"You were trying to hit him in the hands?"

"Yes."

"You're good with that thing. But you are an idiot. If you're that good, you could have popped up and hit me in the head and then him."

"Call it a natural revulsion, Frank."

"You've got first aid stuff aboard?"

"Always."

"You're going to get it and fix this foot."

"We're supposed to be in negotiation, aren't we?"

He looked at me and through me, at the narrow vista of his possibilities, his meager chances. He said in a tired voice, "I build that municipal bond business from almost nothing. It was supposed to be a front. But I *like* it. I'm *good* at it. It's what I really want to *do*."

"Frank?"

"I know. I know."

"So the pattern was kill me and the woman and Davis and Meyer, burn this boat with all four bodies aboard, after retrieving the rarities Mary Alice ran off with, and go back and run a very good bluff and hope for the best, hope they don't find out Mary Alice killed Jane Lawson, and then tie you to Mary Alice in the Fedderman swindle. If you can get the goodies back, your best move would be cancel out with Fedderman and retrieve that junk out of the box."

He frowned at me. "How would you know about burning? Just how in hell would you know that?"

"You must have asked Meyer some questions about this houseboat that gave him the idea you were trying to figure out if it would burn well and if it was in a place where there was no chance of anybody putting the fire out."

He thought, nodded, and said, "Then he radioed you."

"So you're still on course, aren't you? Two down and two to go. Get me to fix the foot. Get me to tell you where she hid the stuff. And you should probably have me retrieve that body out there so it won't be floating around with holes in it, making people ask questions. Then we go over and bring the rental around, and you add two more bodies to the pyre and get out of here."

"You're very helpful. Why are you so helpful?"

I had to make it very good. He had to believe me. I had to be casual, but not too casual, earnest but not too earnest. "Haven't you had the feeling, Frank, I've been a half-step ahead of you."

"Maybe. Until right now."

"Once I heard from Meyer that I could count on you making a try, why would I just sit here and wait for it? Would I be such an idiot that I'd figure I would be able to take you with no fuss? I have respect for you, Frank. As a fellow professional. I did what you'd do in my shoes. I took out insurance. I talked to Meyer late yesterday afternoon. I wouldn't exactly say we're going to hear bugles and look up and see the US Cavalry come riding across the water, firing their Sharps rifles. But I wouldn't say that anything you do is going to go unnoticed."

"Then I've got no chance at all. End of the line?"

"Insurance can always be canceled. Maybe I wouldn't make a claim."

He swung his leg out, looked at his shoe. "Stopped bleeding, at least. If it can be canceled, McGee, I can make you tell me how to go about canceling it. I found one man once I couldn't make talk. He had such a low threshhold, he'd faint at the first touch. That's the only time I've ever missed. And I've had more than a hundred people find out they had more to say than they wanted to."

"I'm terrified. I'm not trying to be smart. I really am. You could make me tell you. I'm sure. But it would take as long as I could hold out, and I don't think you could do it without leaving a lot of visible damage, and when you got all done, Frank, you'd find out that the only way it can be canceled is by me, in person, not on the phone, not in writing. By a personal friendly visit to my insurance agent."

"And you want to use crap like that to make a deal?"

"Why not? Disprove it. I can get Fedderman to market the stuff. I want exactly half. I'm a practical man. I'll put myself in your pocket to save my skin and my partner's. I'll write you a confession of where, when, and how I killed Davis and how I killed Mrs. Ray McDermit. I know an island near here high enough so we can bury the bodies, and I'll put that in the confession along with the chart coordinates. Then you own me."

"But you'll keep the insurance in force? We'll own each other, you mean. Can we get this foot fixed?"

"Is the negotiation all settled?"

"Half? Hell, I guess so. Let me see those damned postage stamps."

"Later. Last night I ran over to the village in the runabout and mailed them to myself. Three envelopes."

"Why didn't you start with that?"

"You wouldn't have bought it. But now you do, because if it wasn't true, I *would* have started with it."

He almost smiled. "Half. Harry Harris said he heard that was the way you go. It's a big piece. That dumb jackass, know what he was doing? Going home at night and telling his woman all about what he did all day. Like he was a bill collector or something. If you hadn't tipped me about the leak, I wouldn't be buying you now. Now will you *please* do something about my foot?"

That word was the one which unlatched half the springs which were holding my stomach up against the base of my throat. Please. A beautifully predictive word. Stomach moved halfway back to normal position.

"There's a first aid locker back . . ."

And Mary Alice thumped the door frame with her left hand as she staggered and caught her balance. She was running wet with sweat, head to toe, her face pallid, mouth open, eyes dazed with the near-fainting state the heat had brought on. She had her little automatic in her big right hand, but it was at her side, pointing at the floor.

Frank Sprenger swung the rifle toward her, and she

tried to lift the little automatic to aim it at him. The rifle shot whacked, and her blue eyes bulged and broke, and she dropped straight down, very strangely, as if she were a bundle of clothing slipping off a hanger. But the little gun was coming my way, floating in the air with the momentum from swinging it up to fire it. But instead she had released it. It was moving so slowly in the air that I had time to change my instinctive reflex to pick it out of the air with my right hand and try instead with my left. My hand was still numb, and some feeling was coming back, with enough pain along with it to tell me it was broken in some way.

I could see it turning, floating, and as I reached and took it out of the air, taking it properly by the grip, beyond it I could see Frank Sprenger, out of focus, standing transfixed with the rifle still aimed down the companionway, at the empty air where her head had been.

I pointed at him and the little automatic snapped a little louder than a cap gun, and he spun and yanked the trigger of the rifle while some spectator in the back of my mind peered at him and told me that the fool had forgotten to work the bolt action. Keep firing, the spectator said. Hurry!

He came at me. Bounding. Stone-brown face under the orange cap. Huge brawny arms reaching for me. A caricature of a muscled chest, carved of hickory, moulding the black T-shirt. Bowed legs, massively thewed, bounding under the white shorts, springing him toward me, while his little nightmare blueberry eyes looked remote, impersonal, totally assured. No favoring of the smashed foot. I backed away, pointing my stupid left hand at him, the little automatic saying its futile bang, bang, bang, making no impression on him at all. He smashed me like a truck, bounced me against the bulkhead and off it to fall under him, and see that sledge fist rise high and come smashing down toward me. I rolled my head to the right, rolled it into blinding brilliance and over and over and off the edge of the world and down, the brilliance turning to a tiny white dot way above me and then winking out.

Twenty-one

I was in a big old bed that sagged in the middle. It had a tall dark headboard. There was a window over to my right. Double hung, with an area of flawed glass in the bottom pane that warped the green calligraphy of the banyan that reached so close to the window it muted the light in the upstairs bedroom.

The bedroom door was opposite the foot of the old bed. It was always open. The closet was off to my left. There was a chest of drawers beside it. There was a huge conch shell on top of the chest of drawers. There was a framed lithograph of Venice on the wall over near the window. With a gondola in the foreground. The bathroom was out the door into the hall and to the left, just before the stairs going down.

I had been there a long time. I had heard heavy rain on the roof and roaring down through banyan leaves. At every dusk the tree screamed with its full passenger list of small birds. Sometimes I could hear surf, far away. I could hear traffic, closer than the surf, high-speed trucks droning by in the night. Something with a noisy old engine came in and out during the day, dying somewhere below my window. I could hear outboard motors sometimes, much closer than the surf. Once a great blue heron landed in the banyan, so close I could see his savage yellow eye.

I could hear young voices in the house, laughing. They played music, banged doors, roared away on motorcycles. I saw and heard these things and accepted them. They were there. I had no questions.

I could not open my mouth. My tongue tip traced the bits of wire and the new hole where it felt as if two teeth were gone in the upper row on the right, near the front but not right in front. And one tooth below them. That was where the glass straw went. It had a bend in it, to make it easier to suck while lying down.

For a time, vaguely remembered, there had been a broad starched woman in white, who had strong and gentle hands and clicked her tongue a lot. Bedpans, back rubs, changing dressings. And before that a different place, corridors, stretcher, shots.

Now there was only the small woman with the ruff of blond hair turning gray. Gentle brown eyes. When the wheelchair was first gone, I was afraid to lean on her as hard as I had to, when we made the endless journey down the hall to the bathroom. But she was strong, much stronger than she looked. I remembered that I used to see her in the night, in the rocking chair over there, always awake when I woke up.

It was my face in the mirror, but not my face. When the leg began to hold better under me and when the dressing was gone from my face, I would lean on the sink and try to decide just what was wrong. There were two long, healed incisions, stitch dots still apparent, dark red against the yellow pallor of the lost tan. It was something else that was wrong, not the red wounds. Something subtly out of balance, the way the bedroom was not quite true, with no corner exactly ninety degrees and the doorframe and window frame not parallel to either ceiling or floor.

I accepted, but I began to superimpose a question atop the acceptance. I had another world somewhere else, but the shape of it was murky. I did not want to try to bring it into focus. But it seemed to be coming nearer of its own accord.

It was easier to stay in this world. I knew what the little wire cutters on the bed stand were for. I had asked the woman, and she had said that if I vomited, I could choke to death unless she was there to cut the wires that held my jaw together. It had been broken in three places. And the cheekbone had been crushed.

It was easier to stay in this world where I knew that in the middle of the morning and in the middle of the afternoon, I had to sit in the rocking chair and slowly lift and lower my right leg. From ten times at first, with no weights, to a hundred times with the gadget she had made, a sailcloth wrapping with strings to tie it on and with pouches for the lead fish weights. The leg grew stronger, but it did not feel right. It felt numbed and prickly, as a limb does when it has gone to sleep and has started to come awake. Sometimes there were needles of pain from my toes into my hip. Sometimes the area around the ankle and the top of the foot would feel very hot or very cold or even as if it had a soaking wet stocking on it when it was dry and bare.

The doctor came. He snipped the wire. He made me work my jaw while he watched. He told me the woman would get me gum to chew. It would condition the jaw muscles. He shone a bright little light into my eyes. He made me strip and walk away from him and toward him while he watched my right leg. He told me to put the pajamas and robe back on. He said the leg was doing fine. He asked me my name. I told him it was Travis. He asked if there was more, and I said I wasn't sure. I didn't know my address. He made me count backwards, add figures in my head, spell long words.

One day she came to my room a little before dusk, as the tree was beginning to fill with birds. I had been sitting in the rocking chair by the window, watching the birds come home, watching the sky change. She pulled a footstool close to the rocking chair and put a hand on my arm and looked up at me in a way that was half mischief and half sadness. "Who am I?" It was her familiar question, and I knew the familiar response.

"You are Cathy," I said.

In the last of daylight I took her hand and looked at it, at the weathered back of it, the little blue veins, the country knuckles. It seemed a very dear hand indeed. She knelt on the footstool and was closer and taller. I kissed her and felt the ridged area where the inside of my mouth had been stitched. Her brown eyes glinted in the last of the light. It was all strange and sweet and unemphatic, as though it were an inescapable extension of this unquestioned world, as natural and inevitable as all the rest of it.

I looked at her and said in a shaking voice, "You *are* Cathy! My God, I have been . . . What has . . . Oh, Cathy! Cathy!"

The whole back of my mind had been nailed shut. There was a creaking, straining, and the barrier tumbled, and it all came spilling out. The watery weakness ran out of my eyes and down my face, and I couldn't make words. But she knew what had happened. She hugged me, laughing, crying, snuffling.

Candle Key. Cathy Kerr. That sagging, weathered old bay-front house of hard pine and black cypress.

She said, "Your houseboat, it's tied on up to our old dock out there like before. And like before, there's handyman stuff that's piled up, when you're feeling up to it."

"We used to go out in your skiff and take Davie fishing."

"Remember that day he caught into that shark and got mad at you for cutting it loose? He wasn't even in school yet." She touched her hair. "Now he's near thirteen. I'm an old lady now, way over thirty, Trav."

"Where's your sister? Where's Christine?"

"Just down the road. She married that Max fellow, and she had four more, six in all. The kids are in and out of here all the time. I tried to keep them quiet, but you know how it is. Max got into the land business, and you wouldn't believe what he got us for the land that daddy left us the other side of the main road."

"How many times are you going to have to put me back together?"

"This is only twice. And it was both of us needing it the first time. It could be forty times and never make up to you for what you did for me and what you lost of your own a-doing it. I've got to call Meyer right now! I shouldn't even have waited this long. He was closer to believing that fool doctor than he was me. I said it would be just a little time, and the doctor said maybe never."

She gave me a quick kiss as she stood up. "Because you had a terrible terrible concussion and they thought there could have been some bleeding inside of your skull that cut off what you knew before somehow. Meyer being here three times and you not knowing him was terrible for him."

She went swiftly to the door, and I saw the well-remembered way she moved, that quick light way of the professional dancer, quick of foot on those lithe, sinewy, lovely legs.

"What's the date?"

"Hmm. The man on the television said this morning it was nine more shopping days til Christmas."

She was gone, leaving me to try to fit my mind around that huge hole in time. Sprenger had killed me on the twenty-eighth day of September. Over two and a half months ago.

When she came back upstairs, she said Meyer said he would leave in ten minutes to drive down. The day was gone. She turned the lights on. I felt emotionally exhausted. I got into bed, and she sat beside me on the bed and held my hand and told me how Meyer had arrived in a rental boat the afternoon of that day with me in the bottom of the boat, wrapped in blankets with the left side of my face so horribly bashed in that my eye seemed to be out of the socket. I seemed to be alive but barely. Not alive enough to go through the routine of phoning an ambulance. They put me in her old pickup, and she had driven like a madwoman while Meyer had stayed back in the truck bed with me to keep me from bouncing around too much. They took me to Doctor Ramirez. The one who looked like a Swede. I suddenly realized it had been Ramirez who had been coming to see me here in Cathy's house. He remembered me from before. Back when he and I started putting Lois Atkinson's head back on. He treated me for shock. The three of them watched over me that night. The next day I was moved by ambulance to the little hospital in Homestead, where there was a surgeon Ramirez believed in, who could rebuild the left side of my face. Cathy told me I was full of alloy pins and plates and special wire. When I was well enough to be moved, I was brought back to her house by ambulance. She had quit her job in the village to take care of me.

"What did Meyer tell you about what happened? What did he tell Ramirez?"

She licked her lips. She wore an odd expression. "What happened, you and Meyer had come down into Florida Bay to do some fishing. You went out from the *Flush* in your fast little boat, and you went up on the bow to make something fast and gave Meyer the wheel, and he was going between some little islands when the steering cable broke, and he veered right into the island, you got threw headlong into the mangroves."

"What's the matter with my leg?"

"Your back got wrenched up, and it tore a nerve some. The si-sciatic? That's it. But it's coming along real good."

"So where did Meyer get the rental boat?"

She straightened. "Any questions like that, you better ask him. I just wouldn't know a thing."

She fed me well, and I slept and was awakened at ten-thirty when she and Meyer came into the bedroom. He was beaming like a pumpkin with a big candle. I didn't want him to notice the damned water running out of my eyes again. He didn't notice because he kept turning his back to blow his nose.

Cathy left us alone and closed the door. He said, "The absolutely worst part of it, believe me, is to have nobody to tell."

Nothing could have stopped him telling me. Davis had come aboard the *Keynes* at one in the morning, roused Meyer, and driven him down to Miami, where they picked up Sprenger and drove on down to Regal Marine. Sprenger and Meyer had waited near the public boat ramp while Davis drove to Regal and eventually arrived with the rental boat. Sprenger carried an elegant leather case, the shape of a gigantic dispatch case. It was custom fitted for two rifles, two scopes, ammunition, slings, cleaning equipment. Meyer managed to delay their arrival at No Name by routing them across flats where they could not risk planing speed. Sprenger had left Davis with Meyer in the boat behind the nearby island. He waded to the south end of the island and waited there a long time. He had fired one shot and then, at varied intervals, three series of six shots each. He came back to the boat and had Davis tie Meyer's hand behind him, with one arm through the steering wheel. They left him alone.

"Distant firecrackers," Meyer said. "And then nothing. One hell of a lot of nothing. Except heat. And bugs. Finally I wormed around and stood up on the seat and got my fanny on the edge of the steering wheel. I bounced on it three times, and on the third time it broke off. I got out of the boat and found a mangrove stub covered with barnacles and backed into it and rubbed until I frayed the rope in two. And lost some skin. There was an old gaff in the boat. I took it along. Where do those bluebottle flies come from? How do they know? They were so thick on Davis's face, I couldn't tell who he was until I scared them off.

And the lounge was full of them. I thought you were dead. He was lying across you. Then I wondered why you didn't have your share of flies. I put my ear next to your mouth and felt the exhalation. So I lifted him off you."

"Thanks."

"Don't mention it. I wasn't tracking well. I didn't know where to start. I should have got on the horn and called a Coast Guard chopper in. I never even thought of it. Everybody . . . everybody was so damned *dead!* You know? It makes it hard to think."

"What killed him?"

"Five little holes in his chest, right through his black shirt. Centered, but just a shade to the right, I think. You could have covered them all with a playing card. Fantastic."

"He shot her. Where did he hit her?"

"I don't know. There was a hole right at the base of her skull, big as half an English walnut."

That fitted the way she had gone down. Her mouth had been sagging open. So that was where the little slug had gone, into the back of her throat and on out.

"I got the boat and had a hell of a job getting the steering wheel back on. I never did. I had to push down on it to turn it. I got you into the boat. I couldn't go back to Regal Marine. I hadn't rented it. I'd taken time out to pull Davis inside and close everything I could and shove clothes into the broken ports and spray those damned hungry flies. I remembered Cathy and figured I could find this place from the Candle Key water tower. So I told her—"

"She picked it up from there. I know about Ramirez and Homestead. But what did you do then?"

"Okay, I had the feeling then that you were going to

live. But I couldn't think of any good way to explain what had gone on. I didn't even *know* what had happened. So on the way back from Homestead, I stopped at Regal Marine. They weren't worried about their boat, not with Davis's car parked in their lot. I told them I was a friend of Davis's, and we'd decided to keep the boat longer. I gave them two hundred dollars and said he was having good luck further down the Keys and sent me up to get his car. I showed them his car keys. I said it might be another few days. I went out and told Cathy not to wait. I drove Davis's car to Miami and left it in a shopping center lot with the windows down and the keys in it. I took a bus to Homestead to see how you were and took another bus down to Candle Key. It was too late to do anything. I slept in this room, and in the morning I took the rental boat back out there. I tied a towel around my face. I had a little bottle with gasoline in it. It paralyzes the sense of smell. Every time it started to get through to me, I'd put a little on the towel. Even so, I wasted a lot of time running for the rail."

"Jesus, Meyer!"

"By then it was self-preservation. Where would I fit if it all broke open? I'd fit in a cell somewhere. I kept thinking it was what you'd do. It was a McGee solution. But not my kind of thing. I wrapped them in that blue canvas you had, that roll of it. I sewed them in with that curved needle and that waxed twine. I wired that big rifle case of Sprenger's to his ankles. After he was in the rental boat. Bodies are heavy. I cried once, Sprenger was so heavy, and I thought I couldn't get him out of the lounge even. Not tears of sadness. Tears of rage. I kicked him. That's a bad reaction. Were you saving that thirty feet of chain for something special, with the big links, this big? I wrapped it around and around her waist and wired it. It won't come off."

His voice was too thin and fast and high, and his eyes were strange. "Meyer, Meyer."

"The thing I used for the third one, Davis, you'd described him, the moustache, Joe Namath haircut, I don't know what it was, down in the aft bilge, heavy, like the end of an iron cage. Then when they were in the boat, I covered them with that big net, that gill net. I put two rods in the rod holders."

"Take it easy."

"I drank some of your gin. Out of a cup. Warm. A whole cup. I gagged and gagged, but I kept it down. Then I went across and under a highway bridge, and I went outside. I don't even know what bridge. I wanted it to be calm out there, but it wasn't. Whitecaps. I had to throttle way down, and it took forever to get out to where the Keys were just a line on the horizon. What do you say when you dump over three people in blue bags? My head is full of things. I couldn't find anything I wanted inside my head. Then I remembered something. I looked it up later. From the Book of Mormon, the Book of Ether, chapter three.

" 'And the Lord said, For behold, ye shall be as a whale in the midst of the sea; for the mountain waves shall dash upon you. Nevertheless, I will bring you up again out of the depths of the sea; for the winds have gone forth out of my mouth, and also the rains and the floods have I sent forth. And behold, I prepare you against these things; for ye cannot cross this great deep save I prepare you against the waves of the sea, and the winds which have gone forth, and the floods which shall come. Therefore what will you that I should prepare for you that ye may have light when ye are swallowed up in the depths of the sea?' Why did I remember that? I wish I knew.

"So I said amen and tipped them over the rail, and they went down. That cage thing caught in the net, and it took it along too. I had some headway, and the steering was stiff, so it held into the wind until the last and it started turning. When I got to the wheel, the wheel came off and before I could get it back, a wave came in and filled it half-full. The engine started missing, and I turned it toward land and opened it up. It drained the water out. I bit my tongue. I lost my lucky hat."

"The Lion Country hat?"

He tried to laugh, but his face twisted and broke, and he put his head down into his hands and sobbed. It is the gentle people who get torn up. They can cope. They can keep handling the horrors long after the rest of us fade out. But it marks them more deeply, more lastingly. This was role reversal at its most bitter. I knew what he had to have, and I wondered for a moment at my own hesitation. Life seems to be a series of attempts to break out of old patterns. Sometimes you can. I reached and touched him on the shoulder.

"You did well," I said. "You really did a hell of a job. You did exactly what you had to do. It was the right choice."

So he straightened up, dabbed his eyes, blew his nose, smiled in a wan way. In a level, unemotional voice he told me the rest of it. There had been time to intercept the letters he'd left with Jenny Thurston, but he knew I hadn't signed them. So let them go. Let the people look for Sprenger and Mary Alice. Take the chance that there were only five people who knew Mary Alice had left via Lauderdale aboard the *Flush,* and three of them were dead.

He had returned the rental boat, paying for the broken wheel, and had used Cathy's old skiff to get out to No Name, day after day, cleaning up the evidence of violence, repairing the places where bullets had struck. He got the generator and the airconditioning operational. He threw out the perishables, which had spoiled in the heat. He did not get rid of Mary Alice's belongings until he had found the treasure in the hidey hole he himself had invented. He had floated the *Muñequita* the hard way, with a hand pump. He had taken the lights off her, the fittings that had been damaged by Sprenger's sniper fire, deep-sixed them, bought replacements, and with Davie Kerr's help, rewired them. They towed the *Muñequita* to Candle Key, to a small marina with a good mechanic. The engines had been in the salt water too long. He had pulled them, rebuilt one, was nearly finished with the other. On an especially high tide they had left Christine, Cathy's sister, to watch me, and Cathy, Davie, and Meyer had gone out and brought the *Flush* back and tied it up at the dock near the old house. He and Davie and Cathy had done a lot of work on it.

I asked him about Hirsh and the murder investigation.

He shrugged. "The guilty flee when no man pursueth. The law leaned on my old friend, but he had nothing to say. Yes, he had an investment arrangement with a Mr. Sprenger, who was in the bond business. The amount invested was a matter between the two of them. If Mr.

Sprenger was dissatisfied, the money would be returned. Hirsh had to go to the bank when the tax people opened the box and took what was in it. He had to sign a release saying the contents were Sprenger's. He gathered from the tax people that every single piece of paper relating to Sprenger's personal affairs had disappeared along with Sprenger. When I gave him those three brown envelopes and he opened them and saw what they were, he asked me three times how I came to have them. I told him if he asked me once more, our friendship was over. He asked me what he was to do with them. I said that because, according to his own explanation, they were not sufficiently unique to be traceable as individual items, they should go back into stock. He said they would go into his box at the bank, in case somebody should come to claim them. He was eighty years old when I got there. When I left, he was fifty, going on forty-nine. He and Miss Moojah are running it alone."

"Didn't Goodbread come looking for me?"

"Oh yes. And Captain Lamarr. They came down here together, the two of them, after you were out of the hospital. They went to the hospital too. They were sorry you were so badly hurt. I think I had to tell them six times how you got hurt. When they talked to Ramirez, he remembered picking mangrove bark and splinters out of your face. It was a big help to have him remember that. There was a big fuss about the murder. General Lawson made a thirty-second television spot, offering a hundred thousand dollars for information leading to the whereabouts of Mrs. McDermit and/or Mr. Sprenger. It's quieted down. It was a long time ago. The universe continues to unfold."

It was after midnight. We were both exhausted. He stayed over, sleeping aboard the *Flush.* When I saw him at midmorning, he showed me what he had forgotten to show me the night before. He had a little folding viewer in his pocket, and he unfolded it and put a 35mm slide in it. I turned it toward the segment of sky in the top corner of my window. It was Hirsh's photographic handiwork. It was the same lady I had seen in another world. In that world she had been in profile. On these three stamps, a strip of them without the little holes to tear them apart, she was turned and looking out at me. What had she said before? "Oh no, *not you* again!" She was in a different color this time, curiously close to the same color as that hat Mary Alice said Sprenger would recognize.

The lady in the stamp had a small, sulky, oddly erotic mouth and an expression of arrogant challenge.

"Who is she?" I asked.

"A gift from Hirsh to you. A personal, private gift."

"I mean, did the lady have a name?"

"Are you serious? Her name was Queen Victoria!"

"Pardon me all to hell, Queen."

"Here is the certificate of authenticity from the Royal Society. It's an unlisted error, a double error, the wrong color and printed on both sides."

I looked at the certificate. New Zealand Number 1, a horizontal strip of three, printed in scarlet vermilion instead of dull carmine. Recess printed. Fainter impression in same colour on reverse. Unlisted. Unique. Authentic.

"What's it worth?"

"Ten years ago an appraiser from Stanley Gibbons said forty thousand dollars. Hirsh says if you want currency, there is an auction coming up where it should be entered. I forget the details. For a while I thought you really needed the money."

"You think I don't? I'm down to—"

"I know, I know. I was going to buy you an apartment near Bahia Mar. A legal address. Near where your roots are. We've both been there too long to get rousted now by politicians."

"Something changed your mind? You want to move away?"

"No. We had it wrong. You know how rumors are around Bahia Mar. It affects the squatters, that new ordinance. But it doesn't affect commercial marinas. It doesn't affect us. There's been a celebration ever since Irv set us straight."

"The *Flush* is at a good anchorage right here, Meyer."

He looked very thoughtful. "I know. A man in your condition shouldn't make too many decisions, maybe. Should I put Hirsh's gift in the auction?"

"I . . . I think I'll hang onto it for a while."

"That means you'll have to find a salvage job pretty soon, doesn't it?"

I sensed the very first small tingle of anticipation, very faint, buried very deep. But authentic. "I just might," I said. "I just might."

There came a cold day in January, cold and fiercely bright, when I put on the sweater and wool pants she had brought me from a clothes locker aboard *The Busted Flush,* and I went downstairs with her and out through the wind. I was lighter than I had been since the operations long ago on my leg. I felt as if I was made of cornflakes, stale rubber bands, and old gnawed bones. I had come out of an endless old movie into arctic glare.

We went out to the *Flush*. She wanted to get me inside, out of the wind, but I wasn't ready for that. I climbed the steep ladderway to the sun deck with convalescent care, crossed to the starboard rail, and stood looking out across the steel-gray bay under the hard blue sky. The old house-boat did not welcome me. It was not my boat. It had a problem in its guts, blood and stillness and bluebottle flies.

Cathy sensed something wrong and put her hand over mine where I grasped the rail. Something in her touch told me to remember the sweetness. I turned and looked down into those brown eyes, into that strange mix of humility and knowingness and pride.

I had to bend nearer to hear her as the wind tore at her words. "Like before," she said. "Like it was if that's what you want, what you need, when you're ready. I could say it didn't matter to me, I'd be lying." She lifted her chin a little. "But either way, it wouldn't be no obligation to you, Travis."

"Cathy, I—"

"Don't say about it now. Wait until you're up to it."

She heard her own words and looked startled and then blushed a marvelous pink and hid her face against my sweatered shoulder. It took her a few seconds before she could join my laughter. And right then I felt the deck change under my feet. The *Flush* seemed to shrug off her grisly preoccupation and look around and recognize me. She made us welcome. She had been as far away as I had, perhaps.

Cathy and I went below and had mugs of hot tea with cinnamon, and then she walked me back to the old house.

Over the sound of the afternoon game on her television set, I could hear her out in the kitchen, singing as she fixed dinner, as far off key as she used to be, the last time I had lived here on Candle Key.

About the Author

JOHN D. MacDONALD, says *The New York Times,* "is a very good writer, not just a good 'mystery writer.' " His Travis McGee novels have established their hero as a modern-day Sam Spade and, along with MacDonald's more than 500 short stories and other bestselling novels—60 in all, including *Condominium* and *The Green Ripper*—have stamped their author as one of America's best all-round contemporary storytellers.